# THE CAT LOOKED BACK

# THE CAT LOOKED BACK

A MAPLES MYSTERY

**LOUISE CARSON**

DOUG WHITEWAY, EDITOR

EDITIONS

© 2023, Louise Carson

All rights reserved. No part of this book may be reproduced, for any reason, by any means, without the permission of the publisher.

Cover design by Doowah Design.
Cover icons: The Noun Project and Doowah Design.

This book was printed on Ancient Forest Friendly paper.
Printed and bound in Canada by Hignell Book Printing Inc.

We acknowledge the support of the Canada Council for the Arts and the Manitoba Arts Council for our publishing program.

**Library and Archives Canada Cataloguing in Publication**

Title: The cat looked back / Louise Carson ; Doug Whiteway, editor.
Names: Carson, Louise, 1957- author.
| Whiteway, Doug, 1951- editor.
Description: Series statement: A Maples mystery ; 6
Identifiers: Canadiana (print) 20230501990
| Canadiana (ebook) 20230502008
| ISBN 9781773241258 (softcover) | ISBN 9781773241265 (EPUB)
Subjects: LCGFT: Detective and mystery fiction. | LCGFT: Novels.
Classification: LCC PS8605.A7775 C384 2023
| DDC C813/.6—dc23

Signature Editions
P.O. Box 206, RPO Corydon, Winnipeg, Manitoba, R3M 3S7
www.signature-editions.com

*for dear Trudy Frey,
my most appreciative reader*

CONTENTS

PART 1
DENIAL
9

PART 2
ANGER
63

PART 3
BARGAINING
115

PART 4
DEPRESSION
169

PART 5
ACCEPTANCE
227

# PART 1
# DENIAL

The cat paused outside the low wrought iron fence in front of his house and listened. Painted white, the bars gleamed in the glow cast by one of the few streetlamps in the village.

The lamp gave off a faint hum; the moths that gently battered themselves against its smooth surface made soft little noises. In the surrounding houses various machines whirred on and off. The cat heard the distant mutter of a television set and its canned laughter. A sprinkler spun rhythmically. It was very late. The village was still. Yet—the cat continued to listen. He sat under a waning moon and surveyed his home.

White like the fence, two rooms up and two down, and attached to its twin on the right, it was a modest dwelling. The tin roof that sagged in the middle covered the porch that ran along the front of the building.

The cat inhaled. Behind him, delightful odours came from the now closed french fry and hamburger restaurant. To his right, from beyond the neighbours' attached house, behind a tiny café, the smell of coffee roasting tickled his nostrils. He wrinkled his nose in distaste. French fries and hamburgers and the grease they were cooked in— yes. Coffee—no.

The lawn also hummed—with life. Insects thrummed and clicked their coded messages. One—brown, stick-like—hopped up to the fence. The cat pounced and missed. The insect took flight, becoming a larger target. The cat pushed between two of the fence's verticals. The insect had gone. The cat listened again.

Odd. She usually called for him to come inside around this time. His outside errands accomplished—traces of other cats carefully sniffed, his own saliva added on; a bit of careful digging in someone's garden; perhaps the bark of his favourite shrub in the churchyard shredded a bit more—he'd return, and, hidden, wait for her call.

*"Luc, Luc, Luc," it would sound, soft yet clear. And he would make his way back to her, always careful to wait a moment, so that, once she'd caught sight of him, he could run to her the last little bit of the way. She'd bend over, pick him up and cuddle him, say "Ah, mon Luc, mon petit Luc." And he'd begin his mightiest purr, push his head up into the hollow place under her chin and mark her as his own.*

*But tonight, nothing. He sat for a few more moments, grooming his short grey and white fur, then walked up the straight cement path to the front of the building, climbed the one low step and paused to look in either direction along the porch. She was not sitting on any of the comfortable old pieces of furniture arranged there. On the other side of the partition that separated his house from the neighbours', he saw a figure sitting. It shifted its position and something creaked. It wasn't her. She wouldn't be over there.*

*He mewed tentatively at the front door and waited. In the distance he heard the sudden sound of cats fighting, or mating, which was sometimes the same thing. But he resisted the temptation to run and see who it was. After a few seconds, he left the porch and trotted around to the left of the house. Perhaps she was in the back yard where she grew her few vegetables.*

*As he trod the soft grass, he thought he heard "Luc, Luc, Luc" but it was only a mourning dove cooing sleepily to its mate up high on a wire.*

*He rounded the back corner of the house. There she was. But not upright, reaching for him with greedy affectionate fingers. She was on her stomach, her nightgown spread out on the small lawn.*

*He crept up to her face. It was turned sideways, her mouth open. "Luc," he heard. He licked her cheek. Usually, she would laugh and flinch away from its roughness. Not tonight. "Luc," she breathed out. He heard the neighbours' back door open quietly then close. He crouched and waited. Soon she would get up. Soon, surely, everything would be all right.*

# 1

It had been a beautiful wedding. The bride had been radiant, as brides almost always are, in a pale-yellow summer suit and pillbox hat with tiny veil, the colour complementing her dark hair. The groom had been quietly happy; happy and proud, as the bride, accompanied by her much shorter sister dressed in a similar suit and hat of pale green, the two of them beaming from ear to ear, advanced across the lawn towards him.

They hadn't bothered with flowers, except for the bride's bouquet, which she'd cut and fashioned herself early that morning from the assortment that surrounded the wedding party in the garden of The Maples, a more-than-two-hundred-year-old home on the waterfront of that part of the Ottawa River known as The Lake of Two Mountains.

The bride had selected bluebells, large white Shasta daisies and pink bee balm, filling in with sprays of white baby's breath and lavender, finishing with a few red bee balm, sprigs of feverfew's tiny white daisies and light pink marjoram flowers, as well as fern leaves and that feathery elegant grey plant that rejoices in the common name of wormwood.

High summer it had been, the first weekend of August, and the garden had been at its glorious peak. Tiger lilies competed with black-eyed Susans to see which could be the hottest orange. Goldenrod swayed on tall stalks. A dark purple-red phlox, which hadn't been visible the day before the ceremony when people had been busy tidying the edges of flowerbeds and cutting the lawn, had suddenly opened its blooms. Shasta daisy heads floated above and mediated the clash of colours.

A month had passed. Prudence Crick replaced the wedding invitation, already curling from summer's damp, back on the mantelpiece and went to make a cup of tea.

She stood in the kitchen at The Maples and waited for the tea to brew. It was mid-afternoon, a Saturday. The garden bore little resemblance to its previous glory. There was no sign of lilies or daisies, though white and pink phloxes were holding their own. The goldenrod had mostly turned from multiple yellow flowers tightly packed together, to brown fuzz with maybe a bit of yellow at the top. The black-eyed Susans were still a bright eye-catcher. And the little white and larger purple asters were beginning to open. The purple coneflowers had faded to pink but here and there a late bluebell showed its delicate spire. There was glory still but it was softened, muted.

There hadn't been many guests. The bride, in her fifties, had been brought up in Lovering, a small village of five thousand inhabitants on the western side of the river, northwest of Montreal, but had moved away when young, only recently returning. The groom, a quiet man, had lived there all his life; at present he owned the cottage across the street from the much larger property of The Maples.

So, beside their family members, the guests had included only a few of the couple's friends, and that had been a good thing, because after the ceremony in the garden, the reception under the white tent rented for the day having just begun, the heavens had opened, wind driving the rain sideways, and the hostess, The Maples' owner Gerry Coneybear, had invited all twenty-five or so guests into the house, which had been meticulously cleaned by her part-time housekeeper.

Good thing too, Prudence, that same part-time housekeeper, congratulated herself silently, permitting a thin smile as she remembered the giddy crowd, all grabbing whatever food tray or bottle they were nearest to, depositing wet shoes on the back porch of the house and dispersing noisily therein.

Her tea brewed, she poured a cup and took it out onto the back porch, screened on three sides, ivy-covered, and listened to the Saturday sounds of the neighbourhood.

Lawn mowers, inevitably. More cars than usual slowly passed the house as people from other towns toured along the river road to and from the gift and antique shops, cafés and ice cream parlours of Lovering. The cars were audible but not intrusive. The bulk of the old house efficiently blocked their noise.

Insects hummed. Wasps, sensing shortening days, buzzed angrily in and out of holes under the eaves. Spiders likewise spun their last webs and waited, centred, for prey.

Prudence breathed deeply through her nose and then slowly and contentedly out. She sipped her tea. A few sailboats, a few motorboats moved through the view. The sun shone on the dark pine forest on the water's far shore. Her thoughts slipped back to another summer, fourteen years earlier.

Nerve-wracking was how the then owner of The Maples, Maggie Coneybear, had described it. Prudence, not living on the water but a scant mile inland on Station Road above the tracks, heard the same military and police helicopters patrolling the river day and night as Maggie did. Like Maggie, she got used to seeing police cars driving back and forth along the river road and was even waved over one day when she was pedalling her bike to work at Maggie's.

The cops wanted to know who she was, where she lived, and what her purpose was. With a feeling of unreality, she'd told them and then been allowed to continue on her way.

But she hadn't heard and seen the police boats cruising the river in front of The Maples at night, as Maggie had. And as Winnifred Catford, the aged recluse who'd lived next to Maggie, certainly had.

With the inability to sleep at night that often plagues the elderly, Winnifred had, according to Maggie, been outside her house one evening, in her garden, when Maggie had been similarly placed. Maggie'd heard a "Psst!" coming from the thicket between the houses and had jerked her head in surprise, and, it must be confessed, fear, wondering, as she'd told Prudence later, if she was going to see a soldier. There had been talk of camouflaged tanks along the shore, though why they'd have been deployed on this side of the river made no sense.

"Psst!"

Maggie had focused on the small crouching shape. "Yes?"

"What's happening?" the shape had asked in a voice raspy from disuse.

"The government is fighting with the Mohawk."

The figure had paused then asked, "Why?"

Maggie had snorted. "Something about a golf course being built on sacred land."

"Oh." The figure had added, "Thank you," before retreating back to its house.

Maggie later confided to Prudence that, if she hadn't been so astonished by speaking to the woman, to whom both she and Prudence were distantly related, she would have tried to establish a rapport. "She must not have a television or radio, the poor old thing," Maggie had said.

Prudence had shaken her head in sympathy and wished she could do something for Winnifred. What, she hadn't been exactly sure, and to her regret, she had ultimately done nothing.

"Now what made my memory go down that road?" she queried Mother, the large marmalade long-haired tabby cat who'd followed her out onto the porch to sit, sphinx-like, on the grey painted floor.

Mother blinked inscrutably (like the incarnation of the goddess Bastet that she was) then, her attention caught by buzzing, got up and walked over to where a wasp was brushing against the outside of the screen. She sat and followed the wasp's futile pushing with her head.

Prudence closed her eyes with a sigh. It was good to rest. She should rest more. She was going to be fifty-six this October. October sixteenth. Her body was starting to resent stirring from its bed early every morning. She was even starting to skimp on the thoroughness with which she cleaned the homes of her clients. After twenty-five years, her heart was no longer in it. And now when she lost a client, she didn't bother looking for a replacement. She was down to two: Gerry, who'd inherited The Maples more than a year ago when her aunt Maggie had died (The Maples *and* its twenty feline residents who'd been Maggie's companions); and Edwina Murray, who'd inherited the house next door from Winnifred Catford just last winter. Gerry needed Prudence two or three days a week but Edwina only required her services once every two weeks. Since her husband had died, she'd been doing little entertaining.

Dead husbands. There'd been a rash of them in Lovering in the last year. Prudence could think of three immediately, numbered her own long-estranged one among them. That drug dealer who'd been killed in the house next door just before Edwina had moved in. He'd been someone's husband. Geoff Petherbridge, dead by suicide last fall, made the third.

She sighed. So unnecessary, that death. And yet perhaps he'd seen his death as a release: his wife had so disappointed him; his daughter had so sickened him. After all, it wasn't as if he could ever have pardoned what his daughter had done.

And now his son Andrew is married. To Markie. Markie Stribling. She smiled, remembering the marvellous food at the wedding feast. Cathy, Markie's sister, was a caterer and owner of the nearby Fieldcrest Bed and Breakfast, and if she had not exactly made everything, had certainly supervised its preparation and presentation. Except for the cake it had all been finger food, lovely little creations one could pop in one's mouth in one bite. The cake had been a gorgeous yet simple three-tiered chocolate one with vanilla buttercream frosting.

And the music had been fun. Gerry's boyfriend, Doug Shapland, had found a jug band—a violin, bass fiddle, drummer, and yes, jug player who doubled as guitarist—to keep the guests dancing and cheerful. Once it began raining, the band had set themselves up in the large foyer at the centre of The Maples where guests had supplied them with food and drinks as the evening unwound. It had been wonderful.

Markie and Andrew must have had a wonderful honeymoon too, she thought. A Mediterranean cruise for ten days followed by a further two weeks driving around Italy, sampling wine and food and soaking up the scenery.

Not that she knew any of the details; only that they'd returned to Andrew's cottage across the road a few days previously. They'd need time to sort themselves out in their new life together. Andrew and Markie—who'd have thought?

"Well, Mother, is it cat feeding time?" Mother, who'd resumed dozing, opened one eye as if to say "Lady, it's *always* cat feeding time," yawned, stretched and followed Prudence back into the house.

As they moved towards the kitchen, they added various members of The Maples' feline community to their procession. Three grey tiger-striped cats and a smaller thin white shorthair dashed ahead down the hallway that led from the porch to the foyer. In the formal dining room two giant black and white "cow" cats jumped with thuds from two of the chairs around the huge (it could seat twenty) table. Others could be heard coming downstairs.

Prudence marched through the living room into the small kitchen, slamming its door in the face of the top cat who led the pack—a black and white tuxedo who rejoiced in the suitable if undignified moniker of Bob.

Automatically, Prudence prepared the saucers of canned meat and topped up the tub of kibble. Odd that Markie had just married, she idly thought, as she set the saucers on the floor. She and Prudence were the same age. Markie had waited until middle, late middle, age, whereas Prudence had married young. And Prudence's marriage to Alexander Crick had blown up after a couple of years. She'd never had the heart or stomach to do it again. Never even divorced him, not officially, kept his name as a talisman to ward off other men perhaps.

She opened the door and the savage beasts, who'd been encouraging her in her labours by mewing and scratching, but who she didn't even notice anymore, streamed in, tails high. An odour of fish permeated the room. Prudence smiled at their pleasure and left them to it.

They'd behaved fine at the wedding. No one had tripped over one of them. No cat had snagged a smart pair of trousers or shredded stockings. There had been no hairballs upchucked at just the wrong moment. The shy ones had retreated while the extroverts enjoyed themselves. Kind of like humans, she ruminated.

This is where Gerry, if she were here, would notice my pensive face, and ask me what I'm thinking about. And I'd tell her about the cats at the wedding but not about Alex and me. And then Gerry would pause before ever so casually bringing up Bertie.

Bertie was Bertie Smith, an antiques dealer Prudence had met a scant four or five months earlier. Since then, they'd spent some time together, mostly in Montreal where he lived. Neither of them had a car and, really, while there wasn't much one could do in Lovering without one, unless one was prepared to ride a bike, in Montreal, the lack of a car didn't matter.

And so, her inner voice prompted, what would you tell the ever-inquisitive Miss Gerry about Bertie? Would you tell her he was planning on shutting his shop and taking a couple of weeks off work? And that he was planning on spending them in Lovering? In order to see Prudence? And that his sidekick, Marion Stewart, who'd been to school with Gerry's grandmother and was old enough to be Bertie or Prudence's mother, was coming too? And that all of this had you in quite a flutter?

They'd be staying at Fieldcrest with Cathy, just across and down the street from where Prudence was housesitting at The Maples. Actually, it was kind of amazing that she'd been able to keep the fact of Bertie and Marion's visit a secret from Gerry; Cathy was a notorious gossip.

Prudence hoped her surprise would be ready by the time her friends arrived for their vacation. She smiled. It should be an interesting two weeks. Not that she thought of Bertie as anything more than a friend. No. Meanwhile—

She removed the hairy towels that covered most of the upholstered furniture in the house and replaced them with clean ones before doing a laundry. She'd usually do laundry in the morning on one of the days she cleaned for Gerry. Then she'd vacuum, eat lunch, vacuum some more, wash the kitchen floor and clean the two bathrooms.

But now she was in residence while Gerry was away, her schedule had slipped, and she found herself doing a little work here, a little there, most days. Hadn't she found herself dusting after supper last night? More out of boredom than any real need.

Saturday night and doing laundry, she mused. Well, why not? She switched on the TV.

Later, and most uncharacteristically, she went into the kitchen, made a simple sandwich for her supper and didn't do the dishes. The sight of them depressed her. She just filled the sink with soapy water and left her own and the cats' plates to soak overnight. As the water ran she looked out the window at Gerry's car, a cute red and white Austin Mini, parked between the house and the shed. A brown leaf slowly drifted down and, out of nowhere, the thin white cat named Ronald skittered after it. Dead leaves falling. But it was still summer, wasn't it? Rather drearily, she went to bed.

# 2

Hi, Prue!

We made it! Gosh, the flight was long. It didn't help that it was overnight too. So tired the next day, which is today! We got in around 8:30 a.m. and gave up on our idea of taking the slow train down the coast from Dublin to Kinsale—I just wanted to sleep—so bought two plane tickets instead. The tiniest passenger plane in the world—like they shrunk a bigger one down ninety percent! I felt like an old-style movie actress, walking from the air terminal out onto the tarmac to the plane. We went up a rickety little stepladder to get into it. When we landed in Cork we took a half-hour taxi ride to our B&B. The taxi driver wanted to know if we would like to buy his house!

Anyway, we conked out as soon as we arrived. Kinsale is lovely and our hostess is kind. Fed us and let us go to sleep.

We were outside before, enjoying the harbour and sea wall, and now in an internet café, and then we'll look for somewhere for supper. (Lunch? What time is it?) Our B&B is in upper Kinsale. I expect I'll be puffing on the climb back up the hill. But we have a view of the sea from our bedroom window!

I'm so hungry all the time! Thank goodness I'm not nauseous anymore. The ham here is fantastic—there was some at brunch. And the bread is good too. I'll finish up now. Doug wants to use the computer for a quick message to the boys and doesn't want to spend another euro for an extra fifteen minutes. Tomorrow we hire a car and really start exploring! Will write more soon. Lots of love to you and the cats.

Gerry

Prudence switched off the computer in Gerry's studio. They'd flown out Friday night. Ireland was, what? five hours ahead? so now it was three in the afternoon. And that had been typed yesterday on Saturday, so now today they must be off in their rented car seeing the sights.

She replied briefly, just to tell of Andrew and Markie's return from their trip and some of the cats' doings. As she dressed for church she wondered again why the wedding hadn't been a double one.

Doug and Gerry were obviously in love. Gerry was five months pregnant. Why wouldn't they get married? Then she paused, remembering her own reluctance to re-engage emotionally after her personal fiasco so long ago. Maybe Gerry was willing but Doug —?

Long divorced, his wife criminally insane, and he still responsible for his three almost adult sons, maybe he was afraid to experiment again, to change his life.

Prudence tilted the cheval glass. She was using Maggie's room at the back of the house. Maggie, who had been her greatest friend in the world. She stepped back from the mirror, checking her appearance. Grey dress pants, white short-sleeved shirt with lace collar, black sweater. She frowned. Was she satisfied to look like this for the rest of her life?

She removed the black sweater and replaced it with a light beige jacket. After all, she wasn't going to a funeral.

She let herself out the side entrance of the kitchen and walked briskly up the slight rise in the road that led to the little stone church of St. Anne's, three minutes away. The call-to-worship bell was ringing as she slipped into a back pew.

It was a morning prayer service, which was a relief. Something in Prudence's puritanical soul always felt a bit uncomfortable during Communion. All that sinning and confessing, guilt and forgiveness; and then the public loitering in line as one advanced self-consciously toward the altar rail. And how was one supposed to look afterwards? Divine? She always felt faintly sheepish.

No, she thought, give me a good old service of praise and thanksgiving anytime, and reached for the hymn book.

She knew almost everyone in the sparse congregation, was related to many of them. There were the two Shapland sisters, Jane and Bette, quite a bit older than she, who were her cousins on her father's side. They would be Doug Shapland's aunts, named for movie stars, she'd always thought. She wondered if Doug was at all close to his extended family, his parents being dead.

There were many members of the large clan that was the Parsleys. Prudence's mother, Constance, had been one before she'd married Edward Catford. Catfords and Parsleys and Coneybears and Shaplands had been intermarrying for almost two hundred years since their ancestors had emigrated from Devon, England. And Petherbridges and Muxworthys, she added, seeing all these names on brass memorial plaques on the church walls.

There was one person she was happy not to see at the service—Mary Petherbridge, née Coneybear, another cousin from her father's side, and Gerry Coneybear's last remaining aunt. Though Prudence and Mary had managed a truce of a kind the last time they'd been together, it had been more for the sake of Gerry, who'd engineered the meeting, than from any true sense of reconciliation. They'd avoided each other at Andrew and Markie's wedding. You can't do away with half a century of enmity, Prudence grimly concluded.

Besides, Mary wouldn't be worshipping at the "poor" church in the "poor" end of town. She'd be at the other end of Lovering at St. Martin's, which was near the large country club she belonged to, near the luxurious house her husband Geoff had provided for her.

Not the place to be having such thoughts, Prudence reminded herself as the sermon concluded and the congregation rose for the offertory hymn. It was only when she was unlocking the door back at The Maples that she realized she had forgotten to visit her mother's grave.

It has been twelve years, she argued with herself, feeling guilty. Not that her mother was actually buried at St. Anne's. No. Prudence's mother's ashes reposed in an urn at her own home. But her name was inscribed on a plaque on the memorial wall at the back of the tiny graveyard. And Prudence usually visited it.

She cleaned the cat boxes—seven of them lined up in the downstairs bathroom—checked the level of kibble in the kitchen tub, and again left the house. She cut a few black-eyed Susans from the garden and put them in her bike's basket.

The ride to Lovering proper, where the shops and restaurants, the grocery and hardware stores clustered, took fifteen minutes. As it was a lovely Sunday afternoon, traffic was moderately heavy. There'd be no cars for a few minutes, then a steady stream would attempt to pass her on the winding narrow road.

Bicyclists dressed in shiny bright spandex suits whizzed past her. Prudence kept pedalling serenely on. She reached Mackenzie Avenue and turned left, continuing to a pleasant-looking narrow Victorian house painted blue with white trim. A low hedge of neatly trimmed honeysuckle shrubs stood in for a front fence. She left her bike in the narrow driveway, parked behind the compact car.

Her friend Lucy Hanlan was rocking on her porch and got up when she saw Prudence. "I hope you're hungry, 'cause I made lots. Come in!"

"Starved," was the terse response, accompanied by a smile. "These are for you." She handed Lucy the little bouquet of flowers.

"Oh, thank you, Prudence. They're sweet."

"There's not much left at this time of year," Prudence apologized.

Lucy dished out homemade mac'n'cheese and salad. "There's blueberry lemon pound cake for dessert, so save room."

"Thank you for going to the trouble. I haven't felt much like cooking lately. Or baking."

Lucy shot her friend a worried glance. "That's not like you, Prudence. Are you eating?"

"Oh, I'm eating. I'm just not fussy what. I'm tired, I guess. I'm just tired."

"You *are* a perfectionist, you know, and that must be exhausting. I wouldn't know. I've never been one."

Prudence looked around the tidy kitchen. "You keep a clean house. You don't let clutter pile up. You made this nice meal."

"Yee-es," Lucy said grudgingly. "But when I get busy with my costumes, on top of work, well, I've been known to heat up a TV dinner or open a can of something." Lucy, a seamstress, owned Lovering's little fabric store and volunteered to make or alter many of the costumes required by Lovering's various amateur dramatic societies.

"I had a sandwich for supper last night," Prudence said dreamily, "and I don't even remember what kind."

Lucy gave her friend a hard look before clearing their plates and putting on the kettle. "Well, it's good you came here today for a proper meal." She changed the subject. "We had a bit of a fuss this morning on the street."

"Oh?"

"Well, it must have happened last night but they found her this morning. One of my neighbours died, I think. Another neighbour found her. Poor thing."

"Who? The neighbour who found her?"

"What? No. *She's* as sour as vinegar, if it's the neighbour I think it is. Madame Ménard is the poor thing. Found in her backyard. Someone at church told me. Very sad."

"*Is* she dead?" Prudence asked.

"I'm not sure. Well, probably. That is, I didn't hear an ambulance siren at any point. She was just lying there apparently. On the back lawn. With her cat." Lucy shivered and Prudence put out a comforting hand. There's always a cat, she thought.

"Well," Lucy said with a haunted look in her eyes. "It's what we're afraid of, isn't it? All us old ladies who live alone? Keeling over and no one but the cat around to help, or rather, not help. At least a dog might bark and be heard if you were outside."

"First of all, you're not old." Lucy was approximately the same age as she was. "Second, you don't have a cat to not bark for help." Lucy smiled. Prudence continued, "Third, let's take our tea outside and enjoy the mild weather while we can."

They walked down the house's long hallway to the front porch and sat. "Good cake," Prudence complimented.

"Thanks." Lucy craned her neck forward and to the right. "That's Mme Ménard's house, the little white one on the left—of the two attached ones."

Attached houses were rare in Lovering. Prudence looked down the street at the two little cottages side by side. "They're quite cute."

Lucy, who knew a lot of the area's history, and who was descended from Irish workers who'd arrived a hundred and fifty years previously, nodded. "Probably originally for servants or labourers. See how low to the ground they are? No basement. Not even a crawl space. Just big stones with timbers laid on top for a foundation. Actually, they're sinking. Mme Ménard was worried about that. She said the linoleum floors had big cracks in them and you can see where the roofline sags. Well, not from here, you can't. Subsidence. She didn't have the money to fix it. Ah, well, her worries are over now."

"Did you know her well?"

"Just as a neighbour. You know, to chat with when one of us walked past the other's house. Or at the store. And I'd see her at St. Pete's." St. Peter's was the Catholic church around the corner from Lucy's house. They could see its silver spire from where they sat.

"I see." Prudence paused. "What about the cat?"

"The cat?"

"Mme Ménard's cat. The cat that was sitting with her when she—died."

"*I* don't know. Perhaps the neighbour—no, she's too mean. Perhaps one of the other neighbours—"

"*You're* one of the other neighbours," Prudence reminded her. Then she added, knowing Lucy's good heart, "It would be a kindness. It must be scared."

Lucy sighed. "Oh, all right. You and your cats." They rose, put away the tea things and walked down the street. They're not *my* cats, Prudence thought. They're Gerry's.

As they drew near Mme Ménard's home, the building's shabbiness became apparent. Paint flaked off the walls. The tin roof was rusty, and one of the eavestroughs had become slightly separated from its neighbour, hanging down on an angle right above the front step, presumably, on a rainy day, sending a cascade of water down onto anyone unfortunate enough to pass under.

The friends paused outside the gate where the over-long grass pushed through the fence. The fence's wrought iron, which had once been painted white, and which sported a proud *fleur-de-lys* atop each second vertical, was also rusty and flaking. "I don't see it," Lucy said.

"It's probably nearby. This is its home. It may be hiding," Prudence replied. "What's its name?"

"*I* don't know! We were neighbours, not friends."

"All right. Don't get testy. You say Mme Ménard didn't get on with her neighbour?" Prudence jerked her head to the right, where the twin of Mme Ménard's house stood, in somewhat better condition. Its paint was not flaking, nor was its roof rusty, and its lawn was short and neatly trimmed. Its roofline still sagged however, and, Prudence supposed, inside it might have the cracks in floor and wall which indicated the ground's sinking.

But where the house on the left was cheerful with a few pots of pink geraniums near the porch, ceramic bunnies on the lawn, a bird feeder on a pole and a concrete birdbath, the yard of the house on the right was sterile. On the porch's freshly painted grey wooden floor stood two straight-backed kitchen chairs either side of the front door. "No soul," Prudence muttered as Lucy replied to her query.

"*Nobody* gets along with *her*." Lucy snorted. "She obviously wants to be left alone and we are happy to comply."

"That's sad," Prudence commented. "For her, I mean."

"She has her son. They stick together." Lucy looked around. "I don't see the cat."

"What does he look like?"

"Uh, black and white, I think. Maybe grey and white. I've never really paid him much attention." Like Mme Ménard, Prudence thought, but didn't say. Lucy continued, "He patrols the street, sits under my honeysuckles sometimes."

Prudence called the cat. "Puss, Puss, Puss," and sucked her lips.

"Come on, Prudence. It's not around. I promise I'll keep a lookout for it, make sure it's not starving. Let's go home and have another cup of tea. Did you know the Gilbert and Sullivan Society is doing *The Mikado* this year? You can imagine the lovely fabrics we'll need. I've got some costume designs to show you."

And so, distracted by their discussion of Lucy's activities, the women failed to notice the grey and white cat on the porch, peeping from under a distressed leather armchair. Once they'd gone, he crept out and scratched timidly at the front door, uttering a few mews. When nothing happened, he returned underneath the chair.

It was after four when Prudence got back from Lucy's. Usually, she prepared the cats' twenty individual dishes alone, then admitted them to the feast. Today, not really paying attention, she let them stay in the kitchen with her.

This was a mistake. They swarmed her, jumping on the counter as she spooned a bit of food onto a plate, then enveloping the plate when she put it down. Finally, after one dropped and broken plate and one pair of claws (she didn't know whose but suspected one of the three tiger-striped boys) clasping on to her calf (even through pants, it hurt), she gave up and just whacked two large cans of food onto two large plates and let them have at it.

"It's going to be a long month," she said through clenched teeth and went to clean the litter boxes. By the time she'd finished the first two, customers had started queuing up. She worked as fast as she could, filling up two shopping bags with ordure, spraying a big blast of air freshener into the room and retreating outside.

She dumped the bags into the garbage and went back into the kitchen to wash her hands. The two large plates had been licked clean. She washed them, thinking, why didn't I do that years ago? Much easier than washing twenty individual ones. Twenty plates had been Maggie's method when Prudence came to work for her. "Sheesh!" she said, suddenly sick of all the cleaning and washing, the tidying she'd done. Taking a basket from the counter, she went out to the garden. "Got to get the stink of cat food and cat poop out of my nostrils," she muttered. Walking over to the vegetable garden, she inhaled the good clean air. What would be left for her to pick at this time of year?

Lots of tomatoes, both cherry and full size; a few green beans; the travelling onions had made some new little plants with fresh green shoots. She looked doubtfully at Gerry's hot pepper plants, laden with green and red jalapeños. No. She'd cook an omelet for her supper. She pinched off a few of the onion greens, one from each plant, and a handful of basil. Nice. With the beans and tomatoes on the side, bread and butter.

As she straightened, she remembered the garden her family had had when she was a child and teenager. Their house had been perched almost all the way up the big hill of Side Road, which led from Lovering to the highway, the new highway, the Trans-Canada. That hadn't been there when she'd been young. In those days the two-lane highway between Montreal and Ottawa was down at the bottom of the hill, between her home and Lovering.

She'd been isolated as a child, cut off. Theirs was one of a few farms up and down Side Road, each with a lot of space between it and the next. So her closest companions had been her parents.

She walked back to the house and sat on the steps, her chin in her hands, and stared at the lake. Various felines pushed through the cat flap behind her. She let them go about their business and they accorded her the same courtesy.

Up until she turned fourteen, she'd been closest to her father. Edward—Ted—Catford was a big quiet man. He farmed a few sheep, a herd of dairy cattle. An apple orchard's trees marched down the slope behind the house. Bees hummed in and out of their white boxes beneath the blooms.

There were chickens and ducks and geese for eggs, and in the autumn half the fowl would be slaughtered to go into the deep freeze in the old house's cement-floored basement. People from Lovering used to drive up to the Catford farm for fresh eggs in the summer, or for poultry in the fall.

And the garden. Row after row of potatoes, carrots, turnips. Tomatoes—people didn't grow their own peppers back then, and

Prudence doubted if either of her parents ever tasted an eggplant. They ate cabbage though, and her mother made sauerkraut that lasted all winter.

She also made jam. From all the berries, one by one, as they appeared. To Prudence as a child, summer was marked off not by months but by fruit seasons. Rhubarb in May, gooseberries and currants in June, also strawberries. Then blueberries, raspberries. And in autumn, apple or pear butter, peach preserves. For six months, their house smelled of sweet fruit, cooling.

Not that at first she was allowed to help make the jam. She was sent out to pick the fruit, and she topped and tailed many a gooseberry or peeled apples. Her mother was very particular and liked to oversee the jam-making and conserving herself. So she would say to young Prudence, "Go find your father," as she readied her jars, put her great cauldrons of fruit and sugar on to boil.

And off Prudence would skip, glad to be released from her mother's strict methodologies, glad to go from inside the house to outside, and bask in her father's genuine pleasure in her company.

She fed the chickens and gathered eggs. Well, they trusted her to do that alone. With her father she washed the dairy cattle's udders and applied and removed the automatic milking machines that saved so much time. He let her ride with him up on the tractor and later drive it while he followed behind, throwing bales of hay up onto the flat trailer.

She also took her turn walking and tossing the hay and straw for the animals to eat and bed down on in winter and grew into a wiry teenager. Her father called her "his big strong girl" though she never exceeded medium height.

They mulched strawberry plants together, using the animals' rotted manure. They pruned gooseberry and currant shrubs and burnt the raspberry canes down to the ground every two years to control pests. Her mother helped with this, as they had to stand at the sides of the raspberry patch with brooms and rakes to control the fire. She doubted that sort of thing would be allowed nowadays.

And so Prudence had no time to really dwell on the fact that when other teenagers in Lovering were swimming in the lake or playing tennis, she was learning how to be a farmer. "I should have been one," she said, standing and stretching. And went inside to make her supper.

# 3

Monday morning Prudence checked the computer in vain for a message from Gerry. They must be living in the moment, she thought, enjoying the different sights, sounds, tastes and smells. She didn't think of sending her own message. What was there to say? That she'd gone to church, had lunch with an old friend; that an old lady neither she nor Gerry knew had died? She decided to bike over to her own house.

The temperature had cooled overnight so she wore a sweater under her jacket. The sky was overcast as she pedalled along the river road in the opposite direction from yesterday, away from "downtown" Lovering.

Monday. Labour Day. The road was quieter than usual—no one heading off to work. No school buses. But the traffic, if you could call it such, would, she knew, pick up later as people visited each other; or tourists, fresh from their ride across the river on the ferry, streamed into Lovering.

So for now she enjoyed the quietness. A small flock of geese flew low overhead and landed on the water to her left. They would fly in from the north for months, massing in ever larger groups until they decided it was time to leave, fly south for the winter. Perhaps they used the Ottawa River as a guide.

The great blue herons that stalked the shallows of the lake seemed to already be gone. She wondered where they migrated as she puffed up the steep hill just past the Parsley Inn. Her head down from the effort, she didn't see the pickup truck coming out of the driveway of the old stone house that was being renovated. Its driver saw her though, and braked just as she crested the hill. She nodded at the familiar face, kept pedalling. Those who were self-employed, like that contractor, like Prudence, worked when they needed to, holidays included.

She approached the little ferry landing and heard, hitting the dock, the double crash of the two boards used for cars to drive on and off. She turned right just as she caught a glimpse of the docked ferry itself and pedalled up Station Road.

She passed the property that flooded every spring when the stream that ran behind the house overflowed its banks as meltwater hurried to the lake. She passed the yard where a previous owner had lovingly planted masses of daffodils every fall, weeding around them in spring so their yellow popped into eyes weary of snow; the daffodils that now, years later, the owner dead, the garden neglected, grew, barely peeking above the weeds in spring. But still there. Yes, still there.

She passed the place where the railway station had been before it and its platform had been torn down and replaced with— nothing. She had a sepia-tinted photo of the building in a frame at her house. The photo reminded her that things remembered almost always seemed larger than they'd been.

The station had been a brown hut. Its peaked tiled roof had a wide overhang, so, on all four sides, it offered shelter from rain and snow. And it was snowing in Prudence's photo. The snow made the sky and fields and parking lot, the platform, even the tracks, blend so the brown wooden hut was the only thing one noticed. The snowflakes closest to the camera assumed a larger-than-life-sized dimension, one blurring as it melted on the lens at the moment the photographer snapped. She wondered who he or she had been.

Could it really be that she remembered standing, a toddler, hand clasped in her mother's, on the platform as a steam engine chugged terrifyingly to a stop? She remembered the churning noise, the squishy sound of its brakes, the hiss of air escaping. Were there steam engines still plying the line between Montreal and Lovering in the 1950s? Or was it a fanciful projection; something she'd read about or seen on TV? As a child she'd picked up coal on the tracks...

They'd only left Lovering for Montreal to go to the dentist. Prudence remembered those expeditions with terror and fondness. Terror, as the dentist didn't use anaesthetic when he drilled; fondness because the reward for bravery was chocolate-iced doughnuts, unattainable in the country.

Now Lovering was down from three train stations, necessary back in the days when people walked to the train to get to their jobs in Montreal, to just the one, at the centre of the town, the one Prudence and her mother would have used, nearest to their farm, and far from Station Road. And the service was down from multiple trains all day to a few in the morning out of town and a few in the afternoon and evening back.

She passed the bungalow where the drunken neighbours lived, its grass unkempt, curtains drawn; another large and turreted house that had never been fully finished in thirty years; the house that sported a raven mounted on its mailbox, the owner's name painted in flowing black script.

Everybody is so different, she thought, the one from the other, but they mostly all want the same thing—to be left in peace.

She passed the house where Mrs. Worth had lived, knitting and crocheting dolls' clothes to give to neighbour children or donate to church sales. Mrs. Worth, who had befriended her mother in her trouble after her husband had died, who had been so kind to Prudence all those years ago.

She drew a deep breath as she pulled into her own driveway. Her bike tires crunched familiarly on the gravel. She was home.

A neat white cottage where she'd lived for the last twenty-five or so years. When her marriage ended her romantic life ended. Besides, with her father dead, her mother needed her.

The builders had done a good job. She wouldn't have known which half of the house had been damaged by a falling tree last winter if it weren't for the slightly brighter colours of the roof tiles on the right.

She stepped onto the grass and poked the soil in one of the two window boxes. Dry. The salmon-pink geraniums and variegated ivy still looked fine. She made a mental note to water them before she left.

Her hand shook slightly as she unlocked the door and stepped into the tiny vestibule. It must be the effect of the bike ride, she thought, of that hill, of almost being hit by that truck. She wiped her feet, hung her jacket on a hook, then opened the inner door.

A four-room cottage, its central hall opened on the left into the living room. There was her apricot sofa facing the small television set, her light green wing chair where she liked to read, with its mahogany footrest with the embroidered top, the walls of the room painted cream to highlight the northern light that calmly entered through the sheer curtains of the room's one picture window. There were recessed bookcases in the two far corners. Sugar, she remembered. The paint colour was called sugar.

I have been looking out almost my whole life, she thought, observing the window. I have been silent, in here, all my adult life, watching other people for clues on how to live.

She shook herself and went into the kitchen, a pleasant cheerful butter-yellow room; its ell-shaped counter with cupboards overhead; its little table by its one window; the back door at the far end. She put the kettle on and walked back into the hall, stood irresolutely, then entered her bedroom, the one at the back of the house. Originally her parents', then her mother's, it was slightly larger than the front room, so after her mother's death Prudence had taken it for her own— after a decent interval during which she'd methodically sorted her mother's things into the usual three piles—keep, donate, toss—then scrubbed and painted the room a pale sage green.

She wondered who would go through the house of Lucy's dead neighbour.

She found the few things she needed (Gerry had driven over the previous week and they'd loaded the car with Prudence's clothes and toiletries, enough for a month) then walked back into the hall.

Thinking to air the spare bedroom, she opened its door. Really, the room was superfluous to her needs. She kept a single bed there, neatly made up, though it had never been used, and a desk and chair where she did her modest accounts.

She thought of the two-room apartment over the paint shop she'd shared so briefly with her husband, now dead. That would have been enough space if she'd been alone. Kitchen along one wall, a table, chairs, a couch, TV. But when his friends arrived to drink and smoke, the apartment had seemed claustrophobic and often Prudence had retreated to the small bedroom to read or try to sleep. She thought of the time when she'd been so ill—then remonstrated with herself. Better not go there.

Back in the hall she went to the narrow table where she kept the phone and answering machine. A red light blinked silently. She pressed play and listened.

"Hi, Prudence. Bertie here." She heard the familiar sniff and smiled—Bertie suffered from allergies. "Anyway, it's Friday afternoon. I guess you're already cat-sitting at Gerry's." Sniff. "I'll call you there next week to talk about when Marion and I arrive." There was a pause then he added, first clearing his throat, "I, er, miss you, dear. You know—" She waited but he must have decided to save the thought for he continued with, "Anyway, I'll—we'll—see you soon. On Saturday. All right. Take care. Bye." Click.

Before she could process how she felt about this call, the next one began. More throat-clearing before a different male voice began. "Ah, Mrs. Crick, yes. Well, your purchase has gone through and will be ready on Tuesday this week. If you'd care to pick it up. Thank you."

That was it. The machine had finished. The kettle whistled. Prudence went to make a cup of tea. While it brewed, she carried a watering can to the front of the house and tended her flowers. On the north side of the house, they didn't dry out *too* quickly.

She carried her mug across the road to Rita's. Rita would be in. Rita was almost always in except for Thursday nights when she got her husband Charlie to drive her to the IGA for the weekly shop and they ate at Lovering's family restaurant, Johnny's. Rita liked to say, "Thursday night in Lovering. That's enough excitement for me." The couple was retired and loving it.

Prudence walked down the short driveway, edged with terracotta tiles stuck into the dirt either side. She no longer noticed the numerous garden ornaments: the one shabby plastic pink flamingo tilting unnaturally; the faux rabbits, squirrels, posed, here under a sun-burnt hosta, there next to one of the miniature garden lanterns. The driveway was free of Charlie's old blue pickup and the door to the ramshackle red garage that served as his workshop was closed. If he'd been home, it would have been open. She knocked at the house's side door and waited.

"Happy Labour Day," Rita said through the screen, holding up floury hands. "Come in."

Prudence let herself in to the kitchen. The little transistor radio blared a phone-in talk show from the table. Rita thumped her bread dough. Rita always made bread on Monday morning.

Prudence sat down at the table with a sigh, leaning to turn the radio's volume down. "Charlie out?"

Rita half turned and said, "Yep. Gone to see his cronies," then tossed her head and pulled down her mouth. "As usual." There was a pause.

Prudence sipped her tea. "Bread?" she asked.

"Rolls, I think. For a change."

Prudence nodded and let her gaze travel around the kitchen's clutter. Several sets of matching storage containers—three stainless steel, three brown pottery jugs, three shaped like vegetables, all in graduated sizes—were ranged along the countertops. (Prudence knew other trios were hidden in cupboards. Rita was something of a collector.) A large ceramic tomato was open near where Rita's hands worked the dough. She reached in for more flour, flung it expertly on the counter.

Small cooking appliances competed for space with the containers: a grinder, various blenders, a mixer, a Crock-Pot and even a deli-grade meat slicer. A bird clock sounded ten o'clock—a blue jay's screech filled the kitchen. Gaily, Rita, as Prudence knew she would, said "Blue jay o'clock!" Her voice mimicked the bird's cry.

On the radio show the topic was the terrible rush hour traffic in and out of Montreal. People mostly phoned in to complain. "It took me fifty minutes to drive from my home in St. Paul to the General—" (The General was the Montreal General Hospital.) "—to visit my mother Sunday morning. Fifty minutes! Do you know how long it took on Monday morning?" "Two hours?" the host guessed. "Two hours!" the angry listener confirmed. "And the hospital parking was full so I had to find a spot on a side street fifteen minutes' walk away!" It went on and on.

Prudence tuned it out. "You busy tomorrow? Charlie busy?"

Rita half-turned, still thumping away at the dough. "Eh? Busy? I don't think so. Why?"

"I need a ride," Prudence stated. "Maybe the last one from you ever." She smiled at Rita. "To the car dealer."

"Oh, Prudence! You bought a car! You passed your test and bought a car!"

Prudence nodded, smiling. "Did my practical in Gerry's car last week." She didn't add that before the test she'd almost thrown up.

"Well, congratulations! Now you'll be able to buzz all over the place. It'll be good for you." This from someone who didn't drive and rarely "buzzed" anywhere.

Prudence nodded again, if a trifle uncertainly. Just where exactly would she go in her new car? She cleared her throat, then spoke, thinking aloud. "I figure I'll use it more in winter, for work and shopping. I'd still like to bike in the other seasons. Biking's good exercise and you see things you miss from a car. Especially when you're driving."

Rita, who didn't drive, turned to face Prudence and nodded. "I know. When I say 'Oh, Charlie, look at that funny whatever-it-is', he always misses it. 'Gotta keep my eyes on the road,' he says."

"And a good thing, too," Prudence responded primly.

Rita smiled fondly at her friend. She wished Prudence would loosen up a bit, get *on* with things. Like that Bertie fella. But she knew better than to ask about him directly.

She put the dough in a large metal bowl and covered it with plastic wrap. "There!" She washed her hands, poured herself the last inch of old coffee from the drip machine's carafe and plunked herself at the table. "Now, tell me all about this car."

When Charlie came back from the Lovering coffee shop where he preferred to take his morning coffee with the men he'd known for most of his sixty-five years, he found the women deep in discussion. "Any coffee left?" he boomed.

"You can see there isn't," Rita snapped.

"Eh?" He reached between the two women to increase the volume of the radio.

Rita leaned toward Prudence and whispered, "Selective hearing." Prudence smothered a smile.

The radio callers-in were now complaining about the bridge that connected the island of Montreal with the mainland to its west, where Lovering was. "…going to collapse one morning with me on it! All those heavy trucks! I don't know why we pay—"

Charlie sat down heavily at the table. "Make us a coffee, eh, Reet?" he wheedled.

Rita clucked her tongue as she got up to comply. As she worked she threw little snippets of conversation over her shoulder at Prudence. Charlie, who was genuinely hard of hearing, would say "what?" or "eh?" and Prudence would repeat what Rita or she had said. This pattern of communication was so familiar to all three that they hardly noticed it anymore.

Rita brought Charlie his cup of coffee and loudly informed him "Prudence wants a ride tomorrow morning, Charlie, 'round this time. Okay?"

Charlie blew on his beverage and nodded. "Okay. Don't have to shout." Rita and Prudence exchanged a look. "Where to?" There ensued a repetition of the conversation Prudence had just had with Rita, but more detailed. What kind of car? What year? What was the mileage? When Prudence had satisfied Charlie as far as she could, he nodded and got up. "Going to the workshop."

Prudence also rose. "I should be going too. My library books are due." As she and Charlie left the kitchen she heard the radio's volume diminish.

Marriage is certainly a mystery, she reflected as she let herself in to her quiet, well-ordered house. Those two have managed to rub along together for nearly fifty years. Why couldn't I?

She had lots of time before the library opened. Oh. Today was a holiday. It wouldn't *be* open. She checked her library card in the back pocket of one of the books stacked on the phone table. Huh. Tomorrow's date. Her sense of routine outraged—she always went to the library Mondays between 2:30 and 5:00—she muttered her dissatisfaction. Tuesdays, the library, run by volunteers, only opened at seven in the evening, until nine. She didn't fancy riding her bike on the road in the evening. Then she remembered, and a slow smile spread across her face. Tomorrow she could *drive* to the library.

She picked up the books and looked around the living room. There was nothing to do here. It was strange, living between two houses. Unsettling. Oh, well, she thought, the cats need me.

# 4

Dear Prudence,

Hey! How are you? Did you get your car yet? Knowing you, you'll take your time and buy the perfect most *sensible* best-maintained car ever.

It's evening here, Tuesday, and the landlady of the B&B, whose name is Benny, short for Berenice or something, is letting us use her computer. I am so tired. I didn't think jet lag was a real thing but it is. I go along and go along, looking at Ireland from the rented car's windows, then all of a sudden (so Doug says) there's a silence, he looks over and I'm asleep. Then at night, I can't sleep. It hasn't hit Doug so hard.

How are the cats? Our B&B has two fine moggies (How do you like that word!?)—a pale ginger tom with a stub of a tail who stalks around the place, and a petite black female shorthair, Benny's baby, who rides around in the crook of her arm, or on her shoulder.

But you don't want to hear about cats! We're in Ireland! Kinsale has these little narrow brightly coloured buildings down by the harbour—like the ones you see in ads for Newfoundland back home. So many cute little restaurants, cafés, a smoothie bar where we go each day—my favourite so far is the mocha chocolate banana—even a tiny bookstore. I bought you a collection of short stories and Blaise one of contemporary Irish poetry.

On Sunday we took in the local sights. There are two old forts: one is in good repair—a massive star fort—where we ate a wonderful buttery raisin cake (Gerry's culinary tour of Ireland!), sitting outside in a fine sea mist, the sun still shining.

I preferred the other fort however, a run-down pile of rocks with a small, ancient, fenced cemetery crumbling away in a field of high weeds. No raisin cake there but loads of atmosphere.

Yesterday we drove for several hours into the west, to Killarney, a big park. As we approached through flat land we could see its mountains in the distance, then in the park fantastic vistas were visible from the car. There are lookout points where you can stop. The mountains are rugged and old, pointy, with deep green valleys between them, waterfalls.

(The highways in Ireland are just like ours, but when you get onto the secondary roads they wind narrowly between hedgerows which grow tight to the side of the car, or so it seems to the passenger—me! And the Irish buzz along them like mad bees. I was just praying there wouldn't be a walker or a parked car around the next corner.)

Well, that trip took all day as we stopped for a pub lunch before Killarney (more of that terrific ham in sandwiches!) and then when we got home I just had to sleep but told Doug to wake me in one hour, which he had a great deal of difficulty doing.

But he persisted. We went out for fish for supper then drove to the Old Head, which is a promontory where you can park and walk at the top of flat cliffs far above the sea crashing below. And the sun doesn't set until after eight here, Prudence, in September! I didn't realize Ireland is so much further north than Quebec.

Today we kept our touring closer to home. Went north to Cork City. I loved the bridges across the river connecting the two halves of the city. Then we went up a hill and found the world's quaintest bookstore. I'm not kidding—the books were piled all higgledy-piggledy on tables and floors and the bookstore owner was up a long ladder poking around at the tops of shelves at least fifteen feet from the floor. You could see the dust floating in the air. You'd have hated it. We toured some art galleries too.

It's seven o'clock now and we're going to walk down to the town to see if there's anything going on, grab some supper. Benny said we could rent videos if we want—the store is open till eleven! Driving to Dublin tomorrow.

Much love to you and the furry ones,

Gerry

Prudence rubbed her eyes tiredly and leaned away from the screen. She switched the computer off and got up. She would reply tomorrow, was too exhausted. It had been a long, long day.

She yawned, retrieved her new library books and trudged upstairs. The usual cats followed her. Funny how some of them seemed to need human companionship, touch, while others were indifferent.

She got into bed and retraced her day.

Rita and Charlie had arrived at nine-thirty; Charlie grumbling at Rita for something; Rita, bright-eyed with anticipation of this unexpected outing, ignoring him.

It took about a half-hour to get to the used car dealership, the radio talk show blaring, Rita shouting at Charlie on her left, chatting quietly with Prudence on her right.

Prudence handed over a certified cheque for nine thousand dollars as though she dealt in such sums every day. As the salesman screwed on the new plates, she silently thanked Maggie for leaving her ten thousand. The exact amount needed to pay for the driving course and the car. It was as if she had known what Prudence might use it for.

With a sick feeling, she got behind the wheel of a five-year-old white Toyota Corolla, immaculately maintained with a mere fifty-six thousand kilometres on it, while Rita snapped a few photos. Then, with a smile and a wave, Prudence drove away.

Charlie and Rita followed her all the way back to Lovering until she pulled into The Maples' driveway, then they sailed by, Rita waving out the window.

Prudence had sat for a moment, staring at the lake. It all felt a bit unreal. She glanced to her left at Gerry's Mini then at her own hands still clenched on the wheel. Well, she thought, I did it.

Inside the house she'd felt her energy rise and spent the day cleaning. Every time she passed the kitchen's side window and caught a glimpse of her little white car, she wondered who was visiting. After supper, she carefully drove to the library, selected four books and drove herself home. That had been when she'd thought to look for an email from Gerry.

She looked at the cats who still slept on Maggie's bed, the cats who had perhaps been closest to her dead friend.

Blackie, a fluffy female; Whitey, her brother, a pale beige, also fluffy; Mouse, another female, a grey and white tiger; and Runt, *another* female, a small grey tiger. Maggie's moggies, Prudence thought. Some of the sweetest of the motley crew assembled at The Maples through the workings of her friend's kind heart. She wondered if Whitey thought of the three females as his pride. The cats, warm lumps strategically disposed on the bed, blinked at her.

The window was open and a cool breeze ruffled the trees, made giving in to sleep easy after the sweaty nights of July and early August. She shifted on the bed and the lumps shifted too. She sighed and slept, her book, a biography of Virginia Woolf, barely begun.

When the sun woke her, she counted the lumps pressing against her body. One, two, three, four—five? She looked down and found that Mother had added herself to the group. Prudence reached out from under the covers to pet her. "Mother?" The cat opened its golden eyes briefly, blinked slowly once and re-closed them. Prudence shivered and got up to close the window.

After morning ablutions, feeding the cats, cleaning the cat boxes, and replying to Gerry's email, in which she finally mentioned that Bertie and Marion would soon be staying at Fieldcrest for two weeks, she checked her shopping list. Yes. She would do groceries. And maybe drop in on Lucy, show off her new car. She peeked out the kitchen window. Yup. It was still there. She phoned Lucy at work and left.

She drove carefully, observing the speed limit, forty, slowing to thirty when she reached Lovering's core. One of her fall jackets needed a new zipper so she'd brought it to the fabric store to be repaired. She chatted with Lucy and Doris, the eighty-year-old woman who was the store's previous owner and, who, after selling it to Lucy, still worked there. Prudence agreed to meet Lucy at her house in half an hour. Then she got her groceries, instructing the bag boy to put all the perishables into one bag.

When she turned up Lucy's street, she looked at Mme Ménard's house. No activity. But two people were standing in front of the neighbouring house. An old woman, short and dumpy with wisps of hair, and a man about Prudence's age, tall and stooped, his head hanging on his chest. The woman was talking and pointing around the yard. The man was looking and nodding.

Prudence arrived at Lucy's and removed the bag containing milk, cheese and meat from the trunk. She went around to the side door and knocked. Her friend admitted her. "I made a spot in the fridge for you," Lucy said, this routine of shopping then visiting being long-established from when Prudence would arrive on her bicycle.

"I think I got more than usual, now I have a trunk to fill. I bought those cookies you like." She laid a small box of chocolate-covered ladyfingers on the kitchen table.

Lucy, trying to hide her shock that for once Prudence hadn't baked, cheerfully said, "Oh, *thank* you. We'll have them with a coffee later. Doris will hold the fort at the shop. I thought it's such a lovely day we might go for a walk." After a few practical compliments paid to the car gleaming in the driveway ("White's a good colour—you'll see right away if it starts to rust."), they turned left to walk up Mackenzie Avenue's slight slope.

It must have been morning recess at the nearest school, because they heard children's happy shouts coming from behind a screen of trees. The sound faded as they walked, to be replaced by birdsong and squirrels chattering.

"Squirrels are busy," Lucy commented as one rushed by them across the road.

"Almost fall," was Prudence's terse reply. "Got a nice long email from Gerry yesterday."

"Oh? She okay?"

"Seems so. Jet lag bothering her. They're zipping around seeing the sights."

"Nice. I guess I used to want to visit Ireland—my family heritage and all that, like Gerry—but now it seems like it would be such a bother."

"Mm. And expensive too. A once in a lifetime trip, I suppose."

Lucy, sensing her friend's reluctance to talk, subsided into silence. They reached the top of Mackenzie, where the driveable part of the road ended, and a little dirt path descended into a forested dell. A wooden bridge crossed over a small deep stream. They paused. Sounds of cars and children disappeared, replaced by the stream's delicate song.

"It's nice here," Prudence said.

"Yes," Lucy agreed. "Shall we go on?"

They walked up the hill to where the path met the road. Another school, another playground's occupants could be heard but not seen. They turned right, down, right again onto a bike path, passing a pond where ducks glided among rushes and purple loosestrife, then climbed a steeper hill. At the first crossroads they turned right again.

"Do you remember Mrs. Ballands?" Prudence asked as they passed in front of one of the few multiple-unit dwellings Lovering possessed, a square white stucco four-plex. "Mrs. Etta Ballands?"

"No," Lucy said. "Who was she?"

"She was my music teacher."

Lucy turned to stare at Prudence. "I didn't know you took music."

Prudence nodded. "When I was ten. I had a nice singing voice so I started with that, then added piano lessons. I used to bike all the way from my house to here on Saturday mornings." She added dreamily, "Mrs. Ballands wore party dresses and fancy little shoes when she taught. She spoke with an English accent. She gave me a pretty amethyst necklace." She walked on, saying, "I really enjoyed those lessons."

"So, what happened?"

"Oh, you know. I turned thirteen and got all shy, high school started, Dad and Mother needed me more on the farm. The lessons just petered out."

Sensing her friend's regret, Lucy refrained from further comment except to say, "No. I never met her, which is funny considering we lived down the road."

Prudence shrugged. "She kept to herself I guess. She was a widow. No children. And then she moved away." They turned left onto Lucy's street. "Do you mind if we walk down to Main Road?"

"No."

As they neared the Ménard house, Prudence asked one of the questions that had been bothering her. "Who's going to clear out her house?"

When she responded, Lucy sounded surprised. "Why, I don't know. She's without family here but maybe somewhere. Why do you ask?"

"I can't help thinking, what if there's no one to do it? What then? And what about the cat?"

"Well, we can't do anything about the house, but I bought some kibble and left it for him last night. Let's go see if it's gone."

They walked through the gate looking for the cat. A creak alerted them that the neighbour was sitting on her porch. "Whadda ya think *yer* doing?" she asked in a querulous voice.

"Hello, Mrs. Lester," Lucy replied cheerfully. "How are you? We're just checking on Mme Ménard's cat. Have you seen it?"

"Seen it! It kept me up half the night with its prowling and meowing, scratching at *my* door for some reason."

"Well, it's upset," Prudence chimed in, thinking of Maggie's cats' reactions after Maggie's sudden death. "It misses its owner, its home."

"And who might *you* be, sticking yer nose in, I'd like to know!"

"Mrs. Lester," Lucy replied in a tone of reproof, "this is my old friend, Mrs. Crick. I put some food down here—" She picked up an empty bowl from the porch's floor.

"You put food outside, we'll be having every cat, skunk and raccoon in Lovering nosing around! You've got no right—"

"I hear you found Mme Ménard, Mrs. Lester," Prudence cut in.

"Maybe. What's it to ya if I did?" Then the penny dropped and Mrs. Lester smiled maliciously. "I know you. You're the one married the bank robber. Finally got what *he* deserved, didn't he?" Prudence faced the woman silently, her heart pounding.

"You don't know what you're talking about!" scolded Lucy. "I will continue to feed the cat until some plan can be made for its disposal."

An unfortunate choice of words, Prudence thought, and sure enough, Mrs. Lester jumped on it. "Ha! *I'll* dispose of it! Get my son to put down some rat poison, I will. That'll take care of it! At least I don't have to hear her calling it every night." She mocked a woman's high-pitched voice. "'Luc, Luc, Luc' she'd call. It used to drive me crazy! Sounded like chickens clucking."

Lucy made herself speak calmly. "Mrs. Lester, if any harm comes to that cat, I will know to whom to direct the police. Goodbye!" They made as dignified an exit as they could.

"Well," Prudence said, "now you've really got to make a plan for that cat, and soon. Or she'll kill it." She sucked her lips coaxingly as they walked, hoping the cat would appear. She even tried a tentative "Luc, Luc, Luc."

Lucy, back straight, fuming, strode quickly toward her house, saying merely, "Coffee?"

When Prudence turned her head to see if the cat was responding to her calls, she looked back at Mrs. Lester's house. She saw the son come out of the front door and his mother talking and gesticulating with her hand, pointing up the street at her and Lucy.

If it was in the vicinity, Mme Ménard's cat—Luc—wisely kept out of sight.

# 5

Prudence got back to The Maples after a hurried coffee in Lucy's kitchen. (Lucy had been in a hurry, not Prudence. "Doris could run the shop all day but she *is* eighty," was her excuse.) Prudence unpacked her groceries, feeling aimless. She had absolutely nothing to do.

She made her customary peanut butter and sweet pickle sandwich and took it and the usual single-serving-sized bag of chips onto the back porch. She never tired of this combination of flavours for her lunch. The stickiness of the smooth peanut butter was lightened by the crunch of juicy bread-and-butter pickles. The salty potato chips added another layer of flavour. She'd thought it perfect back in grade one when she'd opened her lunch box that first miserable day; and she'd continued to think so for the last fifty years.

She smiled as she wondered what had made her mother construct such a meal. *She* didn't eat peanut butter and pickle sandwiches. And including the little bag of chips had been a stroke of genius, raising shy Prudence in the other children's estimation. *They* might only have a box of raisins or an apple. And by luck she'd sat next to Maggie Coneybear, who had all the status of an upper middle-class Lovering family built in, who *assumed* people would like her, and who quickly made their table one of happy chattering girls.

School hadn't been so bad after that, Prudence reflected.

The sound of hissing and growling came from somewhere on her right. She got up to look but whatever the kerfuffle was, it was happening in the shrubbery. When it amplified, turned into high-pitched cries descending into terrible low howls, she left the porch to investigate.

The lawn was over-long and still wet from the previous night's rain. Her house shoes got wet and she paused in annoyance, but the intensity of angry noises grew so she advanced again, through the gate between The Maples and Blaise Parminter's back garden.

Unlike Gerry's property, Blaise's had been *really* let go. Jewelweed, waist high, lined either side of the dirt path. The grass had long since given way to weeds and moss, though Blaise paid a local boy to keep the front yard looking neat.

Sure enough, the usual culprits were duking it out, fangs bared, ears pinned back: Bob, the big tuxedo cat, Gerry's favourite, on one side; and Graymalkin, Blaise's hostile-to-almost-everyone-but-Blaise grey cat.

Blaise could be seen, standing outside his kitchen's sliding glass door on a little flagstone patio, looking helpless. At ninety-four, he had the excuse of not wanting to risk a fall by intervening.

"Oh, Prudence!" he said, his voice sounding more than usually quavery, "What should we do?"

Prudence marched past the two creatures, now locked together on the patio, a spitting ball of male aggression, and grasped the broom leaning against the house's wall. Fearlessly, she batted at the cats with the idea of chasing Bob toward home. "That's enough, Bob!" she said severely, feeling like she was talking to a bad little boy. "Scat! Scat!" Eventually, both cats, not liking the feel of bristles poking into their skin every which way, broke apart, Bob heading back toward The Maples while Gray, having successfully defended his territory, sat on his haunches and began grooming, licking all those raised hairs back into place.

"I *hate* when they do that," Blaise said.

"It's cats, Blaise. They fight. And those two have never liked each other. To be continued, I'm sure," she concluded wryly, replacing the broom.

"Oh, I hope not, Prudence. I hope not." He entered the house together with his cat and closed the door.

Prudence walked back to Gerry's house looking for Bob. She found him, like Gray, nonchalantly grooming near the huge hydrangea bush that grew next to the pink stone path paralleling the back of the house. She picked him up and found blood oozing out of a deep gash on the back of his neck. "Now, what has Gray done to you, Bob?" She carried him into the house, to the upstairs bathroom and closed the door. She dabbed at the wound with a wad of toilet paper. "I don't think this'll hurt—much," she said as she poured peroxide into the wound, holding the cat over the bathtub. Bob struggled free, landed in the bathtub and shook. Cat blood thinned with peroxide spattered the tub, the wall and Prudence's slacks.

She waited to see if the wound stopped bleeding, blotting it from time to time. It did, more or less, rather quickly. When she was satisfied Bob wouldn't be decorating anywhere else in the house with his blood, she opened the door. He shot out, but only into the hall, where he sat and resumed his grooming. Prudence cleaned the bathroom, changed her slacks and returned to her interrupted lunch on the porch.

A grey squirrel frisked its way across the lawn. Two cats—a black shorthair and a tortoiseshell without a tail—froze in their tracks, lowering themselves into the grass. Seymour and Lightning.

A black squirrel suddenly ran down a tree, chasing the grey one. The cats jerked in response but only sank lower, ears flattening, watching as the rodents disappeared into the neighbour Edwina Murray's thicket and from there up into one of her trees.

The black cat got up and approached the tortoiseshell; they touched noses. Then they wandered down toward the wildflowers growing near the shore.

Even cats, Prudence thought, even cats have figured out how to pair off.

She finished her meal and went inside. The cat boxes needed her attention. She noticed a light flashing on Gerry's answering machine. "Hi, Prudence. It's Bertie again. Just about to open the shop and thought I might catch you. I'll call later." Click. She dialled his number but it went to his machine. She didn't leave a message. I know, she thought, I'll bake something.

She opened the kitchen drawer where Maggie had and Gerry now kept recipes. She took out Maggie's old folder and sat at the table in the living room facing the lake.

The recipes, handwritten, or clipped from papers or magazines and pasted onto sheets of paper, were stained and yellowed. Prudence's hand stroked the pages. She knew most of them, of course. Ah, here was one she hadn't made in years. Butter fingers. Buying the commercial ladyfingers for Lucy reminded her how much better the homemade ones were in comparison. She'd make some and take them to her friend. And she should really bake some nice things to serve Bertie and Marion when they visited her at The Maples.

Suddenly, she felt cheerful. Friends—one of them special—were coming to spend two weeks with her. She spent the rest of the afternoon making the buttery shortbread fingers, setting aside favourite recipes and adding ingredients to her shopping list.

Thursday she gave the house a good cleaning. It wasn't very dirty but Friday she was due to clean Edwina Murray's house. She finally spoke to Bertie Thursday at noon. On Saturday, he and Marion would catch the 12:30 train in Montreal, to arrive at Lovering's station by 1:30. Yes, they would want lunch. No, she wasn't to make it; they would eat with her in a Lovering restaurant. He said he was looking forward to his holiday.

Prudence hung up the phone feeling—yes, what was she feeling? A bit fluttery in her stomach was how she could best describe it. A bit fluttery. Or even a bit flustered. She frowned. She didn't enjoy feeling uncomfortable.

Her eye caught sight of the tin of homemade cookies she'd set aside for Lucy. Perhaps her jacket was ready.

Parking on Lovering's one commercial cross street, she gave a thought to Saturday's lunch. Soup and a scone at the Two Sisters' Café, which she could see across the street from Lucy's shop, or a more substantial meal at Johnny's on Main Road? She knew Bertie didn't care what he ate as long as it tasted good. But Marion Stewart?

Prudence entered Lucy's shop, smiling (as usual when she noticed it) at the sign. Not original, but funny.

Sew What? inhabited an old house. It had an enclosed porch along the front, where Lucy casually displayed odds and ends, things she purchased at yard, church, and rummage sales and marked up, just a little. Lucy knew the people who shopped for fabric were mostly like herself, thrifty, and she liked bric-a-brac, didn't she? Prudence, who didn't, rarely gave the collection of plates, bowls, and ornaments a second glance. I'll have to expose Bertie, who was used to buying and selling fabulous furniture and *objets d'arts*, to this stuff, she thought mischievously. Have him "appraise" it. Now, now, don't be mean, Prudence, she cautioned herself. She went through into the main showroom.

This part of the store was all business. Fabric hung or was stacked in rolls. Displays of hooks, buttons, clasps, pins and needles, threads of many colours, a selection of wools, all vied for the eye's attention. Prudence, who only attempted simple sewing repair jobs, a bit of knitting, still looked around appreciatively. This part of the shop appealed to her—more professional.

Doris sat behind the cutting table. Grey-haired, with bright eyes behind glasses, she beamed at Prudence. "And what can I do for you today, Miss Prudence?"

"Hi, Doris," Prudence replied with a smile. "How are you?"

"Oh, you know. Gotta keep busy. Want to see a picture of the latest great-grandson?" Prudence waited while Doris reached under the table and brought out a photo obviously kept there for sharing with customers.

After the young man (he was about two months old and swaddled so there wasn't much to admire) had been commented on, Prudence asked, "Is my jacket ready, do you know, Doris? It's beige."

Doris chirped, "Did it myself yesterday," and went to get it.

Meanwhile, a clumping on the stairs above them announced Lucy's arrival. Her arms were distended as she clasped a huge plastic bag full of cushions. She dropped the bag next to the cutting table, opened it, and began handing Prudence cushions. "Put them on the table, Prudence. Please."

"Good to see you too, Lucy," Prudence said a bit snippily, then, relenting, brought the tin of cookies out of her tote, whacking it down on the table.

This got Lucy's attention. "Doris!" she yelled, "Put on the kettle!" In a quieter voice she asked, "What are they, Prue?"

"Butter fingers," Prudence replied primly, putting cushions first into piles, then, when they kept coming, arranging them on their sides like records in a collection.

"There! All done." Lucy reached for the tin.

"Better not," Prudence warned. "Not until we've finished with these." She indicated the cushions with her head. "Greasy fingers."

"Right, right," Lucy muttered. "Well, I want to sort these by colour, the way the yarn and thread is, and then put them by the door. You know what?" she said as Doris approached with a large brown teapot in a hideous orange, cream and brown striped knitted tea cozy. "Let's carry them over to those shelves now and I'll sort them later."

"If you were going to do *that*, you could have just carried the bag over *there*," Doris commented before she left to bring the other teatime accoutrements.

Lucy stared after her, her eyes narrowed slits. "One day, Doris," she murmured as she compressed a row of cushions and lifted. "One day."

Prudence, attempting to compress some cushions, misjudged, and the whole armful of ten or so cushions exploded upwards, creating a soft fountain of colour around her head.

The shop's doorway chimes tinkled. "Customer!" yelled Doris as she plunked the tea tray down on the table. Catching Lucy's eye, she meekly said, "I'll deal with her, shall I? I put Prudence's jacket by the cash."

A red-faced Prudence, scrambling to pick up cushions, said, "Maybe I should—"

"No, no," Lucy scolded, hastily stacking cushions on the shelves. "You're fine. We'll take our tea in the back." And, after pouring Doris and the customer (a short stout woman who was looking for some fine yarn for baby clothes) two cups of tea and leaving them some cookies, Lucy and Prudence retreated.

The room in the back had been the little house's kitchen before it became a shop, and a kitchen it remained, albeit also a place for the overflow of stock. Lucy placed the tea tray on the table, removed some boxes from two chairs and motioned Prudence to sit. "Phew!" she exhaled. "You wouldn't think a village fabric shop could get hectic, but sometimes—" She bit into a butter finger. "Ahh. Just as I remember them. So good, Prue."

"They are a bit of a spoiler, aren't they?" Prudence agreed as the buttery shortbread snapped in her mouth and mingled with the taste of bittersweet chocolate in which one end had been dipped.

"Oh!" Lucy exclaimed, surprising them both. "I have to tell you! Father Lackey called me last night." Father Lackey was the long-time incumbent at St. Pete's, Lucy's church. "He asked me if I would organize cleaning out Mme Ménard's house."

Prudence put down her tea, a cold feeling overtaking her. It was as she had feared. "She had no family then?" she quietly asked.

"No. Yes. Well, not close family. A nephew or great-nephew or something—Father Lackey said the man was in such a hurry he hardly understood what he wanted. He already visited the house and doesn't want any of its contents, wants to put it up for sale as soon as possible. But he doesn't live near here and he asked Father Lackey if the church would like to distribute or sell Mme Ménard's possessions—the furniture, everything—and keep the money. So Father Lackey asked me if he thought St. Pete's women's auxiliary was up to the job." Lucy sat back and took another cookie. She was the current president of that group.

Prudence nodded. "I see. What did you say?"

Lucy leaned forward. "Well—and I told Father Lackey this—most of our members are so old, they wouldn't be able to do any meaningful physical work—packing, lifting and so on." She leaned back and looked at Prudence. "So I asked him if it would be okay if I pulled in some help from ladies of other denominations. Of course he agreed. Well, he doesn't really have a choice."

Prudence smothered a smile. Lucy had been president of St. Pete's women's auxiliary for at least a dozen years. She suspected her friend would give up the position only on her deathbed, and then kicking and screaming. And Father Lackey himself was shrewd—shrewd enough to know when to compromise.

"So I thought of you," Lucy concluded.

"Me!?"

"Yeah. You only have two clients, one of whom is away and the other only needs you once every two weeks; you've got a car, which would be useful for hauling stuff away; and you're looking for something to do."

"I am?"

"Please," Lucy begged. "I really need your help, Prudence. We could have fun."

"If you consider picking over the earthly possessions of a dead old woman fun. All right. But you know my other friends are going to be here for the next two weeks, right?"

"Yes, but they won't want to hang around you *all* the time. Thank you for agreeing." Lucy began to clear the tea things from the table and Prudence understood her friend was anxious to get back to work.

"Call me when you need help then."

"I will. And thanks for the cookies."

As Prudence drove down Lucy's street she eyed Mme Ménard's little house. She'd forgotten to ask Lucy about the cat.

"Good boy, Shadow. Thank you." The big black Labrador retriever rose resignedly from his dog basket and plodded out of the room. Prudence lifted the padded cushion from the basket and shook it before vacuuming it. The dog still liked to sleep in his dead master's den. Probably hoping he'll return one day, thought Prudence. Well, if he never saw the dead body, how would he know Roald was dead? She felt a sudden pity for companion animals, living as adjuncts in their owners' lives.

Not that Shadow wasn't well looked after by his owner's widow. Every day in the morning, Edwina Murray and Shadow got into her car and drove to a trail where he could be loose. He had a lovely big yard behind her house to sniff around in the rest of the time. No, he had a comfortable life. But—he still preferred to sleep in Roald's room. Prudence paused. Come to think of it, Edwina hadn't changed the room in the four months since the death. What do I know? she thought. Maybe she likes to come in here too. She shrugged, turned off the vacuum and began dusting Roald's pipes, jars of tobacco, cigar cases. He'd certainly enjoyed his life, she thought sourly, remembering how he'd sponged money off his wife, even invited his girlfriend to his and Edwina's parties. "Push the clear button, Prudence," she said out loud, not really knowing the origin of the saying but understanding its meaning.

The dog, who had silently returned to his basket, lifted its head at her voice, then turned to look at the room's doorway. "Almost finished, Prudence?" asked Edwina, looking vaguely at her. A mystery author, Edwina usually looked vaguely at Prudence. Working for her wasn't like working for Gerry, that was for sure. There were no shared tea and coffee breaks, no cozy chats. All of a sudden, Prudence realized she was missing Gerry.

"Yup," she replied. "This is the last room."

"Oh. Good." Edwina crossed over to the dog and patted his head. His tail remained curled around his body but fluttered a little in appreciation. She straightened. "I've left your money on the hall table. As usual." She looked about to say something else, then seemed to think better of it. Or maybe she just forgot what it had been. "Have a nice weekend." She left the room and Prudence heard her cross the living room and enter her study.

She looked at the dog. They're both lonely, she thought, but something's holding them apart. Quietly, she put the vacuum cleaner away, got her money and left by the back door.

She breathed in the cool September air as she took the path through the thicket that separated Edwina's from Gerry's property. She fed the cats and put on the kettle before going to clean the cat boxes. The flashing light of the phone answering machine stopped her. She listened to the message in disbelief.

# PART 2
# ANGER

The grey and white cat felt confused. Food appeared on his house's front porch twice a day, and only once had he mistimed his return to find it gone, eaten by some other creature. But it wasn't the soft nuggets of meat in savoury sauce he was used to; it was dry crunchy stuff that made him thirsty. And the plate didn't smell of her fingers but of those of some other. He sat on a chair on the porch and wondered what had happened to his world.

He'd tried the neighbour's house once during the long days and nights since his woman had disappeared. Only once. After he'd scratched at the door and loudly meowed, the woman who lived there had opened it and given him such a kick. She'd missed, of course, as he'd been quick enough to dodge her foot, showing her his fangs and hissing as he twisted sideways, but her loud bad-sounding words had made him realize no comfort was possible there. Just as there had been no help the night his mistress fell.

The nights were a little colder now, and the rampant insect life of a few days earlier had somewhat lessened, though bugs still clicked and hopped around the lawn, but only on a sunny day. This evening a few chilled moths circled the streetlamp.

Now that the surrounding houses' occupants were closing their windows at night to keep in the day's warmth, he couldn't hear their television sets, their dishwashers; and the season for sprinklers seemed to be over.

The hamburger and french fry restaurant still perfumed the night with its delicate scent of old meat, old grease. The coffee roaster still released its bitter exhaust into the air.

Once the cat was tightly curled on one of the old chairs on his front porch, he quickly warmed. It wasn't as nice as sleeping next to her on her bed, or dozing on her lap as she watched TV on the nights when she couldn't sleep.

*But he didn't understand where she was. She'd fallen in the back yard and been unable to get back up. That was bad, he knew. Being able to move was the basis for survival. But she'd been breathing when the strange people had arrived, lifted her onto a kind of bed and carried her, not into the house as he'd been expecting, but along the side of the house, through the front yard and gate and into a big car with flashing lights. He didn't like cars. But in his experience, before when she'd left in a car, she'd generally returned in one. So he'd been waiting ever since.*

*Later he'd watched two women come through the gate and look vaguely around. One of them even sucked her lips as though she wanted him to come. But he didn't know her. He wanted his woman. He'd stayed hidden.*

*He shifted uneasily on the chair on the porch. He heard the familiar creak of someone sitting down on one of the chairs on the neighbours' side. He raised himself up till he could look over the upholstered arm of his chair.*

*The man who lived next door with the mean old woman sat very quietly. He rested his elbows on his knees and buried his face in his hands. As usual, he gave off an aura of despair. The cat sensed that the man was powerless, unable to help even a small cat.*

*The cat sat back down on the chair and listened, just in case. Just in case she was in the back yard, calling him. Or inside the house, moving around as she slowly prepared for bed.*

*No.*

*He lowered his head, tucked his paws under his chest and comforted himself the best way he knew. He began to purr.*

# 6

"Fore!"

"You really don't need to call 'Fore!' every time you drive the ball, Bertie! It's just for when you think you might hit people with it!" Marion Stewart, dressed in smart white pants, a navy blouse and jacket and a white peaked cap, sat in the driver's seat of their golf cart. She tsked-tsked after her comment. They watched as Bertie's ball went very high then landed to one side in deep grass off under some trees. He groaned loudly.

Prudence and Bertie exchanged grins before he replied. "But I've always wanted to say it, Marion. Playing golf is a dream come true for me. Hobnobbing with the toffs."

Prudence took her turn, her ball coming to rest a good one hundred feet past Bertie's in the centre of the fairway. He gave her a cool look. "I see you've done this before."

She shrugged. "I'm a bit out of practice. It's been a few years." She didn't bother explaining that after her marriage ended and before her father died, she'd tried golf and curling, discovering an athleticism she attributed to her years working on the farm. Or that later, with her husband disgraced, her father dead, and her mother clinging, she'd given the activities up.

They got into the golf cart, Prudence next to Marion, Bertie clinging on the back, as Marion took off to the next tee. Prudence, looking at her face, thought she seemed to be enjoying herself. So far they were having, rather surprisingly to Prudence, fun. She replayed the activities of the last few days.

Saturday, she'd spent the morning cutting the grass at The Maples. It was long and wet and she'd had to keep switching off the mower, unplugging it, turning it on its side and using a stick to scrape mulched grass off its undercarriage.

She'd been in a sweat when she finally finished, just had time for a quick shower before driving to meet Bertie and Marion at Lovering's train station. Bertie had admired her new car; Marion hadn't seemed to realize that this was a big step for Prudence and had taken being chauffeured around as her due.

Both had voted for sandwiches and scones for lunch, so they'd driven the block and a half to The Two Sisters' Café, a large room with local art on the walls (Bertie had grimaced.), and shelves of teacups, teapots and glass jars of tea leaves. Marion had chosen bacon and cheese; Prudence, curried chicken with thin apple slices; and Bertie had simply said, with a grave look in his eyes that made her heart beat a little faster and left her cheeks flushed, "I'll have what you're having, Prue."

They enjoyed their scones with cream and jam and Marion grudgingly admitted that the place certainly seemed to be able to serve a good cup of tea.

Afterward, Prudence drove them to Fieldcrest, Cathy Stribling's B&B, down the road a little from The Maples, where Cathy welcomed them with cries of "Come in! Come in! You must be exhausted! Let me show you your rooms!"

Marion had gone to lie down, and Bertie had spent the afternoon with Prudence, quietly chatting on Fieldcrest's wide veranda, discussing what activities they might undertake that Marion would enjoy and wouldn't be too tiring for her.

That evening they'd gone to the Parsley Inn, another short distance away, and enjoyed a "good, solid meal," as Marion described her steak and kidney pie, washed down with most of their bottle of red wine. Prudence had driven them back to the B&B and said good night.

Sunday, she and Marion attended St. Anne's Anglican service. (Bertie said it really wasn't his kind of thing and he would read the paper in Fieldcrest's large guest lounge, while digesting the marvellous blueberry waffles with bacon *and* sausage Cathy had provided.)

Marion had spent some of the summers of her youth in Lovering, and knew various of the elderly people in the congregation, including Doug Shapland's two aunts, Jane and Bette, having been at school with their older sister, now deceased. Prudence eventually had to tear her away when they were the only four still in the church, the minister nervously loitering at the door, evidently wanting to be on her way.

They'd gone for a drive that afternoon, just to the surrounding villages, where Marion noticed all the changes. Looking at one development after another, she exclaimed, "But this used to be all farms!" And, in front of a strip mall, "I remember picking strawberries here!" On the way back to Lovering, after grabbing a hamburger at a fast-food restaurant, they took the river road and Marion seemed to enjoy this route better. Apparently not much had altered here in the last seventy years. The same farms, the same stone houses, the same waterfront views soothed. A solitary heron, late for the migration, fished in the bay. A few ducks floated calmly.

As they drove past the Crick farm, where Prudence's husband had been raised, she saw a for sale sign with a sold sticker. It was news to her it had even been for sale. Alex's two horrible brothers were probably going to prison, she thought with satisfaction. She supposed some other of the numerous Crick siblings would be in charge of the sale. Eyeing the new sleek glass-fronted holiday homes either side of it, she wondered if it had been purchased by a farmer or a developer. She didn't mention her connection to it to her guests.

When they passed the ferry, Prudence asked if they'd care to take it while they were visiting. They both said yes, Marion adding, "But not today. It's time for my rest." Prudence dropped her at Fieldcrest, then she and Bertie returned to The Maples for another quiet afternoon. They discussed the antique business and Bertie mentioned he might be thinking of retiring.

This was to be, Prudence had understood, the pattern for their days over the next two weeks.

Sunday night Cathy had cooked for them. (This had been arranged earlier in the day and of course, as a special service, cost extra.) A roast chicken with carrots, potatoes and broccoli, and gravy, was served in Cathy's huge shabby dining room. And she made a Charlotte Russe for dessert, which, Prudence could see, impressed Marion. It was a bit too samey for Prudence, all cream and mushy biscuits and strawberry jam. She much preferred a bit of cake with icing or pie with a tender crisp crust. But she ate her portion.

Coffee was served by the living room fire and, after being pressed, Cathy joined them with her dog, Prince Charles.

When Charles's toenails clicked into the room, Prudence had enjoyed Bertie's raised eyebrows and quizzical look in her direction. Marion had seemed to assume that a morose, strange-looking dog was just part of a country house vacation and hardly noticed him, so busy was she monopolizing their hostess's conversation. This left Prudence and Bertie free to converse together.

"Is it part goat!" murmured Bertie, watching Charles, who was slumped in front of the fire, nibbling on a bit of carpet fringe.

Prudence reached down and untangled the fringe so Charles could access the peanut his sensitive nose had detected. "Basset mixed with something, er, shaggy," she replied in a low voice.

"Ah." A pause. "Goats are shaggy." In a louder voice, Bertie asked, "May I smoke?" and pulled out his pipe.

Cathy looked embarrassed. "I'm so sorry, Mr. Smith. The insurance forbids it. And though you are the only guests at this time, some other subsequent guests might notice and complain about the smell. I advertise as a *non-smoking* bed and breakfast. But feel free to use the veranda if you wish."

Bertie returned the pipe to his pocket. "I'll wait," he said amiably.

Cathy, trying to cover her discomfort at having to deny a paying guest any enjoyment, said, "I was just telling Mrs. Stewart about our ghost."

This was news to Prudence, who looked sharply at Cathy. Surely she wouldn't—

Cathy intercepted the look, looked distressed for a moment, then shook her head just a tiny bit. Prudence relaxed. All of which interchange Bertie saw and Marion, helping herself to a bit more brandy from the bottle on the coffee table, did not. I hope Cathy's keeping track of that, Prudence thought with some amusement. Or she's going to lose money on Marion.

"Your ghost?" Bertie said courteously.

Prudence looked at him. That was probably the thing she liked best about him—how courteous he was to everyone, always putting people at their ease, seeming sincerely interested in their lives. Unlike Prudence herself, who was content to watch, who felt powerless most of the time, to effect change. After all—

She surfaced from her musings in time to hear Cathy finish her sentence. "—and so it must be a ghost!"

Marion scoffed. "I don't call a malfunctioning wire proof of a ghost!"

"But you don't understand," Cathy protested. "First my br—sister Markie, who's an engineer, checked it. Then I had an electrician come, open the wall and replace the wire. The same thing still happened. He took the sconce itself apart and tested it. There's nothing wrong with any of the components."

"It just sometimes doesn't work," Prudence said slowly, realizing they must be discussing the lamp on the wall halfway up the main flight of stairs at Fieldcrest. "And sometimes it does. I've experienced it. But I, er, never got the feeling of a *ghost*."

Bertie asked gravely, "And are you sensitive to ghosts, Prudence?"

She hesitated. Now was not the time for a discussion of her past experiences with paranormal events. Nor had she yet confided in him that she'd often, both before and after her mother had died, visited a medium. Cathy, who knew all about these occurrences, came to her rescue.

"Oh!" she laughed. "I wasn't *serious*! You know these old houses—creaky and leaky! I just wanted you to be prepared if you flip the switch and nothing happens. I keep a candle and matches on the little table in the hall just for such occasions."

"Hmm," said Bertie. Marion, bored by the subject, began talking about the old house her parents had owned in Westmount, a wealthy Montreal neighbourhood, and its wonky fireplaces.

Bertie, who'd heard it all before, stood. "I think I'll go smoke that pipe now."

"I'll come with you," Prudence said. She put on her jacket and they spent a quiet half hour on Cathy's veranda, sitting in two cushioned wicker chairs. Bertie had not asked for nor had Prudence supplied an explanation regarding any sensitivities she might entertain for ghosts or, for that matter, anyone living either.

And now they were playing a round at the smallest and cheapest of Lovering's three golf courses, where fifty dollars got you the loan of the clubs and nine holes. It was an extravagance for Prudence, but she'd decided to treat the next two weeks as if they were a vacation for her too.

"Fore!" cried Bertie again. She smiled.

After their round, in the club's tiny bar, he and Marion each had a martini while Prudence contented herself with tonic water. Then they had some rather limp ham sandwiches. As they were not members, they were quietly surveyed by some of the other golfers who were. When Marion was visiting the rest room, Bertie mumbled through barely moving lips, "Am I wearing the wrong-coloured socks?"

Prudence smothered a laugh. His blue and green argyles were a bit…bright, but she'd seen worse. "No, no. It's not you. It's more likely to be me. You know: local cleaning lady; widow of infamous bank robber who was recently murdered." She'd begun lightly enough but found her tone had become bitter by the end of her explanation.

"Perhaps it's time we decamp," he said authoritatively, rising to his feet and stretching out a hand.

"Yes," Prudence agreed thoughtfully, grasping his hand and rising. "Perhaps it is." Marion reappeared and Prudence drove them home.

As he helped Marion up Fieldcrest's wide steps, Bertie said, "I'm going to take it easy this afternoon, Prudence. Shall we take a break until tomorrow?" She nodded and drove away.

Back at The Maples, faced with twenty cats, seven cat boxes and mounting fur-balls in the corners of rooms, Prudence did a quick vacuum, phoned Lucy and checked the computer for news from Gerry. There were *two* messages. Tidy-minded as ever, Prudence read the older one first. It was dated from Friday, three days earlier.

> Dear Prudence,
>
> Dublin is wonderful! What a great city for artists! So many things to look at and do. Doug says I'm doing too much and I *am* tired. But I'm in *Ireland* and who knows when I'll return?
>
> We went to a big art gallery, the Hugh Lane. Mostly modern art. They have Francis Bacon's entire studio there! You'd have a fit if you saw it—paint and rags and

garbage everywhere! The colours were great. Apparently he was a tortured soul. I'm so glad I'm not!

I had no idea the nineteenth-century potato famine was still so fresh and raw in the Irish psyche. A lot of modern artists are exploring it as their theme. I guess it's all part of the Irish drive to regain self-rule, which, thankfully, they now enjoy.

There's a great park in the centre of Dublin—St. Stephen's Green. Our hotel is just off it. The park has winding shady paths, small pools, and loads of birds on and off the water. We bring our sandwiches and coffee there and sit. The weather's been great. Oh! We saw *The Book of Kells* at Trinity College Dublin Library, which as you can imagine, is this great high-ceilinged room just like you see on Masterpiece Theatre.

We were sitting in a great little pub having potato soup with soda bread when I overheard a man say to his companion "That's so cat!" Well, I had to ask, and it turns out "cat" is short for "cat on a melodeon," a melodeon being a noisy keyboard instrument, which, if a cat was treading on it, would make a terrible sound! So something being "cat" just means terrible. Funny, eh?

Well, it's back onto another tiny airplane tomorrow—Dublin to Devon. Enjoy your guests! Love to the cats.

Gerry

Prudence sighed. She felt both envious and exhausted reading all that Gerry and Doug were doing. Gerry must be really distracted to not want more information about Bertie and Marion's visit. She clicked on the subsequent email, dated Monday, just a few hours earlier.

Hello from Devon! Home of the Coneybears! And all those other folks from Lovering, Canada, whose ancestors made the voyage west hundreds of years ago. We landed in Exeter and it was raining. Nevertheless, we have seen all that Exeter has to offer I think, including the medieval underground tunnels that used to bring fresh water right to the city centre; an art gallery; a cathedral. We ate at one pub for lunch (fish) and another for supper (fish). Good thing I like fish!

Sunday we got our rental car and headed along the coast, that's the south coast—Devon has two. We saw Powderham Castle, small but lovely, where the Count of Devon "sits." We passed a sign saying "Cheese" so of course we stopped. They have big orange cows at this farm—they're known as orange elephants! How did I not know that Devon is "the home of cheddar," as one of our holiday brochures claims? Though the owner of the farm, a Mr. Taverner, grudgingly admitted that the village of Cheddar, after which the cheese is named, is in neighbouring Somerset and *may* have been its place of origin. Who cares? What would poutine be without cheddar curds? Then back to Exeter for Sunday night's sleep. You would like this hotel, Prudence, it's an old Victorian rowhouse with big rooms and nice views out into a garden. Right downtown but quiet.

Today we toured more of the South Devon coast, just stopping where we wanted to. We went all the way down to Dartmouth, which is kind of cute, with little houses on the cliff near the harbour, then to Torquay, which is very touristy, with lots of white hotels and yachts in the harbour and palm trees (!). Outside Torquay is where *Fawlty Towers* is supposed to have been set. We drove over to Exmouth, south of Exeter, and along the coastal road to Sidmouth where we got out and walked on the beach there. It's quite a stretch and there's a coastal path hikers can take. We ate our supper in Sidmouth at a strange little vegetarian restaurant that featured seaweed (!) on the menu, then tiredly straggled back to the hotel where we are now. Tomorrow, onward to Lovering! Lovering, England!

All my love,<br>Gerry

# 7

"But, Prudence! What are the chances of something dire happening to two elderly women neighbours in the same week!?"

Prudence shook out another tablecloth, inspected it and refolded it before putting it in the "sell" pile. They'd agreed to begin at the back of Mme Ménard's little house in the kitchen, because of the perishables, and having quickly disposed of most of her meagre supplies in the garbage, had moved on to dishes (Lucy) and cloths (Prudence). "Shush!" she remonstrated. "We don't know how thin the walls are. The son might hear you."

Lucy lowered her voice. "Well, I'm just saying. And I can't hear him, can you? So maybe the walls are thick enough. But one old lady stricken and one dead—what are the odds?"

For it turned out that the sour Mrs. Lester had died, found by her son cold in her bed Friday morning, while Mme Ménard, having survived her catastrophic backyard stroke, had been moved from the hospital to a nursing home, where the prognosis was not good. This according to Father Lackey, who had it from her nephew, who'd phoned subsequent to his in-person visit, to see if the church women were getting on with clearing out his aunt's home.

"Being as how they were both over eighty, I'd say pretty good. I've finished the linen in this armoire. What do you want me to tackle next?"

Lucy's head nodded in the direction of the shelves above the armoire. "Wash and pack those?"

Prudence stifled a groan. Mme Ménard had favoured mostly little ornaments, so the three shelves were crammed—animals, cottages, gnomes—you name it, it was there in miniature. And they were coated in sticky dust. Prudence plugged the sink, ran it with soapy hot water and put the objects in to soak. "Shall I make us a cup of tea?"

"Why not?" Lucy replied with a sigh. While she was waiting for the kettle to boil, Prudence removed four larger ornaments from on top of the armoire and brought them over to the sink to await washing. All pale green stone, they were: a delicate bowl, a heavy teapot, a weird dog-lion, and another bowl, thick-sided, uglier compared to the first, with a bumpy surface that looked kind of like crocodile hide. Minutes later the women each took a chair at the small kitchen table and gratefully sipped their tea. "Lots of stuff for the church rummage," Lucy remarked. "Even though no one from the women's group bothered to show up to help." She sniffed angrily.

"Well, you did say they were most of them older than us."

Feeling their mood somewhat dampened by the sombre nature of their task, Lucy asked, "So what are your friends doing this afternoon?"

Prudence roused herself from her thoughts. "Oh. Marion is resting, as she usually does, and Bertie said we should 'take a break' for the rest of the day. Which is why I'm here."

"Oh." Lucy sounded deflated. Then she brightened. "Well, that's good, isn't it? He's giving you some space."

"Mm," was the uncertain-sounding reply. Prudence changed the subject, or rather, returned to the original one. "What I don't understand is, if Madame Ménard is still alive, why are we getting rid of all her stuff?"

"Oh. Father Lackey told me the nephew has one of those power-of-attorney things—a curatorship. Now she's helpless, he's going to dispose of her possessions and sell her house in order to help pay her other expenses. At the nursing home, I guess."

They could each sense the other felt uneasy talking about such things. "I don't have one," Prudence said. "A power of attorney. Do you?"

Lucy shook her head. "I have a nephew, but not a power of attorney. Do you think we should get one?"

"I suppose. But you'd have to really trust the person you gave such powers to. We'll get them eventually, I guess."

This seemed to make Lucy feel better. She straightened up. "Yes. Eventually. But not *now*."

Prudence smiled slightly. "No. Not now." Then after a pause, she added, "But this disposing of her stuff just feels so rushed."

Lucy nodded. "Well, apparently the nephew already has a buyer for the house."

"What!? How could he? It's been little more than a week since she fell ill!"

"I know." She leaned forward. "Well, I didn't hear this from Father Lackey—I'm sure he never gossips or listens to gossip—but one of our women's group members was buying a fancy coffee at that place down the street—Coco Poco, or whatever it's called—*I've* never been there—anyway, she heard the owner telling one of the girls who works there, once he gets hold of the 'cottages out back' he called them, he's going to extend the café and put in a terrace." She sat back triumphantly. "So."

Prudence reflected. "So long as Mrs. Lester's son is also willing to sell…"

"Exactly!"

"Huh."

They got back to work. After Prudence had washed every ornament in the house and dried it, she began wrapping them in newspaper and putting them in boxes. Her hand hesitated when she began to wrap the heavy ugly bowl. "Lucy, I've just had a thought."

"Mm?" Her friend lifted her head from similarly packing dishes.

"Instead of just hauling everything over to the church, maybe we should get Bertie to look at it."

"Oh! He won't want to look at this junk!"

"Most of it, yes. But I think I've seen stuff like this in his antique shop." She held up the chunky rough bowl.

Lucy sniffed dismissively. "I wouldn't give you five bucks for that! No, wait, maybe it could be a doorstop or something."

"But still. It would be a shame if we undersold stuff. For the church, you know."

Lucy thought for a moment. "All right. If you think it matters. Bring him by. I'd like to meet him, anyway."

Yes, thought Prudence, I bet you would.

Lucy chattered on. "That's a good idea, Prue. He won't mind doing it, will he?"

"He says it's the most interesting part of his job—picking."

"But he's on holiday!"

Prudence responded rather dryly, "I imagine, by now, he's rather bored."

Lucy gave her a keen look. Sometimes her friend baffled her. "Sometimes, Prudence Crick, you baffle me."

Prudence looked surprised. "*I* baffle you?"

"This man comes all the way out from Montreal by train to spend his precious two-week holiday in Lovering just so he can visit with you. *And* he escorts a very old lady so she can walk down memory lane. She couldn't manage the trip without him, could she?"

Prudence remembered Marion's long afternoon rests, her inability to walk more than the shortest distances, her overindulgence in alcohol. The elderly, she knew, sometimes self-medicated. "She must be in pain," she said slowly, "and he helps her distract herself."

"I think he must be one of the kindest people in the world and you one of the luckiest." Lucy snapped, "Wake up, Prue!"

Prudence opened her mouth to snap back, found her cheeks were hot and thought better of it. She got up and returned to the sink. She swallowed, her eyes suddenly full of tears. She thought of Bertie, wickedly shouting "Fore!" even after Marion had instructed him not to, just so she could have something to complain about. And probably because he *wanted* to shout fore. In her chest something tight and aching loosened, slightly. She blinked and cleared her throat and when she spoke it was in dignified tones. "I have listened to what you've said and I shall think on it."

Lucy brought another armload of grimy dishes over to the sink. She smiled at her friend. "And I think Bertie looking at Mme Ménard's junk is a great idea."

Prudence changed the subject. "Have you caught sight of that cat yet?"

"That reminds me," Lucy said, "I should wash the cat dish sometime. It's been a week."

"Our cats' dishes are washed twice daily," Prudence said primly, drying her hands. "I'll get it." She went out onto the front porch. She sat in a chair and blew her nose, heard a creak to her left. When she looked, she saw Mrs. Lester's son about to enter his house. "Wait!" she called.

The man froze, then slowly turned to face her. Prudence was shocked by the expression on his face. He looked utterly weary, beaten down, and what was worse, he seemed to cringe, as though he expected her to be angry.

She spoke softly. "Mr. Lester?" He nodded and his eyes darted nervously away. "Mr. Lester, I just want to say, I'm sorry for your loss." He nodded vigorously a couple of times, his head bobbing. "And, my friend—you must know her? Lucy Hanlan? She lives up the street—" The head bobbed again. The eyes now fixed themselves on a point just above Prudence's right shoulder.

"We're cleaning out Mme Ménard's things. Have you heard? She's in a nursing home. She had a very serious stroke. Oh—you hadn't heard? But I thought—"

His head had come up and steadied itself. He now looked startled. "But, she was dead! My mother said—" He didn't finish his thought and looked around a bit wildly. "We thought she'd died." He let his head sink back to his chest again.

He's not well, Prudence thought with pity. He's not right in the head. "Well, we thought so too, and she very nearly did. It seems she was out there—" She jerked her head in the direction of the back yard. "For a long time."

Without any further conversation, he went back into his house. Rats, Prudence thought, I wanted to ask him about the cat. She picked up the empty dish and took it inside. "Met the neighbour."

"Oh?" Lucy was on her knees, peering into the depths of one corner of the lower cupboards. "You met Boo?"

"Boo?"

Lucy backed away from the cupboard and sat on her heels. "That's what we call him. Just a few of us on the street. After Boo Radley in *To Kill A Mockingbird*." She caught sight of Prudence's face. "What?"

"That's not very kind, Lucy. Anyone can see he's not well."

Lucy shrugged. "Oh well. We don't mean anything by it. We don't say it to his face. He never talks, doesn't like to go anywhere. I've never met him at any shops. So—Boo."

"What's his real name?"

"Would you believe Walter?"

"Walter Lester," mused Prudence. "Walter thought Mme Ménard was dead."

"Well, so did we, remember?"

Prudence nodded. "Lucy, I know we've just had tea, but I have a sudden desire for a fancy cup of coffee."

"Oh yes?" Lucy had her head back in the cupboard, was dragging out an assortment of rusty baking trays and old tinfoil pie plates. "Yuck! Garbage all this, I think. You go ahead. I want to finish as much of the kitchen today as I can. No, wait." Her head reappeared and she was grinning. "If the café has any nice little desserts, I wouldn't say no."

"I'll see what I can do," Prudence said dryly. As she walked past the glass box that housed the coffee roasting facility behind Coco Poco, she saw amidst the gleaming steel appliances a man working at a desk. Perhaps the man who wanted to buy the two houses behind his business.

She continued walking, turned and went up the flagstone path, climbed the front steps and paused. Help Wanted, a sign said on the door. She entered the main floor of a narrow old house. You would have thought there'd be more than one small front room for the café. There were some tables and chairs on the deep front porch, but that wouldn't work once the weather got cold. She could see why the owner wanted to expand. And there wasn't much to choose from in the way of snacks. The *poco* seems apt, Prudence thought, looking at the meagre assortment.

Two moms with babies in strollers were taking up all the seating area at the back of the room. Prudence scanned the chalkboard up high on the wall while the bored-looking young server gazed moodily out the window. The girl's phone vibrated on the counter and she snatched it up. Prudence read about coffee varieties she'd never heard of, their places of origin and taste descriptions. Notes of marmalade? She thought of Rita's bitter brew, scooped from grocery store discount giant cans, run through a coffee machine from the 1970s, and smiled slightly. "I'll have the pumpkin spice latte," she said, adding silently to herself, at least that's one I recognize.

"Size?" asked the girl impatiently as she reluctantly laid aside her cellphone. She was short and plump and her hair, which went straight up, was dyed an improbable orange. She reminded Prudence of one of the little trolls she could remember buying at the Five and Dime when she was a child. A tiny jewel glinted from the side of one nostril.

"Er, small."

The girl tossed the orange hair in seeming annoyance. "To stay or to go?"

Prudence looked around, wondering where the girl would suggest she sit. Out on the porch, she guessed. "Um, to go, please."

"Anything else?"

There was nothing on the chalkboard to help Prudence so she looked at the offerings in a few glass jars on the counter. One contained something labelled gluten-free sugar cookies, one biscotti. She pointed at the biscotti. "Two of those, please."

The girl reached into the jar with tongs and with difficulty extracted two biscotti and dropped them onto a plate. Cranberry-pistachio dipped in white chocolate, they looked delicious. Prudence waited. Then there was the noise of steam under pressure as the girl fiddled with an enormous machine. Next milk had to be heated, what Prudence guessed to be the liquid essence of pumpkin spice poured in from a bottle, and the whole disgusting concoction poured into a small paper cup to which the girl fitted a lid. She pushed the cup to Prudence then noticed the biscotti. Suddenly, she smiled. "Sorry. You asked for to go, didn't you?" She slid the biscotti off the plate into a white paper bag. "There you go." She triumphantly announced the price. "That'll be $15.95."

If Prudence was the sort of person who showed her feelings, her jaw would have dropped. Instead, she paid, took the meagre change from her twenty-dollar bill, saw the tip jar and dropped a dollar in. Then she calmly asked, "Can I see the manager?"

The girl, who'd been further cheered by the clink of change into the jar (and probably by the thought of Prudence's imminent departure), gave her a hurt look and walked to the back of the room. "Excuse me," she said haughtily to the mothers. One repositioned her stroller so the girl could reach the doorknob. She passed through, to reappear in a moment with the man Prudence had previously seen out back.

"May I speak privately with you a moment?" Prudence asked gravely. He gave her a wary look then nodded. They threaded their way between the mothers and strollers and passed into the back of the shop.

He seemed a nice man. He settled Prudence and her purchases in a chair across from his desk then sat down himself. "So," he said, leaning forward and clasping his hands, "what can I do for you?" Prudence thought he looked a bit nervous.

She turned to look behind her at the coffee-roasting equipment. "This is so interesting. To be right where you roast the coffee. I'm Prudence Crick, by the way."

He looked pleased and relaxed. "Thank you, er, Mrs. Crick. Good coffee is a passion of mine. I'm Dan Bartram." They reached across the desk, a minimalist wooden slab on delicate metal legs, and shook. He repeated, "What can I do for you?" He added, "Drink your coffee while we chat. It'll get cold."

Prudence inwardly shuddered and said, "Oh. That's for a friend. And I won't take much of your time. Look, Mr. Bartram, I realize you probably prefer to hire young people to work in your café—"

He interrupted her, anxious again. "Are you here to complain? Was Ginger rude?"

Prudence smiled inwardly. "Oh, no, she was fine," she lied. "No, I was going to ask, if you have an opening, if you would consider hiring an older person. Part-time. Say, two or three days or half-days per week."

Relieved, he sat back and considered the woman before him. Neat, in her fifties, quietly confident, seemed pleasant. She sat composedly, awaiting his reply. He thought of his clientele, mostly young to middle-aged housewives. He thought of the vast majority of Lovering's population—the elderly—people who rarely entered his shop. "Hmm," he said noncommittally.

Prudence saw a tall thin man in his thirties with a worried expression. "I've worked as a housekeeper almost my whole life," she explained, "and I feel that now I need something less physically demanding. Before I was a housekeeper I worked at the IGA as a cashier. And I rose to be a supervisor."

I bet you did, he thought, observing her unflappable exterior. God, it might be nice to hire someone who knew how to behave for a change. Someone he wouldn't be afraid to leave alone in the store. She was speaking again.

"—could just hold off for a week or so as I have friends visiting from out of town and I don't want suddenly to abandon them. I could take more work after they left."

He slowly nodded. "I could try you out. Give you a couple of short training sessions. Then if we are both satisfied—"

They exchanged contact information.

Prudence stood. "Thank you very much, Mr. Bartram." She smiled her thin-lipped smile and made to go back through the shop.

He stopped her. "Here." He indicated a back door that led into the parking lot that abutted the roasting facility. "If you don't mind. You can go out this way. Don't want to disturb the yummy mummies. Again."

She couldn't help thinking, as she walked past the sacks of coffee beans and the roaster, the boxes of small coffee bags waiting to be filled, what a nice café *this* space would make; two sides glassed in, facing the south and the west, just asking to be filled with quiet people happily drinking their coffees; a few floor plants spaced here and there. And more variety in its desserts wouldn't hurt: lots of things besides biscotti were good with a cup of coffee.

Danish. From reading women's magazines, she knew cupcakes were fashionable. Gluten-free cupcakes.

Bartram politely opened the back door for her and she stepped into the narrow walkway that began at Lucy's street and ran parallel to Main Road behind three or four businesses until it stopped at the driveway for St. Pete's.

She looked right toward the church and saw a cat, mostly grey with white on its chest and paws, dart between a small dumpster and some blue recycling bins. She turned toward the church and walked quickly down the path, calling "Puss, Puss, Puss," before changing to "Luc, Luc, Luc," and looking to either side.

Where the path ended, she scanned St. Pete's rear parking lot, then turned and retraced her steps. The cat, if it was listening, was not responding.

She paused behind the café and saw Dan Bartram sitting at his desk on the phone. He waved and she nodded. I hope he doesn't think I'm senile, she thought, wandering past garbage cans then reappearing moments later going the opposite direction.

She turned up Lucy's street, passed the Lesters' and entered the Ménard house. She handed the cup of coffee to Lucy. "Here. I'm afraid to try it."

"Oo, biscotti!" Lucy cooed, looking into the little white bag. "Oh, don't be silly." She poured half of the coffee into a just washed teacup and offered it to Prudence. "How bad can it be?"

They sipped. "Oh dear," Lucy said, while Prudence just made a face. "Sweet, and horrible."

"The girl squirted in a thick orange liquid. It *is* horrible. At least the biscotti look good." They chewed.

"I think these are Cathy Stribling's," Lucy said.

"You may be right," Prudence agreed. "I've tasted this recipe before." She took Lucy's cup and poured all the pumpkin spice latte down the drain. "Guess what? I've got a job."

# 8

After she'd driven back to The Maples and fed the hungry horde; after, feeling grubby from the afternoon's rooting around in someone else's dirt, she'd showered and changed; after making herself a BLT and settling down to eat it in front of the TV with several of the cats gathered around her, the phone rang. She rose and warily answered it, hoping, for once, it was a telemarketer to be easily disposed of.

"Hello?"

"Hello, my friend," Bertie said warmly. "Marion's exhausted from being Mistress of the Golf Cart and wants an early night. Care for some company? I could come over."

"I'm pretty exhausted too," Prudence began slowly.

"Oh. Well, if you're too tired…"

"I guess I can manage to stay up a few more hours," she said. "Can you make a fire?"

"With your guidance, I'm sure I can. Five minutes."

Prudence chewed the end of her sandwich and tried to remember the last occasion when a man (other than Bertie) had wanted her company. The cats hadn't bothered when the telephone rang, but when Bertie knocked heartily on the kitchen door, several of them roused themselves, yawning and stretching, curious for whatever entertainment the humans might provide.

Bertie stepped inside, sniffing appreciatively. "Mm. Bacon for supper."

Prudence, suddenly aware of the two large cat food plates on the floor and the greasy cast iron frying pan on the stove, felt embarrassed. Then, defensive, she said, "I've been out all day." She tidied while Bertie stood awkwardly. "After the golf I helped my friend Lucy begin cleaning out an old lady's home. She's in a nursing home and—" She stopped abruptly. "It's a long story."

Bertie found a dishcloth and started to dry the dishes. "Tell me. If you're not too tired."

So she did, finishing with, "So if you wouldn't mind, before Lucy and I start packing everything away, could you, er, assess Mme Ménard's possessions? They're to be sold for the benefit of St. Peter's church."

"A busman's holiday? I don't mind. I love old things. I wouldn't need to do a written report, would I?"

"Oh no! All very informal." She was feeling better so added with a straight face, "Besides, Lucy wants to meet you."

"Oh, she does, does she? And this Lucy person, she's important to you, is she?"

"Only my best and oldest friend." Prudence replied demurely, taking the now dry frying pan from his hands and putting it away.

"*I* see. A final vetting. Why do I feel like livestock before the auction?"

She gave him a level look then said primly, "Shall we make a fire? The cats will like it."

"Oh, well, if it's for the cats—"

They moved into the living room, Bertie got down on his knees, and Prudence handed him the objects he would need: the twisted newspaper spills, the tiny shreds of wood and bark, a few pinecones from the bowl on the mantel; then the slightly larger slivers of wood; all carefully placed so that air could encourage flame.

He sat back on his haunches as the fire took hold. "Hey, this is fun!"

"First fire of the year," she said sombrely, adding, "winter's coming."

He shot her a quizzical look. "But not yet, Prudence. It's still summer! And then comes autumn. Winter's not for a long while."

She returned his gaze but said nothing except, "We'll have to get more wood from the shed."

He followed her outside. Dusk was settling over the garden. Cats flitted around the lawn, disappearing singly or in pairs. "I saw all this in spring when it was just starting," he said, looking around. They thought back to that May afternoon when they'd met, when they'd wandered down to the water's edge and discovered a liking for each other.

Mischievously, she asked, "Have you been practising skipping stones?"

He turned to her. "Now where in Montreal would I do that, Prudence? My bathtub? If I tried skipping stones on Beaver Lake I'd probably get a ticket!" (Beaver Lake being an ornamental pond in a public park at the top of Mount Royal.)

She smothered a grin and slid back the woodshed's long side door. Inside were the eight cords of wood she and Gerry had stacked in August, though she'd tried at the time to dissuade the pregnant girl from doing much of the labour. A few cats strayed inside.

They each took an armload of wood back into the house, to be carefully laid to the sides of the large fireplace. Behind its screen the fire had subsided so Bertie built it up again with slightly larger logs. Prudence pulled two rocking chairs closer to the hearth and began introducing specific cats.

"In order of seniority, not of age, you understand, but of rank, we have the top cat, Bob, who is Gerry's favourite." The long lean tuxedo cat, stretched out on the hearthrug, blinked and purred. "There's Jay." She pointed to the petite black cat with white legs who was watching the fire. "She's still a—oh, no, I guess she isn't a kitten anymore. She's another favourite." The cat's whiskers twitched as her gaze followed sparks up the chimney. Prudence flicked a hand towards the couch where the marmalade tabby, Mother, sat composedly. "Mother." Then she named the other cats sitting on the sofa, pointing to each one in turn. "Blackie, Whitey, Mouse and Runt—the Honour Guard."

"The Honour Guard?" Bertie sounded mystified.

"They were the cats who slept with Maggie. They still sleep on Maggie's bed. Where I sleep when I'm staying here." There was a painful pause.

"That must be hard for you, Prudence," Bertie said softly.

She shrugged. "Everybody has to die somewhere," she said briskly. "At least she died in her bed surrounded by her pets. Not in some ditch." Her voice quivered on the final word.

Bertie reached over and took her hand. "I'm sorry you've been having a rough time, Prudence. I wish I could make it better."

She blinked and withdrew her hand, standing. "I'll make some tea." From the kitchen she heard the sound of his rocking chair on the wooden floor. While she waited for the kettle to boil, she put some butter fingers on a plate and listened to a cat, Mother, it so happened, crunching kibble from the tub under the kitchen table.

"Here we are," she said brightly, setting a tray down on the coffee table.

Bertie took a biscuit and bit into it. "Did you make these?" He sounded incredulous.

She nodded. Mother returned to her spot on the sofa.

"That cat—Mother?—is following you."

"Is she?" Prudence thought back to the days since Gerry had left. "Oh. Yes. I suppose she is. Must be missing Gerry."

"Mm," Bertie said.

Prudence sighed. "It's funny. Whenever I say her name, it's like I'm saying it to my own mother. She was never Mum or Mom, always Mother. Though Dad was Dad."

"Tell me about them," Bertie said.

"My father was born in 1915, my mother in 1920. They were both from Lovering. My father and Maggie's mother were brother and sister. He farmed one of the Catford farms up on Side Road. He was the only son. His younger brother Andrew died in the Second World War. Dad also served in the army but would never talk about it. That left Dad and his three sisters: Ellie who became Maggie's mother, and Sylvia and Mary. Sylvia married a Parsley and Mary a Shapland. I have lots of cousins." She added silently, who I rarely see socially, at least not on purpose. Bertie was quiet so she continued.

"Mother was a Parsley, a twin. Her twin Mary Isabelle died a few years before my father. My mother took it very hard. Twins have a special bond, they say.

"Anyway, my parents grew up knowing each other, got married, had me. And I grew up on the farm."

"And how was that?" Bertie got up and put two logs on the fire in the shape of an X. The cats shifted then resettled. Two more—a black shorthair and tailless tortoiseshell—joined the group, sitting side by side at the edge of the hearthrug.

"It was great!" Prudence said, her face breaking into a wide smile. Bertie, happening to look over his shoulder as the smile appeared, was surprised. It was the first time he'd seen anything more than Prudence's usual thin-lipped excuse for a smile. He turned back to the fire, poking the logs with the poker.

"There was always something to do, and it was so *interesting*. The animals, the crops, the vegetable garden, the orchard. We kept bees. My father hunted rabbit and wild turkey. My mother preserved the vegetables and fruit. We made jam and bread together." She paused.

"It sounds like a full life," he said simply, sitting back in his chair. He bit into another cookie. "And she taught you how to cook."

"She taught me how to cook," Prudence said dreamily, returning to the winter kitchen where they'd made stews and soups and roasted meats, and to the summer kitchen, a large lean-to tacked onto the back of the kitchen proper, where they'd pickled and jellied, dried herbs, sat shelling peas or topping gooseberries, as the summer breezes blew through the room's three screened sides, the two of them looking up from time to time at the valley stretching down, down, to where the cows and sheep grazed, to where they sometimes caught a glimpse of Edward Catford walking or riding his tractor.

"What?" said Prudence, lost in memories.

"I said, you should have married a farmer. You look so happy describing farm life."

"Oh. Do I? I suppose I must. I *loved* my childhood."

"Lucky," Bertie said dryly.

Prudence focused on his face. "Your turn," she said quietly.

So he told her. How he was the only child of a single woman in a time when that was so frowned on the authorities could just remove the child from its mother and give it to a couple to be adopted. And how that was partly why his mother had moved them from England to Canada.

Born in Liverpool just after the war, he'd never known his grandparents, extended family, or even who his father had been. "She never would talk about it. Stubborn. I suppose they all rejected her. We arrived here in 1950 when I was five, and she got a job as a cleaner at Eaton's department store. And because she was neat and smart, they let her apply for a sales job. She didn't get it, but they moved her from cleaning floors to washing dishes and eventually serving in the store cafeteria. She worked there for the rest of her life. I grew up on Eaton's cakes, stale, of course, because of the reduced price, and meat pies."

"Is she still alive?"

"Oh no. She died in 1970, a few months before her sixtieth birthday. Heart. She knew she was ill but didn't do anything about it. She was in hospital a few days then—just died." He stopped speaking and they both gazed at the fire. The two cats sitting close together shifted slightly, the tortoiseshell turning to lick the other's ears.

Bertie asked, "And who are these two, so devoted to each other?"

"The tortoiseshell is Lightning. And the black one is Seymour. She lost her tail; he an eye." Bertie leaned forward to stroke Lightning. "Don't pat her!" Prudence warned. "She's skittish. *He's* all right though. A bit of a softy."

Bertie petted Seymour's back and Lightning paused in her grooming of him to give Bertie an evil glance. Bertie reassured her. "Don't worry, m'dear, I'm just admiring your friend." Seymour, the object of all this attention, kept his eyelids closed and a steady purr coming.

"More tea?" Prudence asked.

"Why not?" Bertie straightened and looked at her. "Prudence, may I ask about your marriage?"

She put the teapot down. "I was young. I made a mistake. I thought he'd settle down. He didn't. He was gentle but weak and his—" She paused to find the right word. "His associates were bad people, criminals, and he went along with them. Remember the bank robbery in 1972? The one that turned violent?"

He shook his head. "I was travelling. After my mother died, I bummed around. I wasn't reading the papers."

"Oh. Well. A guard at the bank was killed. The thieves got away with a lot of money. To make a long story short, Alex, my husband, was the only one caught and he wouldn't rat the other two out, so—*he* was charged with murder and bank robbery and spent the next twenty-five years in prison." Sarcastically, she added, "You spend more time in jail for armed robbery than you do for murder. Did you know that? Shows what society really values. Or it used to be that way." She turned blank eyes on Bertie and added in a dull voice, "He got out earlier this year, met up with the other two robbers, and one of them killed him."

Bertie said in a distressed tone, "Prudence, I confess I heard some of it from Marion. She remembers the robbery. But I had no idea of the rest! Did they catch his murderer? Will there be a trial?"

She nodded. "Yes. The murderer confessed. But he's not right in the head so probably won't stand trial. I don't know. And his accomplice is accused but hasn't confessed so he'll go to trial, if they can come up with any evidence. At least the murderer implicated him, but again, if he's judged non-competent, his evidence may be thrown out." Her voice dripped venom as she added, "Did I mention they're Alex's brothers? Robert and Jack Crick. Left Alex in a ditch after he'd protected them all that time. A fine family I married into." There was a stricken silence.

Three grey tiger cats streaked into the room and came to an abrupt halt by the fire. Following closely behind them came a little white cat with a thin black moustache. The gang looked around at the cozy scene and decided to join it. Mother left her position by the fire and walked over to inspect the white cat, sniffing him from head to toe before returning to her original spot.

"Mother's favourite," Prudence explained, glad of the distraction. "Ronald. She always mothers the youngest. It was Jay last year, Ronald the year before that. Now she hardly notices young Jay but Ronald—" She shrugged. "She has special feelings for him, I guess."

"Who knew cat relationships were as complicated as human ones?" Bertie said lightly. "I shall never remember all their names, I'm afraid." He pointed to Bob. "That's Jay?" Prudence smiled, a little, and shook her head. He continued, "And that's Seymour?" He indicated Jay.

Prudence named them correctly, pointing. "Bob—large tuxedo. Jay—small tuxedo. Seymour—all black. Start with those three."

"At least I remember her!" Bertie said triumphantly. "That's Mother!"

Yes," Prudence agreed, sounding thoughtful. "That's Mother."

# 9

"Marion!"

"What?"

"Slow down!"

"What?"

"I said, slow down!"

Marion braked abruptly, jerking both Bertie and Prudence forward. "I can't hear you when the engine's running. What did you say?"

Bertie hissed under his breath, "It's electric—there's no sound," then more audibly admonished her, but mildly. "We're here to look at the plants, Marion. Don't go too fast, please."

Prudence, sitting next to Marion, smiled and stared at a topiary of a dog, about ten times life size. The dog was standing, alert, straining at something in the distance. She consulted the printed pamphlet. "It's a memorial to a real dog. Made by the landscape artist."

Marion nodded. "Very nice." She set the cart in motion again along the gravel path.

They were visiting the Dream Garden, a showpiece created by a local landscaper in the next town over from Lovering. Prudence had been before, a few years previously, but in the blazing heat of high summer when all the flowering plants made the garden spectacular.

It was still colourful in September, just different. Instead of yellow water lilies in the pond, she saw lilac-flowered water hyacinths. The flowerbeds where day lilies had ruled were now a blend of differently coloured cone flowers—the usual purple, but also pink, yellow, red. Purple salvia and salmon yarrow here, tall red or golden clumps of grasses there, completed the scene.

And then there were the sculptures. They passed an earth goddess, made from red begonias and succulents, dreaming, her head pillowed on her arm; and another goddess, head rising out of the soil, her hair many plants of purple-black grass, presiding over a bed of pink sedums.

Prudence looked at Marion, who had a fierce look of concentration on her face. She's going to want one of these for the city, she thought of the golf cart, then wondered if Marion already had one of those electric scooters the elderly used, for those days when they just couldn't get going for very long by foot. She half-turned to observe Bertie.

His expression was one of happiness. This must be totally out of his experience, she thought, and realized she hadn't heard much sniffing from him lately. "Are you enjoying it?" she asked.

He nodded. "Very much."

"And your allergies?"

He breathed deeply through his nose. "Cured," he confirmed, nodding. "I was obviously meant for country life."

They passed over a wooden bridge into a field of lavender. Even Prudence, who'd seen it before, was impressed. She'd thought by September the lavender might be dull, faded, or even no longer flowering. But she was wrong. They must cut it at mid-summer, she thought, and it re-blooms.

They breathed in the sweet scent and the view. Bertie spoke: "Marion, why don't you park over there, where the chairs are, and you can sit and rest and take it in for a moment." They bumped over the slightly uneven terrain at the edge of the field. Bertie assisted Marion off the cart and into a seat. "Walk?" he asked Prudence. She nodded. They meandered up and down the purple rows, pausing to rub their fingers on a bit of plant here and there, smelling the results. At the far end of the field was a stand of giant sunflowers. "Let's go in here," Bertie suggested, pointing at a handmade sign: Sunflower Maze.

Most of the plants were three times their height. The stalks were three inches around. Many were bent from supporting the weight of giant flower heads more than a foot across, while some had snapped. While they were in the maze, more than one plant fell with a sudden swoosh, rustling as it was caught by its fellows. It was awe-inspiring being part of the life of a patch of mature sunflowers.

They picked their way slowly along the mud path. It was wet in places and once, Bertie going ahead, turned and offered Prudence his hand to help her around fallen stalks. When she hopped the puddle, she wound up close to Bertie who was still holding her hand with a strange expression on his face.

"Prudence, I—"

"Oh, my goodness!" Prudence interrupted, looking at her watch. "Marion will be wondering where we've gotten to." She turned as if to retrace their steps but found he was still holding her hand.

"Prudence, you must know—"

How ridiculous, she thought, her cheeks flaming. Two almost-old people holding hands in a maze. "Don't embarrass yourself," she said in a low voice.

He looked taken aback. "Embarrass myself?" He dropped her hand.

"Just leave it—the way it is!" she replied vehemently. "Can't you?" Without waiting for an answer, she turned and fled toward where her sense of direction told her Marion would be waiting.

As she broke free of the maze and stepped back into the fragrant field of lavender, all she was aware of was a crushing sense of disappointment.

They were silent as they rejoined Marion, who was lying back in an Adirondack chair with her eyes closed. She opened them, took in the tension with a keen glance and said only, "I want my lunch."

"We'll get something at Cathy's," Bertie soothed. "Or I'll walk to the Parsley Inn for takeout if she's busy."

Prudence said nothing until they were back in Cathy's driveway and Bertie was helping Marion out of the car. Then she addressed Marion. "You're coming to The Maples for supper, remember?"

Marion testily replied, "I haven't forgotten!" Bertie focused on getting Marion's hat, purse and gloves from the car. As he backed away, he cocked his head and gave Prudence one quizzical look. She shrivelled inside.

Instead of driving the short distance back to Gerry's house, she backtracked the way they'd come from the Dream Garden, up Station Road to her own small cottage.

Parked in the driveway, she looked furtively in her rear-view mirror. That was the last thing she needed—Charlie or Rita hailing her from across the road, demanding to know all the details of how her visitors were enjoying their vacation.

As she walked up the arc of the front path, she realized she hadn't pointed her house out earlier to Bertie or Marion when they'd passed—twice. I have to keep *something* private, she reasoned. Once inside the tiny front hallway, she felt her shoulders relax. This house with its four rooms, its clean lines, fit her. It was the house her parents had moved to after her father's second heart attack made selling the farm a necessity.

Prudence had been living in the apartment over the paint shop, but on her own, having separated from Alex, and was still working in the IGA as a supervisor. Her friend Maggie Coneybear had just inherited The Maples after her mother's death at the comparatively young age of fifty-six. Maggie, content to be her mother's companion after her father's death, and studying at the École des Beaux-Arts in Montreal, hadn't had to move. Unlike her older brother Gerald and sister Mary, she'd never left the Coneybear family home. So her solitary life of cats and gardening, baking and visiting friends, drawing and painting, had begun.

None of them had been able to foretell the coming disaster, she thought gloomily. Disasters. Her father's and Maggie's premature deaths; the one so natural; the other, not.

Her father hadn't been much interested in life as an invalid. For her mother's sake, he'd tried to be cheerful, but as inactivity withered his body, so the atrophy soon spread to his mind.

Thinking to give him pleasure, Prudence had dug a small vegetable plot behind the house for him to tend, and it was here her mother found him one afternoon when she'd called him in vain to come in for tea. Prudence had subsequently sown grass seed into the plot.

Preparing cheese and crackers with a cup of tea, she looked sombrely out at the back yard. Everybody dies somewhere, words she'd shared with Bertie, repeated themselves in her brain. No need to fear or avoid any place because someone had died there. Though it was hard at first.

She sat at the little kitchen table where she'd so often sat with her mother after her father's death. His going had bewildered her mother. "Only sixty!" she would say in a shocked voice to anyone who would listen. "Sixty's not old!"

To Prudence, twenty-seven when he died, sixty seemed pretty old, at least numerically. Since her separation from Alex followed by his participation in a fatal robbery and all that shame, she felt she had left youth far behind. She wondered if those events had in some way contributed to her father's early death.

Moving in with her mother and transitioning from cashier/supervisor to cleaning lady (both of which took her out of the public eye) seemed to set the seal on an early middle age.

And her mother had begun to get a bit strange after her husband died. She claimed he was still with her, not in the widely accepted and sentimental forms of in her heart, in her memories, but actually in the room with her.

And neither she nor he, apparently, was shy about this. Constance talked to Ted at home, in the store—she even whispered to him at church, looking sideways down the aisle to shush his imagined voice.

At first Prudence had thought this was going to be temporary, a way for her mother to work through the first stages of mourning. But far from mourning, Constance seemed to simply be carrying on life as usual.

She cooked large heavy meals of Ted's favourite dishes. She baked bread and desserts as she'd always done. She preserved vegetables and made jam, much of which Prudence donated to the local church's sales, as how much jam could two women eat between them anyway?

And then Constance discovered Mrs. Smith.

That her mother began regularly seeing a medium seemed strangely logical to Prudence, and when, after a few months, Constance ceased chatting to Ted in public, she was grateful. The next time Constance went for a private séance, Prudence accompanied her. It cost the same amount—why not?

It grew to be a routine; every second Thursday at twelve-thirty in the afternoon, Prudence would phone for a taxi, then she and her mother would sit silently in its back seat, gazing at the lake as the taxi took the pleasant river road to Mrs. Smith's apartment twenty minutes from Lovering. They'd go up in the elevator and be welcomed into the light-filled room, sit at a round table and hold hands.

Prudence was never a participant. She listened to Mrs. Smith (who she quite liked) ask if there was anyone who wished to speak to Constance. Mrs. Smith always used Constance's full name—Constance Virginia Parsley Catford—because, she said, that way any spirits who might be hovering around would know exactly who had come calling, so to speak. Prudence thought this sounded sensible.

All was well until that Thursday afternoon when Mrs. Smith had introduced Constance's name into the ether and, as the spectral conversation between Mrs. Smith and her long dead twin Mary Isabelle paused, Mrs. Smith had interjected, "Prudence Catford Crick is also here."

Right away, Prudence had felt a tingle of—what? Hyper-alertness was the best way she would later describe it. They waited.

Mrs. Smith spoke. "Ted is here." Constance gave a little sigh of satisfaction. "He says…he says, to tell Prudence that Jimmy just passed. Jimmy just passed, he's seen him, and he's okay."

Prudence and her mother exchanged a puzzled look. Jimmy? They didn't know any—then Prudence's mouth opened. Oh. Jimmy. Jimmy the pony her father had taught her to ride on, who they'd sold to a riding stable when the farm had been broken up.

She blinked back tears. How would Mrs. Smith know about Jimmy? The sceptic in Prudence wondered if the medium just threw out a random name and watched for a reaction. Or possibly her mother had mentioned the pony on a previous visit.

Constance leaned toward Prudence and whispered, "Jimmy. Your pony."

Prudence nodded and said, "Shush, Mother. I know who Jimmy is." She addressed Mrs. Smith directly. "Ask about Billy."

Mrs. Smith sat quietly for a moment then opened her eyes, looking placidly at Prudence. "There's no Billy in your past, Prudence."

Prudence felt that tingle again.

Mrs. Smith paused and her eyes half-closed. "Except—" Aha! Prudence thought. Gotcha! Mrs. Smith continued, "Except, your father says, didn't you go to school with a Billy? One of the Cottles, he says. The ones who set the hay barn on Larson's Drive on fire."

Prudence was dumbfounded. That was ancient history. Unless Mrs. Smith was possessed of an encyclopedic memory and had studied Prudence's personal history back to and including everyone she'd gone to school with, how would she know about Billy and his brothers?

Constance leaned forward and hissed. "You father was so upset! All that good hay—up in smoke! And the neighbour's horses upset."

This time when Prudence shushed her mother her voice was gentle, and when she met Mrs. Smith's gaze she saw the woman's eyes were clear, serene.

They always had a quick cup of tea with Mrs. Smith after each séance, after they'd phoned for the taxi, after Constance had laid the money on the table.

That day, as they sat quietly sipping, Prudence felt a great release as the words "no more sorrow, no more tears" repeated themselves in her mind. She never missed a séance after that, even (or especially) after her mother died many years later.

Until the last few months. Since Alex had died. Her fear of having to hear his words from the afterlife was too intense. It would be too much after their fraught marriage, long shameful separation. She would rather let his shade, and those of her beloved parents, move away from her altogether.

She straightened her shoulders and took a deep breath. That was it. She would eschew the spirit world from now on. She would get on with her life in the world of hard reality.

She tidied her dishes and drove back to The Maples. She had a supper to prepare for her guests.

The evening hadn't turned out as awkwardly as she'd feared. Marion and Bertie arrived at six-thirty, at the front door of The

Maples, of course, as befitted Marion's dignity. Marion wore a half-length natural mink coat with a blue Chinese jacket underneath. She wore a matching mink beret, and though she surrendered the coat, smelling of mothballs and perfume, to Prudence in The Maples' grand foyer, she kept the hat on all evening. Bertie had put on a suit.

Prudence had set three places at one end of the formal dining room's enormous heavy table. She used the good china with its orange and royal blue oriental pattern, the heavy old silverware and the crystal stemware; and she found enough pink phlox, white phlox and silver wormwood in the garden to make an attractive table arrangement.

She served them roasted pork loin stuffed with sage and onion dressing, oven-roasted potatoes, and carrots from the garden tossed with a little sauce of brown sugar, melted butter and orange juice. Bertie had brought a bottle of wine. For once Marion was abstemious, choosing to stay alert to take in the tension between the other two, as well as the surroundings, with bright inquisitive eyes. "So, this is where Ellie Catford lived after she married." Marion and Ellie had attended the same private girls' school in Montreal. "Very nice. Too bad she didn't live to enjoy it very long. Dead in her fifties, eh?"

"She was my aunt," Prudence said quietly.

"Oh?" Marion seemed startled. "I didn't know that. On what side?"

"My father was her brother. Edward Catford."

"Oh. Ted Catford. I remember him. Big strong-looking fella. Going to be a farmer." She took a sip of her wine and reassessed Prudence. "So, you're one of *those* Catfords. Had a lot of farmland up on Side Road, I seem to recall. Must be worth a lot."

"All sold," Prudence said calmly, "long ago."

"Oh." Marion seemed deflated. "Oh, well. Things change. And your mother?"

"A Parsley. Her twin married John Coneybear, Ellie's brother-in-law."

"What a small world you live in out here in Lovering. So, you're twice connected to the Coneybears, to this house. You're almost Lovering royalty."

Prudence didn't know how to reply to this so didn't. "I'll get the dessert. Tea or coffee?"

"What's for dessert?" Marion asked. You had to hand it to her, she wasn't shy.

"Chocolate cake with vanilla frosting."

"Hmm. Well, coffee then. Coffee with chocolate."

"Coffee for me, please, Prudence," Bertie said when she looked at him. He'd hardly spoken all evening.

Prudence went into the kitchen and put on the kettle. Mother followed her in, sat on the floor next to the fridge. "What do *you* want?" Prudence said rather aggressively.

"Just to help carry things," Bertie replied meekly, appearing in the kitchen door.

"Oh! I wasn't—I was talking to the cat."

"And what did the cat reply?"

Prudence smiled, a little. "I don't know. We were interrupted."

There was a pause. "Cake looks nice," he said. Prudence had laid on the buttercream frosting thickly then taken the tip of a blunt knife to the top of it, making little waves. He added, "Lovering royalty, eh? Who knew?"

Prudence smiled, a little more broadly. "Marion is exaggerating."

Bertie continued in a bantering tone. "Now I understand why you repelled my advances." He picked up the tray with their coffee. "I'm just not good enough for you." Before she could speak, he added, "But I already knew that, Prudence."

She had tears in her eyes when she carried in the dessert.

## 10

Marion sensed the relaxed atmosphere immediately. "Well, I'm glad you two made it up. We're only halfway through the first week of this visit." She accepted a large piece of cake and greedily dug in.

"Marion, your bluntness is exceeded only by your insensitivity," Bertie teased sweetly.

She swallowed. "Hah! If I can't say what I'm thinking now, when will I? Your little misunderstanding is nothing. Why, I remember—" And here she launched into a long rambling retelling of a memorable weekend she and her dead husband had spent at the country home of a member of parliament. As it involved the member's member, and how it got him into trouble with not only his wife, who Marion knew from the University Women's Club; his official mistress, a married woman with whom Marion had played tennis; and the wife of the then prime minister, it made their hair rise.

At its conclusion, Bertie craftily asked, "When was this exactly?"

"Hah!" Marion reiterated. "Wouldn't you like to know? Sometime between the end of the war and 1975. When my dear Fred died." She pushed her cake plate a little away from her. "That was delicious. He was ten years older than me and had a bad heart. They didn't do the heart surgery back then that they do now. He might have had another twenty years. He just got sicker and sicker." She brightened up. "Still, before all that, we had fun! I remember—" And she was off again telling another story, this one about a charity ball they'd attended in the 1950s, who'd been there, what they'd worn, and who she'd flirted with.

Prudence, listening with only half her attention, contrasted the lives of Marion and Fred Stewart with those of her parents. Royalty indeed! If anyone had lived a royal life, it was Marion, not Prudence's mother, Constance Catford. Presumably Fred Stewart had worked but it appeared Marion had just swanned around enjoying herself.

She couldn't imagine a life without work. Which reminded her. There was a lull in the conversation into which she inserted, "I've got a new job."

Both of them stared at her.

"What do you mean?" Bertie asked. "A new house-cleaning client?"

"No. Something different. I'm going to work in a little café in Lovering. Just to do something else before I retire."

Marion looked at her keenly. "Bored, eh? Good for you. I enjoyed my working years. Nice to get up in the morning and have somewhere to go."

Bertie looked at her in surprise. "You? Worked?"

Coolly, she replied. "Clerked for Fred for twenty years at his law practice. Once we realized we weren't going to have any children. Made us closer."

"Shall we move into the living room?" Prudence asked. "There's a sofa there and perhaps Bertie could make a fire." She raised her eyebrows at him.

"Yes, yes. Delighted to."

They transferred themselves to the living room. Cats, who'd been quietly observing during the supper hour, trickled through the passageway that separated dining from living room.

"I hardly noticed them when we were eating," Marion observed. "How many are there anyway?"

"Twenty. Now. But the numbers have varied over the years."

"Why would Ellie allow her daughter to have so many cats?" Marion mused.

"Well, she didn't really. Most of Maggie's cats were outside cats. She had one or two inside as pets when she was a girl. But after her mother died, the cats just seemed to drift into the house. The ones who live here now are her last cats. Gerry's added two since she inherited."

Marion snorted. "Must have inherited the cat-collecting gene as well," she said, and promptly fell asleep.

"I've never had a pet," Bertie said from the hearth. He'd managed to build an acceptable combination of log house and pyramid as Prudence had previously shown him, and now set a match to it. It flickered nicely into life. "So, what's this about a new job?"

"Nothing," Prudence said defensively. "What Marion said: I'm bored cleaning houses over and over. It'll make a change. I start tomorrow, just training for a few hours."

"Hmm," said Bertie doubtfully, and tended his fire. The cats crept closer to its warmth. The wood's crackling and Marion's gentle snores were the only sounds in the room.

Prudence parked at the town parking lot across the street from Coco Poco and took a deep breath. Something new. Something different. She climbed the front steps and greeted a man she recognized as one of Lucy's neighbours, sitting on the porch at a miniscule table drinking a coffee. His golden retriever slumbered at his feet. "Nice day," she offered.

He wasn't having any of it. "Bit cold," he complained, and scowled.

"Yup. But sunny. Gotta keep moving," she encouraged.

"I suppose. Come on, Jazz." The dog got up slowly and together they progressed stiffly down the stairs.

Feeling depressed by the encounter, Prudence straightened her back and took another deep breath. She pushed on the door. A bell tinkled overhead.

The café was empty. Well, it was only nine o'clock, a bit early for mid-morning coffee. "Hello?" she said tentatively.

There must have been a corresponding bell or alarm in the back room, because Dan Bartram appeared looking flustered. "Oh, it's you," he rather unflatteringly said. He went to the front window and peered out. "You haven't seen—oh, never mind." He too took a deep breath and smiled. "Sorry. It's just we had some windows broken in the back last night, and I'm kind of rattled. And now Ginger is a no show, *again*. I was going to get her to train you. Well. Let me show you the basics."

Prudence took off her coat and draped it on one of the hooks meant for customers. Dan showed her where everything was and explained the mysteries of the espresso machine and the cash. "Do you think you can remember all that?" he concluded, scribbling the day's special blend—Quetzalcoatl's Gift, With a Hint of Chocolate—on the chalkboard above the counter.

"Perfectly," she responded crisply, wondering if Quetzalcoatl was pronounced as it was spelled. "And if I forget, you'll be in the back, right?"

"Right. I'll be phoning for a glazier to come and repair my smashed windows."

"Ah. Good luck with that. It's sometimes difficult in Lovering to get workmen to come right away. This number—" She rummaged in her purse for a card and wrote the number on a piece of paper. "These are the Hudsons. And I speak from experience about broken glass. I had to get a door repaired last spring. It took at least ten days, I seem to remember. Meanwhile, these two are odd-job men. They'll cover the broken glass with plywood in the meantime."

Dan took the paper ruefully. "I thank you. I've only lived here a little while. All right. I'll leave you to it." With one desperate look at his fledgling business, he disappeared into the back room.

The front door chime tinkled and a stroller appeared in the open doorway. Prudence straightened her back again, twitched her sweater into place, and smiled.

As she walked the few steps from Coco Poco to Mme Ménard's house, she felt exhausted but stimulated by her first half-day at work. She left by the front door, going down the steps and around the corner of the building onto Lucy's street. As she passed Coco Poco's side she saw the damage for the first time.

Someone had wielded a bar, or perhaps thrown rocks against both of the glass sides of the extension. Because the glass was thick, aside from one gaping hole, the miscreant or miscreants had only managed to make starbursts that marred the clear surface.

Prudence clucked her tongue and shook her head. What a waste.

She passed the walkway with its garbage cans, the Lester house, and opened the Ménard house's gate. Something brushed past her legs as she turned to shut it. "Luc!" she said. "Why don't you come in?" She went quickly to the front door and opened it. "Look what the cat—" she began then stopped.

A man with a disgruntled expression came toward her. "You must be Lucy Hanlan," he began.

Prudence shook her head. "Actually, I'm not. I'm helping her, though. I'm her friend." The cat ran into the kitchen. "I'll just—" She sidled past the man and followed the cat. She found the bag of kibble and scooped some into a bowl. Automatically, as she would do at The Maples, she put the bowl under the kitchen table so the cat could eat in peace. She noticed Luc had a notch in his left ear— an old battle wound, she assumed. And his front legs were white up to the elbow whereas the rear ones were only white pawed. The man had followed her and stood, watching the proceedings.

"I'm Mme Ménard's nephew," he said, adding, with what sounded like satisfaction, "That cat'll have to go."

Prudence straightened and considered him. He wore a gold shiny suit. The jacket buttons strained against his ample stomach. His shoes were light brown, shiny and pointed. His two-day-old beard was unshaven but had been fashionably trimmed. She said, "Oh. You don't have to worry about that. We'll attend to it." She made a mental note to query Gerry in her next email about adding to The Maples' collection. That is, if Lucy wouldn't— Her thought was interrupted by the woman herself coming in the front door.

"How do you do, Monsieur Ménard?" She shook his hand. "I'm Lucy Hanlan. Father Lackey told me you'd be along about now. You've met my friend Prudence Crick? She's been kindly helping us."

The man nodded shortly in Prudence's direction then addressed Lucy. "This is all you've done?" He jerked his head indicating the kitchen.

Lucy looked a little affronted. "No-o. We've already sorted the clothes and linens upstairs. Everything has to be cleaned before it's moved, you know."

He grunted. "Yeah. She's been living in filth, that's for sure."

Lucy took a breath. "Not *filth*, I assure you. Just—the very old can't clean the way we younger ones can. And possibly, as their vision goes, they can't even—"

"Yeah, yeah," he interrupted, waving a hand. "Anyway, when do you think you'll be finished?"

Lucy drew herself up and coolly said, "I couldn't possibly say. I'm on my lunch now, from my own business, and Prudence also works. Perhaps you'd like to pay professional cleaners and packers to organize the household?"

He's considering it, Prudence thought, as she saw indecision flit across Ménard's face. Then he seemed to make up his mind. Cheapness won. "No. You keep at it. There's no rush—so long as that weirdo next door keeps avoiding me." He sighed, rubbed his eyes with one hand, and muttered to himself, "I have to wait until the old woman's will is probated anyway."

"You mean Mrs. Lester's will?" Prudence asked. He nodded. "Oh good," she added. "For a minute I thought perhaps your aunt had died. How is she?"

"The same," he muttered, looking around the room.

"At the Rosemont, is she? I think I heard…" Prudence tried to sound bland, though she was on a fishing expedition.

"The Chest—," he began to say, then appeared to think better of it. "Right." He caught sight of Luc, now washing his face with a paw. "And get rid of that cat. Or I will." He walked heavily to the front door. It slammed behind him.

"Well!" said Lucy, blowing out an excess of angry breath. "Not even a tiny thank you! After all our work!"

"All *your* work, Lucy. I see you've done a lot since I was here before."

"Little Mamzelle Fortin came to help me. Apparently, she was friends with Mme Ménard. Church friends, anyway. We got all upstairs done except for the heavy furniture."

"Do you still want Bertie to come look at everything else?"

"Yes! Yes! How's that going?"

"It's going," Prudence replied laconically. "He's agreed. Hey! I just did a three-hour shift at the café."

"No! That was fast work! How was it?"

"I'll think I'll be able to get the place into shape," her friend replied smugly.

"I bet you will," Lucy said admiringly. "I just bet you will. Now what are we going to do about this cat?"

# PART 3
# BARGAINING

Luc hated being in the box. His heart thudded as he crouched, the box swaying to the rhythm of the walker carrying him. Carrying him away from his home. His tail thrashed from side to side, measuring the width of the box. Through a slit in the cardboard, he could see they were proceeding up his street, passing familiar objects.

There went the lamppost at the corner of his property where his fence ended. There went the row of big-leaved shrubs under which he liked to dig. There went the house that always smelled of fish, and the dangerous house where two dogs lived, who might roar out into their backyard at any moment of the day or night and where, for that reason, no cat ever set foot.

The rocking motion made him sick to his stomach. He crouched, ready to spring when the box would finally be opened.

They passed the place where there was a path that led to a big green open area that was usually empty except for when screaming children with a ball ran aimlessly back and forth. He could hear only a few faint voices now. Surrounded by woods, it was easy to skirt. A cat didn't want to be caught out in the open.

Across from that path, another street began. They passed it. They were leaving behind his territory, carefully marked with his urine and saliva. This was bad.

The smells were the same but different. Different trees and shrubs, different earth, dug up by different cats. Cats who would question Luc's right to be there. Cats he would have to fight. The ear with the notch twitched.

The box veered left past a row of sweet-smelling shrubs and into a driveway, then up a few steps. The person set it down on a flat surface and Luc began to push against the top. "Oh, no you don't," *the person said and put a foot on the box's top as they fumbled with keys.*

*He felt the box being lifted briefly then again set down. It opened. He jumped out and skittered from the room, stopping abruptly.*

*He didn't understand. He already had a house. Why had they brought him here?*

*The person called, "Luc! Supper!" and snapped open a can. He re-entered the feeding room and accepted the meal. Smooth chunks of meat in gravy. This was more like it. He ate quickly. But—when the person briefly opened the door to put the box outside, he dashed between their feet and ran away back down the street towards his real house.*

*He threaded his way between the bars of his fence and paused for a thorough grooming. That was better. It had been an alarming experience. He was supposed to wait for her here, not somewhere else where she couldn't find him. He'd learned that you couldn't trust anyone but your own person. Well, he would be more careful in future. If only she would come. He climbed onto a chair on his porch and fell asleep.*

*He was woken by the sound of the neighbour coming out of his house. It was dark. The neighbour moved uncertainly down his front steps and fumbled with his gate before walking toward the main road where Luc never went.*

*Luc remembered with satisfaction that the old woman from that house, the one who used to swear at him, who'd refused him food, had been taken away as had his woman. But she, the neighbour, had been in a bag, unmoving. He dozed.*

*And was woken again, this time by the sound of smashing glass. The sound, accompanied by grunting human noises, was repeated. Then the neighbour, moving like a cat, furtively, low to the ground and with speed, appeared and entered the house next door, keeping his head down.*

*Another bigger man came from the same direction, breathing hard, and paused by the gate, nodded his head a few times and continued up the street. The men were no concern of his.*

*The familiar scents of fried food and coffee lulled him back to sleep. He dreamt he was asleep upstairs in the bed, safe in the crook of her arm. "Luc," he heard faintly, and his body shivered.*

# 11

Dear Prudence (and Cats),

Sorry it's been a few days since I sent you a message. We've been so busy! It's Thursday night (so for you Thursday teatime, I guess) and tomorrow we leave Devon for Wales. Let me tell you what we've been up to since last I wrote.

I would say the one word to describe Devon would be hilly. If you're not going up one hill you're going down another. But they're little. Oh my God, we passed a village called Bubbly Sauceton! I am not kidding! I feel another crazy cat book like *The Cake-Jumping Cats of Dibble* coming on! How about *How Treacle the Cat Got His Name*? Doug is shaking his head, so maybe no.

We made it to Lovering! Our namesake village, Lovering, in north-central Devon, is: ten houses and an old church. We checked for names in the cemetery. Parsleys, Catfords, our John Coneybear's parents' and siblings' graves—all resting. I got a real quiet feeling in my chest standing there reading the names of real people, our ancestors.

We passed the farm where Sir Walter Raleigh was born. It had a thatched roof with a thatched pheasant on top. I sketched it from the car and added a thatched cat stalking the pheasant.

The moors don't do much for me. Dreary, I would say, though seeing ponies walking around on the loose is nice. I got more interested when we reached the north coast. Our hotel for the last few nights has been The Chapel, which isn't, but is next door to one. It's in Ilfracombe. We took a coastal cruise to Lundy Island, three lighthouses in various states of disrepair (one good one, obviously), foggy, birdy, very few people. We bought some puffin stamps, which are the island's biggest seller, apparently.

I'm in scone heaven! They are everywhere, with Devon cream and jam. I eat them every day. Doug says I'm getting fat! And that this baby will be born demanding them! Mostly we eat in pubs for lunch and, if I'm tired by suppertime, grab sandwiches and chips (crisps, they call them) or pasties (yum, we have to make some when I get home) to eat in our room. I love watching British TV. Some of the ads are very humorous.

Well, that's it from Devon, I guess. I can't believe our trip is half done! Much love to you all at home.

Gerry and Doug

Prudence closed the computer with a sigh. She had replied, telling of her and Bertie and Marion's adventures (she could imagine how curious Gerry would be for details), even of her new job, and a little about the two unfortunate old ladies on Lucy's street. And the cat, though she'd tried not to sound like she was asking whether he could come live at The Maples. After all, he was Lucy's responsibility, for now. And she confirmed that she was now, officially, with wheels, and using them.

Today, she had lied to everyone. To Dan Bartram, who wanted her to come in to work, she had pleaded the obligation of guests to entertain. To Bertie and Marion, she'd claimed she had to work. Really, all she wanted this rainy day was quiet time at The Maples. So, after she phoned everyone that morning, she made a coffee and sat on the sofa with her book. She couldn't concentrate on Virginia Woolf's early years, though they were interesting and full of intellectual opportunities Prudence envied, and soon found herself with an empty cup, staring at the cold hearth.

The house's other occupants, their stomachs full, placidly drifted here and there. She and they took each other for granted after all these years. They seemed to know that she was committed to their well-being without having a great deal of emotion invested in them. Which suited everybody's nature just fine.

Then, as if to contradict her thoughts, Mother and Min Min jumped up on the sofa next to her. That made sense to Prudence; Mother was a natural caregiver and Min Min, well, he loved everybody. He settled on her lap, purring, while Mother sat on the sofa arm. She should make a fire, drive out the damp. Maybe later.

She wasn't used to constant human companionship. It had been so long since she'd lived with anyone. She'd discovered she liked living alone during those years after she'd kicked Alex out of the two-room apartment over the paint shop and before her father died and she moved to the Station Road bungalow to be with her mother.

She'd made the apartment over the paint shop a refuge. After Alex she'd had the rug and upholstered furniture professionally cleaned to get out the stale smell Alex had seemed to trail around in—cigarettes and grass, a body oozing the yeasty aftereffect of beer for breakfast, beer for lunch, beer for supper. She'd never told anyone he was an alcoholic, but she supposed people knew.

After she'd cleaned the apartment, she'd painted it herself. By then she knew she was pregnant, the result of a last fumbling attempt by her and Alex to make things right between them.

She'd cursed her luck then calmed. It wasn't usual in Lovering, but her child could be raised by one parent. There was no need to be ashamed. She was still married. And maybe the news would sober Alex. Then she'd remembered his blank face during that other, previous pregnancy early in their marriage, when she'd miscarried, spending days and nights bleeding in their bedroom while Alex carried on with his smoking and drinking buddies in the other room.

Why go over it all again? She clucked her tongue in annoyance at herself, and the ears of both cats twitched. She got up and poured a second coffee. The phone rang and instinctively she reached for it and answered, realizing her mistake immediately. I'm not here, she wanted to say, and, please, don't leave a message.

Fortunately, it was neither Bertie nor Dan Bartram, but the company that was going to install a wood stove in the dining room fireplace. Yes, she knew they were coming the next day, Friday. Yes, sometime in the morning. Yes, someone would be home.

She put the phone down and walked into the dining room. She'd prepare it for the workers: push furniture out of the way, roll the rug up to the far side of the room.

As she passed the round convex mirror hung to the right of the fireplace, she paused. Why had such distortion of image once been thought desirable? She stared at her face in the gilt-framed bubble of glass—small, pale, far away—and thought she saw some slight motion behind her. When she turned there was nothing there. Must have been a cat on the dining table, she decided.

She moved past the fireplace and paused by the new room—the nook Gerry called it, the old post office and general store uncovered behind a wall in one corner of the dining room, and now a retreat with a chaise longue and a desk—made by Gerry into something of a household shrine to dead relatives. Prudence found this aspect of the room vaguely distasteful. The faded photos on the wall made her uneasy. Not a room she would ever relax in.

Like probing a sore tooth with her tongue, her thoughts went back to her second pregnancy. To distract herself, she began rearranging the dining room in preparation for the workmen and removed the mirror, laying it on the floor against the far wall. Hideous though it was, it was probably valuable, an antique. It wouldn't do if someone scratched or broke it.

But, as she moved the small objects left over from her dinner with Bertie and Marion—silver salt and pepper shakers, a candelabra—from the table to safety on a sideboard, the subject of the baby returned.

The second time, she hadn't bothered telling Alex she was pregnant. He was already gone and she had no intention of reintroducing him into her life. She'd told her parents, her employer. Her mother had promised to babysit when Prudence went back to work. Her father hadn't said much, had turned away after one sad smile. She knew he'd just wanted a happier, better life for her.

Being pregnant had been fine. She'd been nauseous at the beginning but never actually threw up. Being a cashier/supervisor wasn't arduous. She didn't do much else besides work and visit her parents. She wished for a girl; a boy being raised by only a mother might be problematic, but she thought she could handle a girl.

Once, when she was about seven months along, Alex had come into the store, for cigarettes and a two-four. She'd been at the front where cigarettes were kept and had served him.

He'd taken in her changed shape and was beginning to smile, looked as though he'd like to talk about it.

She'd shut that down fast, saying, as she passed him his cigs, his change, "It's nothing to do with you. I'll cope on my own."

She could still see the dullness that had entered his eyes and hear his words. "I'm sure you will, Prudence."

Then she'd had her second miscarriage.

Up to that point in her life, she'd not known that a late-term miss meant the woman had to deliver the dead baby. Well, people didn't talk about those things, did they?

She'd felt ill one night, threw up, had diarrhea, and then, nothing. She couldn't feel the baby moving anymore. She waited a few days feeling heavier and more tired, then went to see the local doctor.

Doctor Barron was newly graduated from medical school, but already possessed a formidable bedside manner. After listening to Prudence's belly with her device for a few moments, she said, "The batteries in this thing must be finished. I'm just going to send you to the hospital for a proper scan. Can someone drive you?"

Still unsuspecting, Prudence got her father to take her to the hospital where they told her the bad news. Drugs were given to induce contractions and sometime that night, her baby boy slipped out.

Prudence gave the heavy dining room table a mighty shove. It shifted—a bit. She went to the other end and shoved again. Inch by inch, the thing moved further away from the fireplace, bunching up and dragging the oriental rug with it.

Those cats who usually inhabited the dining room had tolerated her smaller movements of shifting this and that here and there, but when she started on the dining chairs ranged around the table, where many of them were sitting, they began giving her their full attention. And the table shifting caused some of the timid ones to leave the room, leaving the hardy or curious to supervise. *This* had never happened before, their astonished looks conveyed. The bare floor of the room was revealed.

Well. That made sense, she supposed: a trap door in the floor of the room that had used to function as a store. Obviously those Coneybears from a hundred years ago would have needed a large area to hold supplies. People would have laid by more foodstuffs, candles, and kerosene in winter. And the nook/store area was tiny.

She kneeled. One big rectangular door with hinges on one side. Painted closed. Any handle with which to lift the door was long gone. Hmm, she thought, what would Gerry do? It's not my house, she chided herself, then grinned. Gerry would already be chipping away with a hammer and screwdriver. She'd say, go for it. Anyway, it would be something to email her about.

Prudence fetched both tools from the kitchen drawer that functioned as The Maples' toolbox. Not that there weren't other tools in the woodshed, she mused, probably including a chisel, which would do a better job.

She dragged a hairy cat towel off one of the dining chairs, folded it and knelt again. Cats crept closer. Paint chips flew short distances. Jay and Ronald chased them, Jay chewing one briefly before spitting it out. The older cats watched more sedately.

Prudence shifted the towel to the second side of the door and chipped away. When she reached the fourth side, she said, "Almost there, cats." It was still raining, so many of the twenty feline residents of The Maples were in attendance. Again, she felt as though there was motion behind her, around the level of her hunched shoulders, but when she turned to look there was still nothing there.

Her gaze met that of Bob, who sat on the deep, cleared-of-ornaments marble mantelpiece. He looked alert. She sat back on her heels for a moment, then tried to pry the door up with the screwdriver.

The tool was insufficient for the task and a little bit of wood broke, splintering. "*Now* I need a chisel," she murmured. "Two would be better." Ever methodical, she returned screwdriver and hammer to the kitchen drawer, put on her raincoat and dashed across the parking pad to the woodshed.

She entered by the little door closest to the road, into the tiny room that functioned as a potting shed. She always felt close to Maggie in this space, remembering her friend spending hours sowing seeds in trays, transplanting small plants into larger pots, taking cuttings from favourite houseplants.

She pulled back the hood of her raincoat and passed through the door into the main part of the shed. There was a workbench just inside this room and here all the small and large tools of The Maples were stored.

Ancient tools that were never or rarely used now like sickles and scythes hung on the wall. Where would a chisel likely be? She rummaged in various wooden boxes until she found a couple. Hopefully their broader but still sharp edges wouldn't damage the trap door further.

Something made her look past the cords of stacked firewood toward the back wall of the shed. That back wall and she had history. She heard a small noise and waited. It was notrepeated. Wood shifting, settling, she thought, and shrugged, returning to the house with her tools and a bucket of wood. It was a perfect day for a fire. She hung up her coat in the porch. She should probably eat lunch soon, she thought vaguely, then, grasping the chisels and the bucket, she returned to the dining room.

Who could she tell? Only Gerry. Gerry, who'd been a reluctant witness to previous spooky happenings at The Maples, who believed Prudence was a sensitive, and grudgingly admitted that Mrs. Smith the medium might really be communicating with the dead. But Gerry was so far away. *And* on holiday. *And* five-and-a-half-months pregnant. No. It wouldn't do. Prudence couldn't tell Lucy, though Lucy, of all people, as a believing, practising Catholic, *might* admit to the possibility of a psychic presence, a soul in limbo, say. Lucy certainly didn't approve of any of Prudence's séances with Mrs. Smith. "Leave the dead *alone*," she'd cautioned Prudence often. "Pray for them but let them rest."

But Prudence had seen enough manifestations to convince her that some of the dead didn't rest. So, tell Lucy, or not? Damned if she knew.

Gently she lowered the trap door. She thought for a moment then spread a few cat towels over it. She didn't want Friday's workmen to get curious.

It was a still thoughtful Prudence who got ready to go out for supper.

# 12

"Mary."
"Prudence."

Under Bertie and Marion's eyes, the two women leaned in for the double air kiss that would indicate they were prepared for a civil evening.

"Thank you for inviting us," Prudence said, surrendering her raincoat—the same one she'd worn to fetch wood—to the hat-check girl.

One could be as formal or informal as one liked during the day at this particular golf club, Lovering's oldest, but in the evening, well, let's just say that the club kept a collection of jackets and ties for the gentlemen who may have forgotten theirs, while women were expected to dress to a certain standard.

Therefore: Bertie wore a navy suit, pale pink shirt and navy tie; Marion was splendidly retro in a black and white Chanel suit with a large rimless black cloth cloche tilted to one side, which made it look like she was sprouting a failed soufflé out the top of her head; while Prudence wore her trusty emerald-green dress with a white shawl she'd found in one of Maggie's drawers. She was aware of the competing odours of Mary and Marion's perfumes: Mary's heavy, sweet; Marion's richer, spicy. Prudence wore no scent.

"Mrs. Stewart," Mary said prettily enough, offering her hand. "And Mr. Smith." She batted her eyes and said, "I've heard *so* much about you."

"*Have* you?" Bertie declared, before taking Prudence's arm. This left a disappointed Mary to escort Marion into the dining room.

Prudence felt an unholy pang of pride. I've got a man, sort of, and Mary Coneybear Petherbridge doesn't! Her valuation of Bertie increased and she smiled artlessly up at him as he pulled out first her chair, then Marion's, then Mary's.

"Well," Marion rapped out. "This is nice." They looked about the room.

With long, wide windows on three sides, the dining room at Oakleaf Golf and Country Club could seat over two hundred. Tonight, there were fifty or so patrons waiting for their suppers.

White cloth draped each table, the dinnerware was plain but good, and a tiny vase of alstroemeria decorated each table's centre. It was certainly a contrast to the humble nine-hole course and *its* clubhouse they'd frequented earlier that week.

There was still plenty of evening light with which to see the wooded slope that led down to part of the course. For of course they were by a window. Trust Mary to get a good table, thought Prudence. Well, in fairness, she's belonged to the club forever, but—I bet the staff hate her. She smiled sweetly at Mary. "How are the boys?"

The boys were Mary's grandsons: James, Geoff Jr. (named for Mary's deceased husband), and David. The boys were twenty-one, nineteen and eighteen years old, so while Doug was away, and for the first time, they'd been allowed to stay by themselves at home. In their father's absence, they were supposedly under Mary's supervision. I hope now Andrew's back, he's looking in on them, Prudence thought, and grimly smiled as she envisioned the mess three young men could make in a house over the span of a month.

Mary waved a hand. "Oh, fine. They were here with me a few days ago." She looked impatiently around then snapped her fingers at a young waitress. "Drinks?" Three martinis and one tonic water on the way, Mary went into more details about her grandsons. "And before that we lunched at the yacht club. They come to mine for pizza or barbecue chicken a couple times a week."

When you feel like company in that large luxurious house of yours, Prudence thought sourly.

"I live just across from the golf course," Mary added nonchalantly. "Further up Side Road. Get Prudence to point it out when she drives you home."

Their drinks arrived. "It's not on our way," Prudence said quietly.

"Mm," Mary said. "Well, cheers!" They clinked glasses. "Now, Mr. Smith. Bertie. May I call you Bertie?" He nodded. "Tell me about your business. In Westmount, I believe?" As Westmount was one of the best neighbourhoods in Montreal in which to claim an address, Prudence felt her lip curl, just a little. Mary was such a snob.

She wondered again how it was Mary had invited them for a meal. She suspected Gerry, working on rehabilitating her relationship with her aunt, of trying to extend that throughout the family. Well, Prudence would play along. And no doubt Mary was curious about Prudence's man friend.

She looked across the table at Marion and was met by a slight smile and wink. Of course. Marion, with her vast social experience (Bertie often grumbled about how she knew or had known everybody in Montreal!), could read Mary, and Prudence, like open books. Prudence looked sheepish and smiled slightly back.

Mary was speaking. "I must come in to town some time and look at your inventory." She looked at Prudence to see what effect she was making and Prudence saw Bertie raise his eyebrows sharply as though shocked by an improper suggestion.

She smothered a smile and replied in a bland tone, "Of course. I've been there so often, I take 'the inventory' for granted."

Bertie choked on his drink and all three women looked in his direction. "I'm fine," he croaked and drank some water.

"Shall we order?" Mary suggested.

"I already know what I'm having," Marion said greedily. "The roast beef."

Of course, thought Prudence, the most expensive item. "Good idea, Marion," she said, closing her menu.

"Make that three," Bertie said. Smiles were exchanged, three of them triumphant, one less so.

"I'm having another drink," muttered Mary.

"Me too," Marion chimed in.

"I'll switch to tonic," Bertie added. "Like Prudence." He smiled at her and took her hand.

Mary waved for their waitress.

After the roast beef, Yorkshire pudding, roast potatoes and peas, and the bottle of red wine Marion and Mary split (during the ingesting of which Marion entertained them, and the people at the surrounding tables, with tales of her youth—summers spent all over rural Canada including Lovering, and political intrigues observed when she was a young and not so young Montreal matron), and after the two cognacs each she and Mary put away with their coffee, Mary called for the bill.

"I insist on paying for myself and Prudence," Bertie said grandly, reinforcing the fact that they were a couple.

Mary shook her head, slurring her reply. "Not nesheshary. It's included in the yearly dues. Minimum, I have to spend a couple of grand on food and drink. Gotta use it up." Prudence wondered how that was going; if Mary bothered to check how much over or under her tab was running.

A humming sound came from Bertie's vicinity. He reached into his pocket and looked at the pager. "Uh oh. Is there a phone I can use around here?" Mary waved vaguely back toward the entrance. He headed off in that direction.

Prudence leaned forward. "I didn't know Bertie has a pager, Marion."

"Hah!" Mary interjected. "Don't know him all that well then, eh?"

The other two ignored her. "He only takes it with him when he leaves Montreal," Marion explained. "He *is* a landlord after all."

Prudence sat back. "Oh, yes, the art gallery."

Bertie returned. "Sorry about that. The toilet tank in the art gallery upstairs from my shop has cracked. The tenant discovered it before much water had leaked but wanted to know if I had a favourite plumber. I told her to call the twenty-four-hour guy and pay with a credit card." He faced Prudence. "I'm afraid this means I'll have to go to town tomorrow. Can you drive me to the station?"

"Of course. There's a train at 8:45. Does that suit you?"

"Yes." He rose. "Well, thank you very much indeed, Mrs. Petherbridge, for the good supper."

Mary signed the chit their waitress brought, the women fussed with their wraps, and they made their way to the parking lot.

"Is she all right to drive?" Marion said quietly, then repeated herself more loudly. "Are you all right to drive, Mrs. Petherbridge?"

"Call me Mary. Both of you. All of you." She slipped her key into the lock and waved goodbye.

"All right," Marion said, beginning to walk toward Prudence's car. "If the key goes into the lock on the first try and you're only going a short distance, you're good. That was Fred's rule, anyway."

People used to live much more dangerously, thought Prudence, watching as Mary backed her car out of its spot and swung onto the golf club's narrow paved road. And some still do. She got behind the wheel of her car.

"*Will* she be all right?" Bertie said quietly from the back seat.

"We'll make sure," Prudence replied and turned right on the road when she should have turned left. She saw taillights receding down the big hill and assumed they were Mary's. Sure enough, after the hill bottomed out and began to rise again, the taillight indicated a left turn. As they passed the house with its large circular driveway, formal garden and spouting fountain, Prudence slowed and they all watched Mary exit her car.

"That's all right then," Marion said loudly. "What an unhappy woman."

On a whim, Prudence said, "If we go back the long way, I could show you *my* house."

"Okay. No hurry," Bertie said.

"Fine," Marion added. By the time they'd reached the two-lane secondary highway and Prudence had turned left, Marion's head had drooped and they could hear her gentle snoring.

Prudence idly asked, "What's that perfume Marion's wearing?"

"Strong, isn't it? It's one her husband used to give her on their anniversaries. *Calèche*."

"Romantic," Prudence said, looking at him in the rear-view mirror, envisioning couples taking night rides in the old-fashioned black horse-drawn carriages of Montreal—*les calèches*.

"Very," Bertie replied dryly. "Except, she's got gallons of the stuff and I don't think she knows perfume has a best-before date like anything else."

"Perhaps she doesn't care," Prudence softly suggested. "If it came from Fred."

"Yes, that's probably it." He leaned forward and whispered close to Prudence's ear. "I call it Old Horse."

Prudence allowed herself a quiet snort of laughter. They continued on in silence. "Got to watch for skunks," Prudence murmured, as the eyes of one glowed from the roadside and its stripe became visible.

"Yes, indeed," Bertie agreed. "Don't want to stink up the new car."

Prudence, thinking he was also referring back to Marion's perfume, smiled. She turned left onto Station Road. As they drew up to her address, she said. "And this is my house." She pulled into the driveway but left the engine running.

Bertie said only "Nice" and Marion snored on, so Prudence backed out onto the road.

"I'll have the beef," Marion muttered.

"Look after Marion, eh? While I'm gone?" Bertie bent to look into Prudence's car window. The 8:45 to Montreal waited for its passengers.

"Of course. When will you be back?"

"Depends. I'll certainly try for tomorrow if I can. Hopefully not too much water made it down into the shop. I'll call you." He leaned in and kissed her lips before she could offer him her cheek.

Prudence wondered if any locals had seen; and if they had, what they would think. I have nothing to lose, she realized suddenly, and waited to see Bertie's face at a window as the train pulled away.

Now for Gerry's wood stove. When she got back to The Maples, there was the van just arriving in the small circular driveway at the front. She parked on the side and hurried to the front door. "Right," she said, unlocking it. "Let me show you where it goes."

After the men had left, Prudence made her lunch and took it into the dining room, eating at the big table, trying not to think about the trap door, and staring at the new wood stove.

It was strangely small. It looked like you'd barely fit three logs in at a time, and when she'd commented on this to one of the workmen, he'd said, "I bet you grew up with one of those big old square monsters that gobbled up wood." She'd nodded, remembering such a beast inhabiting the kitchen at her parents' farm.

The man had reassured her that this smaller narrower stove would not only burn fewer logs, it would do so far more efficiently, having a second chamber in which the smoke's particulate matter would burn. "You'll see," he'd concluded. "You'll be hauling much less wood."

Prudence crunched away on her dill-flavoured potato chips. The dill gave an unusual savour to her peanut butter and bread and butter pickle sandwich. She watched the cats. Every few minutes, a few appeared to inspect the wood stove. Bob leapt onto its skinny top, while the three grey-striped brothers—Winnie, Frank and Joe—skulked underneath it.

The cats who slept on Prudence's bed—The Honour Guard—a timid bunch—crept into the room for a look. And the cats who liked to sleep on the dining room chairs, once their initial disgust at the disturbance of *their* space had dissipated, could be seen returning, checking out the new object then settling on their perches for well-deserved naps.

Prudence crumpled up her empty chip bag and went to phone Marion. Cathy Stribling answered. "Fieldcrest Bed and Breakfast. How may I help you?"

"It's me," Prudence stated. "How are you, Cathy?" While not a friend exactly (after all, Prudence really only numbered three of those: Lucy, Rita, and Gerry; no, four, if she included Bertie), since Gerry had come to live at The Maples and kept throwing wonderful parties, Prudence had socialized more with Cathy in the last year and a half than she'd done in the previous fifty years. But they'd known of each other all their lives.

"Prudence? I'm fine. Tired. It's different having guests stay for weeks rather than weekends. I'm *quite* tired. And Charles is exhausted. All that extra attention."

Prudence smiled. She could imagine Prince Charles, his plump body tensed, nose aquiver, as he begged from Bertie and Marion for whatever morsels of Cathy's delectable cooking they cared to drop his way. She contented herself by saying only, "I can imagine. May I speak with Marion?"

"She's had her lunch and just gone up for a nap. Should I call her?"

"No. Just get her to phone me when she wakes up. Tell her she's invited to tea and I'll pick her up around three. Or whenever she wants."

"All right. Bye."

Prudence thought, replacing the receiver, now, what shall I bake?

Eccles cakes, an inner voice prompted. She found the recipe in Maggie's folder, prepared the dough for chilling and set aside the currant, butter, cinnamon and brown sugar filling.

She did a quick tidy of the house, dragging a dust mop across the floor, making sure the living room, where she intended to serve the tea, was in order. After the dough had chilled for an hour she rolled out the cakes and shaped the little round flat parcels, before popping them into the oven at two thirty.

The phone rang. Cathy could drop Marion off now, if Prudence liked, as she, Cathy, was off to do groceries. Prudence wasn't sure if Cathy was angling for an invitation to tea, and any other day would have extended one. But she wanted Marion to herself so just thanked Cathy and put on the kettle.

She was taking the Eccles cakes out of the oven when she heard Cathy pull in at the front door. She hurried to assist Marion.

Today, as it was mild, Marion was in a white-flowered blue dress with a dark blue blazer and light blue hat. The hat, stiff and wide-brimmed, perched atop Marion's thin white locks, and Prudence wondered, with a sudden sense of pity, if Marion usually wore hats to cover the sad state of what remained of her hair.

As she led Marion through the dining room with its still pushed-back table and rolled-up rug, the towels covering the trap door still in place, Prudence explained. "I think I mentioned last night that a new wood stove was being installed today." She gestured at the black thing protruding slightly from the fireplace. "I just haven't had time to move the furniture back yet. That table's very heavy."

Marion sniffed at the wood stove. "Always thought them ugly, myself." And once she was ensconced in a padded rocking chair by the living room's large open hearth, she added with a nod, "*This* is more like it."

"I'd make you a fire, but it's so mild today." Prudence went to get the tea.

"Smells good in here. Ah, Eccles cakes! Lovely!"

They had their tea, after which Prudence told Marion everything.

# 13

"So let me see if I understand." Marion transferred another Eccles cake from the cake plate to her own.

"More tea?" Prudence queried.

"Please." Prudence poured and Marion bit into the Eccles cake. It was her third. She smiled at Prudence. "You really are the most excellent cook. I remember those scones you served us last spring."

"Thank you." Prudence topped up her own teacup with the rich Assam and waited.

The assembled cats (not all of them; after all, it was a fine day) having arranged themselves around the room, also waited.

Harley and Kitty-Cat sat either side of the hearth, looking like black and white porcelain ornaments. Mother and Jay, Blackie and Whitey, and Cocoon, sat on the sofa.

"So, you think some spirit opened the trap door while you were out of the room."

"Yes. How else—"

Marion held up a hand. "I'm thinking out loud here." Prudence fell silent and let her get on with it. "You've examined the underside of the door and the door frame from below to see if there's some spring or other mechanism?"

"Oh." Prudence sounded crestfallen. "I didn't think of that. I just closed it again. I was surprised."

"No to checking for a physical cause. You immediately assumed a spirit agent." Marion looked at Prudence and clasped her hands under her chin, her elbows resting on her stomach. "Now *that* interests me. Why?"

"Well. I've experienced these manifestations before, in this house, or near it. In the woodshed. And behind it. Last winter. It felt like someone tapping my shoulder. And—I'm just remembering this now—just before I found the trap door, I thought I saw someone or something moving. In the mirror. Behind me."

"Hmm. And what about the woodshed? What was that all about?"

"Well, it turned out someone had been murdered in or near it. Long, long ago. A servant. Gerry found the skeleton. Actually," and here she pointed at Bob, lounging on the mantelpiece, "*he* found it."

Marion eyed Bob. "Does he knock things off?"

"What? Oh. Remarkably, no. And it's no good trying to get him off the mantel. He just hops back up again. Bob's the top cat and that's his mountain perch, I guess."

"And what did Bob make of the opened trap door?"

"Well, when I came back into the room with the chisels and a load of wood, I was so surprised to see the door already up that I dropped everything and the cats scattered. I seem to recall some of them were sniffing around the opening in the floor but then most of them skittered away."

Marion's mind similarly skittered. "Back to the woodshed," she continued. "How did the, er, body's history become known?"

"A combination of researching local history—Gerry did that—and consulting—" Prudence broke off. This was entering such private territory.

"A detective?" Marion guessed.

"A medium."

"A medium," Marion hollowly echoed.

"Her name is Mrs. Smith. Funny, eh? Same last name as Bertie. Not that there aren't a lot of Smiths. When I was young there were two Smith families in Lovering and they lived across the street from each other. As children we called them Big Smith and Little Smith, due to the size of their houses. Right. The medium. My mother found her after my father died. I've been consulting her for years." Prudence ceased talking, hoping she hadn't blown her credibility and ruined her burgeoning relationship with Marion.

"But you seem like such a sensible person," Marion said candidly.

Mother left the sofa and rubbed against Prudence's legs. She reached down to stroke the soft fur and thought for moment. "I am, I think. At first, after my father died, and my mother started visiting Mrs. Smith, I didn't accompany her. I thought it was—unhealthy, that my mother was trying to deny my father was dead and gone. Then, after her visits, when she'd be chattering about what he'd said to her—through the medium—I realized: she had accepted he was dead; she just really missed him."

Marion cleared her throat. "That's the unsolvable problem caused by death: missing the person." She gazed at the cold hearth. "Your parents must have loved each other very much."

"They were the world to each other," Prudence said simply. "And then they shared that world with me. I had a wonderful childhood."

"And a pretty crappy time since, I've been hearing."

Drat that gossiping Cathy Stribling, Prudence thought, and flushed. Or had Bertie been blabbing to his friend? She merely said, "Yes." Mother jumped into her lap.

"What else?" Marion asked.

"What else?"

"What other happenings have there been that made you veer toward psychic explanations?"

"Oh. Well. Once I was at Mrs. Smith's and she started talking about a child next door who had died, or died young, and where I live there aren't any youngsters for a few houses down, so we—

Gerry and I—we figured out it must be next door to *this* house. And Mrs. Smith mentioned that the child's house was next to the house of many cats, so—" She gestured around the room. The cats blinked their acceptance of her so accurate naming of their house. Their smug expressions seemed to indicate: what else would you call it? "And it turned out there had been a child accidently killed at the big white house next door, oh, almost a hundred years ago. And the person who'd done it, a very old lady of over a hundred, had just died. It's hard to explain," she added lamely, seeing Marion's blank face.

"A hundred, eh? Well, that gives one hope. Anything else?"

"Um. Once Gerry went to see Mrs. Smith on her own—"

"*Gerry* goes too?" Marion sounded incredulous, no doubt that anyone so young and cheerful as Gerry would consult a medium.

"Yes, she does. You know my husband died this past spring. Well, I didn't want to accidently make contact with him. We had a difficult relationship and I was feeling raw. So, without telling me, Gerry went to ask if any spirits knew who killed him."

"And did they?" Marion was interested now. You could tell by the way she was leaning forward. She hadn't even finished her third Eccles cake.

"Not really. There was some mention of Alex sacrificing himself, which led Gerry and me to a certain conclusion. Which proved correct." Prudence had given that last information in such a grim voice that Marion left it there.

Mother jumped down off Prudence's lap, circled once, twice, then curled on the braided hearth rug exactly between Harley and Kitty-Cat and closed her eyes. The two "cow" cats blinked sleepily in tandem.

"So why tell me about this, this trap door occurrence?"

"Well, Gerry's away, and I'm not going to get her all excited by email when there's nothing she can do about it. My friend Lucy shies away from the whole topic of mediums and communicating with the dead. I—haven't told any of this to Bertie yet either. I don't want—" Prudence stopped.

"You don't want him to think less of you," Marion supplied in a crisp tone. "Quite right, too."

Prudence looked surprised. "Really?"

"Yes. Of course. You've presented yourself to him as practical Prudence, a sensible middle-aged person. Safe." Marion looked shrewdly at her. "You don't want to ruin *that* image."

Prudence kept silent, looking at the fireplace.

Marion also fell silent, before adding, "I hope I haven't offended you?"

Prudence shook her head.

Marion reverted to the original subject. "So. What are you going to do?"

Prudence slowly raised her head. "I'm not really sure." She rose. "But right now," and she indicated the growing number of cats slinking toward the kitchen, "if you'll excuse me, I'm going to give the cats their supper."

Prudence shivered and pulled the shawl more closely around her shoulders. It was a lovely evening so she was sitting on the back porch. But, being the middle of September, at night the temperature was beginning to descend.

She made a mental note to visit the vegetable garden in the next few days and pick what harvest was left. There'd surely be a killing frost sometime in the next two weeks.

She wondered how Bertie was doing with his flood. He hadn't phoned so she didn't know if he was coming back on Saturday or not. And she was scheduled to work almost the whole day at the café anyway. Oh well, she mentally shrugged, he can look after himself. He's been doing so for most of his life. Like herself. The two separate thoughts did not warm her.

She left the now dark porch and went into the house, locking the porch door for the night. She entered the bathroom and cleaned out the cat boxes, avoiding the one where furious scratching indicated its occupant was also cleaning—or covering up. She paused after washing her hands and stared into the medicine cabinet's tarnished mirror.

In the room's dim light and with her hair tied back, body enfolded in the white shawl, she might have been an apparition herself, from some distant past. She reached up and removed her hair elastic. The grey locks, still touched with brown here and there, remained pulled back. She tossed her head from side to side, then bent forward and flipped her hair back. She thought of Bertie's kiss that morning.

She tried to imagine her hair dyed its original dark auburn. Cathy dyed her hair. So did Mary. *And* they both wore makeup.

She clucked her tongue at her foolishness and left the room.

The narrow hallway opened into the large foyer. She checked the already locked front door, looking through the sheer curtains that covered it and the windows on either side.

Across the street, lights were on downstairs in Andrew and Markie's house. She wondered if Marion and possibly Cathy, who worked so hard maintaining her large property and business, were already asleep over at Fieldcrest. She yawned. She too had had a long day.

From the foyer, she walked to the dining room and paused by the wood stove. Too late to test it today. Maybe tomorrow after— She sucked in her breath. Surely she had stacked the four logs and the handful of kindling in the recess built for that purpose to the side of the stone fireplace. Yet now they were in front of the stove on the hearth along with one of the chisels. She heard a rustling sound and turned her head to look to her left.

The small black cat so recently adopted by Gerry—Seymour—was batting around a book of matches.

Prudence was shocked. She never left matches lying around, precisely because there were twenty cats sharing the house with its humans. Perhaps Gerry—? She rescued the matches, giving Seymour a quick pat, and put them in the nearby sideboard drawer where the candles were kept.

The matches she could explain but not the wood. "What do you want?" she asked the empty room. Seymour, deprived of his toy, squinted up at her from his one good eye.

No response, though several cats came trotting into view, no doubt drawn by the interlocutory tone in her voice. She looked at the trap door covered in cat towels. "Right!" she said smartly and fetched a flashlight. She turned on the chandelier and every other lamp in the dining room, grasped the chisel and opened the trap.

First to check for a spring around the hinges, she supposed. Something that would account for the door having popped up before.

She knelt and ran her hands around the edges underneath the opening on all four sides. She couldn't *feel* anything. She sat back on her heels, looking into the hole. Several curious cats joined her.

That there was a stone floor came as no surprise. The depth of the room below appeared to confirm her earlier guess that it was for storage. Funny Maggie had never mentioned it.

She retrieved the house's stepladder from a cupboard, opened and lowered it into the cavity. Now. Grasping the flashlight, she backed down the ladder.

Looking up, she was reassured to see the cats' familiar faces. Then she looked down.

First one, then the other foot made contact with the floor. She switched on the flashlight and shone it into the four corners of the room.

It was square, a bit smaller perhaps than the vast formal dining room above. The walls, part of The Maples' foundation, were made of massive stones. Brushing Prudence's head were the equally massive beams, each looking as if it had been hewn from a single tree, and which supported the outside walls and the floor of the house above.

There was little dust or damp, so she guessed the room *had* been used for storage, perhaps of grain and flour. Sealed though it appeared to be, spiders had gotten in, though what they'd find to eat in here, she couldn't think. Many lay dead in their webs, so long dead they and the webs had turned white. Others twitched sluggishly when caught in the flashlight's beam. A cat meowed above her and she jumped.

She looked up and was starting to say, "Now, which one of you—" when the raised trap door appeared in her line of vision, moving, then slammed shut.

Or tried to slam shut. After Prudence's first startled shriek, she saw that the ladder, its length greater than the depth of the room, had prevented the trap door from fully closing.

Though her nerves were aflutter, she remembered Marion's suggestion and shone her flashlight upward, looking for any mechanism that might explain the door's self-agency. There was none.

Cautiously, she mounted the ladder. Cats, who'd no doubt jumped away when the door descended and she screamed, began tentatively returning, their eyes huge, to crowd around the sides of the opening.

Gingerly, Prudence pushed up on the door. It was heavy but otherwise offered no resistance. As she set foot in the dining room again, she announced, "Well! I don't want to go back down there!" and pulled the ladder up before carefully lowering the door.

She began unrolling the rug and inching the dining table back into the centre of the room. She was panting and sweaty once the rug and table covered the trap door again, and she thought, there! That can stay like that until Gerry gets home.

Upstairs in bed, with the usual cats in attendance, she was uncomfortably aware that though the trap door and storeroom were now out of sight, they were most assuredly *not* out of mind.

She took up her book but was unable to read more than a few pages about the earliest days of what would become Virginia Woolf's Bloomsbury group before, to her tired surprise, she fell asleep.

# 14

Prudence could feel Ginger's annoyance from across the small room. The girl tossed her stiff orange hair, bent and retrieved the large bowl of coffee from the tiny table in front of one of the three yummy mummies sitting in the back of the café, and returned it to Prudence.

"Did I make it wrong?" Prudence asked, receiving the cup.

This query was met by further head-tossing, eye-rolling, and even (to Prudence's well-controlled amusement) a tiny stamp of a foot. Then Ginger hissed at her, "She *says* she ordered soy milk, *but I don't think so!*"

"Shush. She'll hear you. I'll drink this one. I was so rushed this morning, I missed breakfast." She proceeded to make another café latte, this time with the thin, drab soy milk substituting for nice creamy cow's milk. "She didn't try it, did she?"

Ginger came around to join her behind the six-foot-long counter. She shook her head. "She said she could tell by the colour. And the smell."

Prudence giggled and softly said, "A very sensitive person."

After a moment's uncertainty, Ginger let her outrage go and agreed with a wan smile. "Don't you get sick of them?" She jerked her head toward the back of the room where the mummies and their strollers monopolized almost the entire café.

"Nah. I try to remember that this is a treat for them before they have to go back home to change dirty diapers, do dishes, think about supper."

Ginger seemed not to be paying attention. "There's that old man again." She indicated with a lift of her chin the pale face bobbing outside the window to the porch.

"That's Mr. Willis," Prudence said. "Don't you remember? He always wants a small regular. I'll take my break now." She handed Ginger the soy latte, prepared Mr. Willis's beverage then joined him on the porch with her own. "Hello, Mr. Willis. Hello, Jazz." She leaned over to pat the ancient animal. "Mind if I join you?" From Lucy she'd learned Mr. Willis was a widower, almost eighty. And that in dog years Jazz was even older.

He grunted. "On your break?"

"Yes."

They sipped in silence for a while. The dog snored. Mr. Willis spoke first. "Miss Hanlan still working on Mme Ménard's house clearing?"

Prudence nodded. "Yup."

"Humph. I heard a rumour. Fella was saying he was going to buy the Ménard place *and* the Lesters'."

"Yes, I believe that's the plan. Dan, Mr. Bartram, who owns this café, wants to expand out the back."

Mr. Willis waved a hand dismissively and shook his head. "Nah. Wasn't him. Some stranger. Said he going to put up condos."

"Oh." Prudence was puzzled. He couldn't be referring to M Ménard, the only stranger she knew of, as he already owned, or as good as owned, one of the properties. "I'm sure Mr. Bartram *said*... Well, I must have got it wrong. Condos, eh?"

"Whole town's going to be condos soon," Mr. Willis grumbled.

"Oh, well, hardly the whole town. A few here and there maybe. Be convenient for older people who want to stay in Lovering after they've sold their houses." She drained her cup. "I've got to get back inside. See you."

"See you," he said gloomily. In its sleep, the dog whined.

Interesting, Prudence thought, rinsing her cup. Ménard must be happy. Two possible buyers for his aunt's property. He can play them off one against the other. She looked at the seating area where Ginger was backing up a stroller to make way for Dan Bartram to emerge through the door from his coffee-roasting lair. He greeted his customers and made his way to Prudence. "Everything all right?" One of the babies was crying.

"Fine," she responded, trying to sound confident.

"Ginger has just informed me she'll be leaving at one. You okay alone until four? I'm going out now but I'll be back then to close up."

"Fine," Prudence said. He looked around the small space, dissatisfaction showing on his face. "Any progress on buying the property out back?" she asked. He gave her a quizzical look. "It's just I appreciate your need to expand, now I work here."

He shook his head. "I made an offer to each of the parties, but I haven't heard back."

Prudence leaned forward. "It's none of my business, but I think others may be bidding."

He nodded. "That's how it works." His brow furrowed but he didn't seem fazed by the idea so she decided against passing on Mr. Willis' gossip. "Well then," he said.

"Well then."

"I'll be back at four."

"All right, Mr. Bartram."

"Call me Dan." After another look at the confusion in the back of the store he let himself out the front. The baby was still crying.

Wise man, Prudence thought, and went to restore order.

Prudence took a breath and surveyed the café. The mummies had moved on and Ginger had left. She was going to a classmate's house to make a video for English class, though how something visual could possibly enhance reading or writing skills, Prudence didn't know.

She wet a fresh rag and wandered around with a spray bottle of anti-bacterial soap cleaning surfaces: window frames and sills, the dusty top of the sofa and the coffee-stained tables, the doorknobs. She finished by removing everything from the customer side of the counter, wiping and replacing. She looked at the day's special coffee doubtfully. VEGAN KOPI LUWAK—NO ANIMALS WERE HARMED TO MAKE THIS COFFEE. What was that all about? No one had asked for it. She shrugged and went in the back to get supplies.

The Hudsons had fitted sheets of plywood where the three damaged panes of glass had been. Prudence loaded an empty box with napkins, wooden stir sticks and bags of sugar. A movement behind the building made her look.

Walter Lester was standing there, looking at the café and her inside it. His hands were in his jacket pockets, and he was hunched over.

Prudence walked to the rear door, half-opened it and called, "Hi, Walter. Can I help you?" in what she hoped were kindly tones.

He shuffled near the door. "Got any food?"

Prudence froze. Then she got worried. "Haven't you got any at home, Walter?" He hung his head and shook it.

Prudence swore under her breath. "Oh, dear. I can't leave the store. You better come in." She leaned harder on the door and he slipped in. He followed her into the café. "Now. Would you like a coffee?" He nodded, but his gaze was riveted to the jar of biscotti. Prudence cursed the place's skimpy menu. She'd have to remember to speak to Dan about that. Then she brightened.

"I know." She rummaged in her purse where her lunch nestled in its brown paper bag. "Here." She handed it over without explanation.

Walter took the bag over to the nearest chair, sat and began to munch Prudence's peanut butter and pickle sandwich and the bag of barbecue chips. Then he ate the banana. Then he returned his gaze to the biscotti. Prudence took two out of the jar and handed him the plate, along with a coffee. "Milk and sugar?" His general nod indicated all would be welcome. She extracted some money from her purse and put it in the till. "Feel better now?" she asked. He nodded. "Now, we've got to get some food into your house, eh? Do you have any money?" He shook his head. "Oh, for heaven's sake!" she said, exasperated. He shrank away from her. "No, no. I'm not mad at you. I'm mad at your neighbours." He looked blank. "I'm mad at myself. For forgetting all about you." For worrying about a cat, she thought, who could probably take care of itself.

Walter must be afraid to go out. Well, Lucy had told her she never saw him leave his property. Probably only hunger and the smell of coffee had brought him to her door. He needed a guardian. Who could she consult? Cecil Muxworthy, of course, Gerry's lawyer. And he lived nearby.

She found the number in Lovering's slender little phone book and called. He would be right over. She breathed out. Now to explain to Walter. "Walter, did you hear me tell Mr. Muxworthy about you and how you need help?" He nodded, looking worried. "He's going to come into your house and look for your mother's will. Do you know what that is?" He nodded. "Mr. Muxworthy will explain what has to happen with the will. It's so you can get money to buy food. You can trust him. Mr. Muxworthy is a good person."

He looked uncertain. "I can't go—go—to the store. My mother used to shop."

"Oh. But you can order food over the telephone and have it delivered. Did you know that? Can you use the phone?" He looked relieved and nodded. "Just go home now and wait for Mr. Muxworthy. He'll be along in a few minutes. All right?"

He stood and moved to the back of the room. Understanding that it would be easier for him to go out this quieter way than onto Main Road, she let him pass through Dan's office again. He scuttled to his own gate, let himself in, and then she lost sight of him.

The front doorbell tinkled and she rushed to attend to it.

"Well," drawled Bertie. "Aren't you something? Left you in charge, has he?"

"Can I help you, sir?" Prudence asked demurely.

The bell tinkled again and Cece Muxworthy stuck his head inside. "Is he at home?" he asked abruptly.

Prudence nodded. "He just left. The first house. Be patient, eh, Cece?"

"Of course." He smiled. "I'll tell you what happens. You did the right thing by the sound of it. Bye now."

Bertie looked at her quizzically. "It's Central Command here, isn't it?"

Prudence made a face. "Just helping a poor soul. Or trying to." She explained some of Walter's predicament then paused. "Um. You're back."

Bertie bowed. "As you see. The flood has been put right, cheques written, the tenant soothed."

"Bertie, would you mind getting me a burger and small fries from the restaurant over there? I forgot my lunch."

"You forgot your lunch? That's not very Prudence-like." She said nothing further so he continued, "No problem. I didn't eat lunch yet either. Is Marion occupied?"

"She was supposed to be visiting the Shapland sisters this afternoon. All-dressed. Not Marion, my hamburger!" she felt it necessary to explain on seeing his grin. "And vinegar and salt on the fries. Please." She reached for her purse but he was already out the door.

Soon Coco Poco's usual smell was replaced by the mingled aromas of the burger condiments and vinegar-soaked fried potatoes. Prudence wiped her lips and fingers and gathered up the garbage.

Bertie burped loudly then looked shocked. "I'm so sorry! I must have eaten too quickly."

Prudence gave him a small smile. "It was good, wasn't it? Buy you a coffee?"

"Thank you." He studied the board over her head. "I will have a medium Americano, please." He watched in silence as she made an espresso then put boiling water and the espresso into a glass mug. He took a sip. "Perfect! But I'm not surprised. You do everything well, Prudence."

She busied herself cleaning her side of the counter. "That's because I only do simple things."

"Really. Like getting and starting a new job in your fifties. Like helping out a 'poor soul' by getting him a lawyer. And like helping a friend clean out an old lady's house. Which reminds me. Does she still want me to assess the house's contents?"

"I expect so," said Prudence, relieved that she was no longer the focus of conversation. "Shall I call her?"

Five minutes later, Lucy arrived at the café. "Nice to meet you," she said as she and Bertie shook hands. "This place smells like a chip shop. Come on, Bertie, I'll let you in to the house. Then I've got to get back to work. Today is the day the cast of *The Mikado* are dropping in to have their measurements taken for costumes. Crazy busy!"

It was arranged that Prudence would drive Bertie back to the B&B around four. Prudence settled down for the rest of her shift.

"She's missed her nap and says she's exhausted—just going to have a hot bath before soup and a sandwich with Cathy. So I'm free."

Prudence stood in The Maples' kitchen with the phone in her hand. "I'm a bit tired myself."

"Don't you want to know how it went at Mme Ménard's?"

She perked up a bit. "Did you find anything interesting?"

"Mayybeee," Bertie drawled the word teasingly. "I can eat here with Marion and Cathy. You don't have to make anything for me."

"I wasn't going to," she said dryly. "All right. How about at seven?"

She returned the receiver to its wall-mounted cradle, then sighed. She was feeling a bit over-stimulated. There had been a steady stream of customers at the café that afternoon, mostly for takeout. Evidently word of Dan Bartram's excellent coffee was spreading. And it *was* Saturday, when people were out and about looking for a treat.

She sighed again. A few cats, their plates of meat distant memories, were still moving around her feet. Jay was standing in the large tub of kibble, crunching away. "Why, Jay? Why?" She lifted the skinny little thing out and placed it on the floor. "With your dirty feet!"

Jay looked up at her, undisturbed, as if to say, "*I* clean my feet five times a day; how about you?" and went back to eating, this time stretching her neck to reach the kibble.

Prudence topped up the tub to make it easier for the little cat then walked into the living room and sat limply on the sofa. Soon, she would make her own version of the soup and sandwich the members of her immediate circle seemed to all be having this Saturday night. But first she would just…

She woke up to hear someone knocking at the side door. "Rats!" She sat up. Her face felt oily and her hair was probably a mess. Oh well, it couldn't be helped. She let Bertie in and yawned. At the same moment he sneezed—hugely, turning his head at the last second. They laughed.

"Must have been the dust at that house this afternoon," he muttered as he blew his nose.

"Excuse me. I just woke up. I'm going to freshen up."

·

In a few minutes they were settled in the living room. "So?" Prudence asked.

"So. Well, of course, most of it is worthless. All of the furniture is. But I have a few questions to be answered about some of the ornaments before I can give Lucy a valuation."

"So, there might be something valuable there?"

"Possibly," he said grudgingly. "But I don't want to get anyone's hopes up. What is it, Prudence?"

For Prudence was looking from the mantelpiece to the table under the back window of the room. "How? I didn't—" She got up and fetched a little golden art deco clock from the table. "This is supposed to be on the mantel."

Bertie didn't seem to be very interested. "Oh? Well, you must have been thinking about something else and just put it down over there. Were you dusting in here recently?"

"What?" Prudence handed the clock, which had belonged to Gerry's mother, to him. "Oh yes. I dusted yesterday before Marion came to tea. Maybe Marion was looking at it."

Bertie turned the clock briefly over before handing it back. "Maybe. But I doubt it. Marion would know this is *faux* deco, probably made in the 1970s. Nice. But worthless."

"Wait a minute." Prudence left the room, Bertie following behind. She stopped in the dining room and looked first at the firewood she'd returned to the recess in the wall, then peered under the dining room table. The wood was where she'd put it, and the rug under the table was flat. The cat Mother jumped off a dining chair, yawned, stretched, and dug into the rug with her claws.

"Prudence, what —?"

She held up a hand and walked toward the sideboard where she'd put the salt and pepper shakers, the candelabra. They shone silver in the room's electric light. One of the sideboard's cutlery drawers was open.

Prudence approached slowly, feeling apprehensive and looked in. Instead of forks, spoons or knives carefully separated and laid out in small stacks, the silverware was jumbled together as if a hand had reached in and stirred.

She stepped back and bumped into Bertie. "Did a cat do that?" he asked, a note of doubt in his voice.

Behind him, Mother jumped onto the table and sat composedly, her tail wrapped around her fluffy orange body. Her golden eyes gleamed.

"Maybe," said Prudence in a tight voice, and slammed the drawer closed. The cutlery rattled.

# 15

"I hate these places," Lucy declared from between clenched teeth.

"Nobody likes them," Prudence confirmed softly. "Probably especially the people who live in them."

The ground floor of the Chestnut Nursing Home included a long foyer where people were lined up in wheelchairs or chairs facing the street in front of the building. Behind the foyer and a glass partition was a room full of small tables and chairs. Sofas and other chairs lined its walls. There was a piano at one end. A huge wall-mounted television, muted, flickered from on high at the other. Many of the people in both areas were dozing. It was early afternoon.

Prudence raised her voice and addressed the woman at reception. "Hello. I phoned earlier? We're here to see Mme Ménard."

The woman looked at them impassively, checked her computer then jerked her head toward the elevator. "She's on four."

"Thank you," Prudence said cheerily. As they waited for the elevator, a bent old man shuffled past. His slippers never lost contact with the linoleum floor, made a swishing noise. As he headed to the common room, they saw the back of his pants were freshly stained high up around the waist.

"Oh no," Lucy moaned, and quickly walked back to the receptionist and pointed to the man. The woman shrugged and Lucy rejoined Prudence.

"Too late," Prudence murmured as the man carefully lowered himself into a chair.

"He doesn't know, poor thing," Lucy replied. "*She* said she'd look after it but—" The elevator bell pinged and they got in. They looked uneasily at each other.

"Why are we here?" Lucy asked

"You mean besides just visiting a sick neighbour?"

"Yes, of course *that*!" Lucy snapped. "Sorry. But you said—"

"You're right. I said I have reservations about Mme Ménard and her nephew's treatment of her. He seemed shifty when we last spoke. He clearly didn't want us to know where his aunt was. Humour me."

"As always," Lucy said lightly as they stepped out of the elevator.

The first thing they noticed was the smell. Prudence felt her gorge rise. Lucy said faintly, "Oh, God. Which room?"

"Four thirty-one." They proceeded down the hallway to their right, peering at room numbers, then, as invariably happens in institutions, realized they were going the wrong way and turned back.

They heard voices coming from some of the rooms, but they were the voices of people talking to themselves, or calling, or simply grunting.

A man lurched by, arms flailing, eyes glazed, babbling nonsense. Both women flinched and shrank back. They came to the fourth floor's common area, in one open corner of the ward, and stopped, aghast.

It must have been part of the institution's policy that people were brought out of their rooms to socialize, or perhaps when their rooms were being cleaned. The area was bedlam.

Bodies in wheelchairs or on gurneys were lined up closely together. As they passed her, one tiny woman, reaching out with frail hands, implored them in an Asian language. Two orderlies appeared, with the glazed-eyed man in a strait jacket between them. He was struggling to be let go but they sat him down in a chair and stood over him talking to each other.

"Is she here?" Prudence asked Lucy.

"I don't see her. Just keep going." They turned the corner back into a hallway. "Are we the only visitors?"

"Maybe people visit in the residents' rooms." Prudence tried to sound calm, though the random storage of these people who'd been blessed with strong constitutions, and now cursed by the same, revolted her. "Ah, 431." She paused outside the door, which was open a little, knocked, then entered.

Mme Ménard lay, a long low lump under the covers with her back to them. Lucy took the lead. "Mme Ménard, it's Lucy Hanlan. Your neighbour. How are you, Mme Ménard?"

The woman must have been sleeping because they saw her supine form suddenly shiver and a choked moan escaped her.

Lucy moved around the bed so she was facing Mme Ménard. "*Bonjour, Madame. Comment ça va?*"

Prudence followed Lucy until she too could see the old woman's face. What she saw shocked her. Tangled hair, eyes crusted with sleep dirt (and not just one night's worth either, by the look of it), dry cracked lips. A plastic glass of water with a straw sat by the bedside.

As they watched, a tear escaped Mme Ménard's eye and ran down her cheek. Prudence saw there was a yellow stain on the pillowcase near the woman's mouth. She took a deep breath. "Okay. It's what I thought."

"What?" said Lucy, who was patting the woman's shoulder.

"Neglect," Prudence said crisply.

Lucy said, "She's certainly thinner than before."

Prudence leaned forward and addressed the frightened-looking old face. "Hello. I'm Lucy's friend, Prudence. Can you move at all, Mme Ménard?" The head dipped toward the chest.

"Good. Your head. Anything else?" A foot jerked under the bedclothes. "Excellent," Prudence said. Under the covers, a hand seemed to slide across the sheet. "Why, Madame, you're getting better, aren't you?"

Another slight nod and Mme Ménard's eyes turned in her head, trying to make contact with Prudence's. "We're going to try to help you," Prudence assured her. "Until then, you know you have to try to move, don't you?" Another nod. "I don't suppose you're getting any therapy?" The head tried to move from side to side. Mme Ménard closed her eyes in exhaustion then opened them.

"L—l—l—" she managed to say. "Moh—moh—moh, sh—sh—" Another tear trickled down.

"She's trying to say *mon chat!*" Lucy said excitedly. "I'm feeding him, Mme Ménard. Don't worry about Luc. He's fine." Lucy looked around the room helplessly. "Stay here, Prue, I'm going to ask for a washcloth."

Prudence sat next to Mme Ménard with one hand on her shoulder. Here was a predicament. Mme Ménard was obviously being warehoused in a nursing home when she should have been in a rehab clinic. And if the nephew had charge of her welfare legally, how could Prudence or Lucy interfere? She was still problem-solving when Lucy returned. Her friend was angry.

"They wouldn't give me a washcloth! Patients have to supply their own. So I went downstairs to the toilet and got wads of wet paper towels." She began washing Mme Ménard's face and hands gently. "Prudence, what are we going to have to do to get her some help?"

Prudence slowly said, "I may have a plan." And on the drive home, she told Lucy what it was.

That evening, after another good meal at the Parsley Inn with Bertie and Marion, trying not to think about what sort of supper

Mme Ménard would be having, if any, Prudence returned to The Maples to a phone message from Cece Muxworthy. She dialled his number. Sunday night at 8:45 shouldn't be too late.

"Oh, hi, Prudence. You want to hear about Walter Lester?"

"Yes. Very much."

"Okay. Well, the good news is I found Mrs. Lester's papers, among which was a copy of her will. And Walter is her heir."

"That's great, Cece. But you said good news as though there was also bad news."

"Mm. Well. Not as it affects the will—I'll handle the probate, get a death certificate and so on. And I've found her bankbook. I'll visit the bank tomorrow and get the ball rolling there."

"But will the bank release the money? Before the will is probated, I mean?"

"No. I'll set up an account for Walter myself."

Prudence was taken aback. "That's very good of you, Cece. I would offer to help but I just bought a car so I'm a bit low."

"No. It'll be fine. Mrs. Lester has quite a lot of money saved up, even just in her chequing account. There are investments too."

"Well, that's a relief. I was worried Walter would *have* to sell his house. Now at least he has a choice."

"*Was* he thinking of selling?"

"There are a couple of people who want the land behind Coco Poco." She remembered Monsieur Ménard's remark about having to wait for Mrs. Lester's will to be probated before he could make Walter an offer on the house. "Mme Ménard's nephew won't be pleased to learn the probate process is just starting. He must know that getting both properties raises the total value to any other buyer. He wants to prevent Walter from selling direct to a developer or to Dan Bartram. I'm afraid he'll try to cheat him."

There was a silence. "I'm beginning to think Walter Lester is the tip of the iceberg. I think we should have an in-person meeting, Prudence. What if I drop by tomorrow morning?"

"Monday? Okay. I have a different yet related matter to discuss with you."

"Interesting. Tomorrow at ten?"

"Fine." Prudence hung up the phone feeling energized. Things were happening! And she was making them happen. She went into Gerry's studio and checked for an email.

Dear Prudence and Hello, Cats!

Well, another half a week has gone by in a flash. I've been scribbling notes next to little drawings in my sketchpad, and a good thing too, or it would all be a lovely blur.

So, last Friday, we drove from Devon to Wales. We drove through Cardiff. Dublin, though interesting, was enough of a city for me, and we still have Glasgow and Edinburgh coming. So we just went straight to our next port of call, so to speak. (Which is accurate really, as we decided to follow the coast north.) This was a little place called St. Donats, forty-five minutes west of Cardiff, right by the seaside. Our B&B was a weathered wood structure. We walked the dunes to a beach, then drove to eat in a nearby village. Early to sleep.

Saturday we were up early, another little walk, then a two-hour drive to the Pembrokeshire Coast National Park and our next hotel, a round stone building. We were on the top floor with views of the sea. Jagged rocks and sandy beaches, and rock arches like they have in the Bay of Fundy in New Brunswick.

We also drove to Little Haven, a cute little old-fashioned former fishing village. We hooked up with the coast path there. All this fresh sea air and walking knocked us both out that night.

Sunday, we dawdled up to Aberystwyth, arriving at supper time, and had *cawl*, a lamb and leek soup—delicious! I'll have to make it when we get home. I should have mentioned the *bara brith*, a fruit cake made with strong cold tea. Also something to bake in the future. I know you love your fruitcakes!

A funny thing happened on one of our walks. We came to a barrow, an ancient gravesite, but one that had been reconstructed, I guess, because you could go in. Anyway, with much huffing and puffing, I crawled in after Doug, but when we got inside, it was so dark that I had a bit of a panic attack, felt that *I* was being buried. I'm all right, but it was nasty while it was happening.

Anyway, going to be in Wales another day or two then the Lake District. Beatrix Potter! Wordsworth! Arthur Ransome's *Swallows and Amazons*! I can't wait.

Lots of love to you and the cats and any of our friends you see.

Gerry and Doug

Prudence typed her brief response, mostly about the wood stove and discovery of a trap door to a chamber beneath the dining room. She left out the other stuff that had been happening, how objects—firewood and cutlery, the little clock—were being moved around the house. She closed the computer with a smile. Gerry, who'd grown up in Toronto, and only lived in the country for a year and a half, was now turning up her nose at cities. Funny girl. The Welsh coast sounded lovely, though the bit about the panic attack was worrying. She hoped Gerry was putting the baby first. She frowned.

Not for the first time, she wondered what Gerry's living arrangements would be when she and Doug returned. Maybe they were taking the opportunity of time spent together on the trip to figure something out. Gerry could hardly expect to bring home her baby to an empty house. And surely Doug would want to be there to help?

But what about his three boys? How to blend two houses and six people? Prudence gave it up. Not her problem except that she cared for Gerry and wanted her happiness.

She ran a finger over the top of the computer. Perhaps she would clean this room tomorrow. Yes. After her meeting with Cece.

She watched a murder mystery on TV then went up to bed. As she fell asleep, she heard the wind rise and rain begin to fall.

Monday it rained all day, so that postponed the next entertainment she'd planned for her guests. After her meeting with Cece, and her lunch, Prudence cleaned Gerry's studio thoroughly. The cats sulked indoors, getting under her feet whenever she emerged from behind the room's closed door. (Precious bamboo wallpaper precluded any feline trespassers.) They were bored. Prudence wasn't. Her mind flitted from one person to another.

Bertie. He seemed amiable enough. Happy to help Marion, help Lucy and Prudence with Mme Ménard's possessions. She thought back to her absolute infatuation with her former husband. What she felt for Bertie wasn't a pale imitation of *that*, but something altogether different. Affection? She set Bertie aside, along with the vacuum cleaner, and got her cleaning rags and polish.

Mme Ménard came to the front of her mind. Cece's plan was first to have a discussion with her nephew, then, if that didn't yield any fruit, begin the legal process of requesting a review of the man's legal curatorship. If it was found he was neglecting his aunt's best interests, they would apply for a judgement of release. As all this would take a considerable length of time, Prudence promised herself she would revisit Mme Ménard soon.

Then there was Walter Lester. Not so much to worry about there—*he'd* be all right. And she could easily check on him before or after work at the café.

She looked around the studio. Nice. All dusted and ready for Gerry's return. She removed her apron, put on a light coat and stepped outside.

*Thook!* Since she'd been a little girl she'd loved the sound of an opening umbrella. It made her feel safe, enclosed under its dome. This one was plaid—red and green mostly. The colours cheered her. Christmas in three months and a new baby to look forward to. She should really make a list of the ingredients she'd need for fruitcake, and the mincemeat for her tarts…

Occupied by such happy thoughts, she barely noticed the dampness rising from the earth, avoiding the puddles instinctively, and soon arrived at Cathy Stribling's wide front door.

Bertie must have been hovering nearby for it was he who let her in. "Hello, you," he said cordially.

"Hello!" For no particular reason, Prudence felt extraordinarily happy. She smiled up at him. "Hello," she said a second time but more quietly.

Bertie's eyes widened slightly. He kissed her gently. As he led her toward the living room, he said simply, "I've missed you."

Prudence was about to say how silly that was—after all, they'd dined together the previous evening—but something stopped her. Could she honestly say she'd missed him since yesterday's supper? She realized she could, but didn't articulate, the revelation leaving her surprised and temporarily speechless.

"Is it going to rain again tomorrow?" Marion querulously demanded.

"They're not calling for it," Cathy cheerfully replied, rising. "Hello, Prudence. I'll go put the kettle on, shall I? You must be feeling chilled."

Prudence relaxed. Bertie rambled on about some reference books back in Montreal that he'd consulted regarding Mme Ménard's pottery. Cathy returned with their tea. And soon it became evident that another two of the company had begun a love affair.

Prince Charles ignored everyone but Marion. His fat bum welded to the floor next to her chair, he faced straight ahead toward the coffee table and its delights, his head following the movements of Marion's right hand.

Now it would descend on his wrinkled bristly brow and scrunch the loose skin there as he slowly panted in ecstasy. His eyes would glaze over, briefly shut, then reappear, greedy slits, as the hand was removed.

Marion would hesitate over which morsel next to choose—a butter tart? a home-made truffle? a ginger snap?—and Charles would freeze, eyes bulging, jaw half-raised, drooling tongue just a little exposed, as she brought the delicacy to her lips. Then, as the last bite was almost taken, instead, remembering the valiant knight so faithfully attending her, whose lower jaw was vibrating with lust, Marion would negligently, as though unaware of what her hand was doing, drop the ort onto the floor at the side of her chair. After much licking of the hardwood and sniffing for crumbs, Charles would resume his post and the whole performance would be repeated.

Two hours, several cups of tea and many assorted treats later, Prudence walked back to The Maples. She was still unaware of the wind driving the rain sideways under her umbrella, adjusting its tilt automatically, but Christmas baking was not what now distracted her.

She was still distracted when, upon returning to The Maples, she got into her car, drove to the library and changed her books. She was on autopilot, her mind elsewhere, though careful as she drove.

Upon her return, she automatically collapsed and shook the umbrella in the tiny kitchen porch and hung her dripping coat to dry. Automatically, she fed the cats their meat and topped up their kibble and water. Automatically, she kicked off her wet shoes, exchanging them for slippers. And all the while, she had a faint smile on her lips, a warmth in her chest.

Humming, she made her supper, after which she read her book, watched the news and drifted off to sleep, the cats of the Honour Guard ranged on her bed, Mother purring on the carpet.

Around her, in the house, some cats slept, while others padded silently from one dark room to another on their particular missions.

Mice, enjoying the newly insulated walls, squeaked and scurried along ancestral paths toward crumbs and cat kibble.

As the night air cooled, the wood of the old house felt it, as it had for over two hundred years. Felt the season almost shift, the nearness of the first frost.

Objects trembled and moved. The sheer white curtains covering the windows either side of the front door fluttered. In the dining room, a cast iron poker, poorly propped next to an ash shovel, slipped slightly, the two metals clanking together. The rug, which covered the trap door under the heavy table, rippled then settled.

And outside, the trees and the wind and the rain continued a conversation as old as the river flowing by at the bottom of the garden.

# PART 4
# DEPRESSION

The grey and white cat was happy. Happier than he'd been for a long time. He purred and his claws gently kneaded the soft woollen blanket over his woman's lap. His stomach was pleasantly full, the room was warm, and he and she were almost lulled to sleep by the dull murmur of the TV's late night talk show. He dozed.

The murmur of voices rose in volume then abruptly stopped. He blinked sleepily at first, then, feeling a damp breeze blow over his body, opened his eyes fully. It was raining.

So, not in the cluttered stuffy little living room. Not in front of the TV. And most emphatically, not safe on her comfy lap. Though the wool blanket the food woman had placed in the cardboard box under a chair on his front porch was soft. And warm. He sat up.

A few moths twirled about the light high in the air. A few ground insects sang from the lawn. Cats were probably slinking around the neighbourhood, though he didn't sense any nearby. He'd had to defend his comfy box from one of the homeless ones. He licked his paw and complacently passed it over the scratch near his eye. Still undefeated.

A dog barked. Human footsteps crunched on the bit of gravel in the narrow lane that led to the large building that clanged noisily at its top a few times a week. A nearby door opened quietly then closed.

He smelled the odours of plants breathing at night, the breathing so different from that of the day. He detected the residual odours from human activity: the level of car exhaust dropping; the smells of cooking food diminishing. Except —

He began to smell a similar scent to that which deliciously filled the little house occasionally, when she would place a small amount of meat in the oven and carefully roast it. She would chop his portion finely, knowing he liked the bloody bits best.

He jumped out of the box and ran around to the back of the house. Yes. There was a smell of cooking meat. Who was in his house? Had she returned? Was she preparing a feast for the two of them?

He scratched at the back door. The metal screen felt warm. He scratched again and heard a faint crackling sound.

The sound grew louder. He retreated a ways into the vegetable garden and sat in a patch of leeks. Their strong odour temporarily distracted him from the one coming from the house.

Then the smell of cooking meat was consumed by the greater one of wood burning.

Light jumped up from the floor inside the house, began to flicker at the windows. It grew until it leapt out of the windows, out of the door. He felt the heat on his face. He fled.

He darted through the back fence into a neighbour's yard, and from there to the field near the large clangy building, where stones were ranged in careful rows. He climbed a smooth polished one and looked back.

His house was a bonfire. He saw a figure come out of the attached house's back door, look at the fire next door, then rush back inside.

The cat crouched on the cold stone and watched his house burn down.

# 16

"Marion! Sit *down*!"

Marion, peering over the side of the ferry at the grey turbulence below, half twisted her body and flumped down on the metal bench next to the railing. She thumped the seat with her hand. "It's cold! And hard!" She gazed again at the water close to the ferry. "I was looking for fish," she explained.

Bertie rose to the bait. "Why would fish be leaping out of the water close to a large noisy ferry?"

"I was looking for *dead* fish," came the dignified reply. "Last time I took this ferry—"

"Back in the Stone Age," muttered Bertie.

She glowered at him for a moment, then reiterated, "Last time, I was with Fred. It must have been in the 1950s. And he'd read about the pollution in the Ottawa River being so high, the fish were dying. Not that we saw any that day. So," she concluded triumphantly, "I was checking to see if things have improved."

Bertie shook his head. "Makes absolutely no sense."

Prudence piped up. "Oh, things have improved. We couldn't swim here sometimes when I was a child." She added mischievously, "Back in the Stone Age."

Bertie's eyes twinkled. "No, you're not as old as Marion, Prudence. You were around in the Bronze Age. Maybe even the Iron Age." He added, "Ow," as she lightly punched his arm.

They stood side by side at the railing. Marion had closed her eyes and tilted her face toward the sun. They'd decided to make this a morning trip, so Marion could be back for a rest by mid-afternoon. It was cool out in the middle of the river and Prudence, thinking of how deep the water was, shivered.

Bertie put his arm around her. "Cold?"

"Not really. What's the expression? I feel as if a goose just walked over my grave."

"Surely, in your case, considering where you're living, it would be a cat who—never mind that. No talk of graves today." He squeezed her shoulder. "It's a lovely day and we're afloat!"

She smiled up at him. "There's The Maples." She pointed to the pile of rocks that marked the tiny beach where Gerry's canoe lay beached. She frowned. Maybe she should drag it up the lawn and stow it in the shed. Surely Gerry was finished canoeing for the season considering her condition.

"Land ho!" Bertie cried. Prudence turned her head. They were past the middle of the river and closer to Oka than Lovering. The yacht club on the left, the few houses, were dwarfed by the church a hundred or so feet from the pier next to which they would land. Thank goodness there was peace there now. No helicopters, army or police vehicles. No Maggie looking across at the conflict from The Maples.

"Better get you back in the car," she said kindly, bending over Marion. She was surprised to see a few tears on the old cheeks.

Marion opened her eyes. "Memories" was all she said, but it was enough to bring a lump into Prudence's throat as she gave her assistance. Memories, indeed.

They watched the pilot in his small tugboat cut the engine and turn, leaving the ferry to gently slide up to the dock. Prudence drove carefully up the ramp, following the majority of cars in turning east. "Well," she asked brightly, "What's first? The gourmet shop? Or a farm stand?"

For, by crossing the river, they had arrived in a place with a strong agricultural heritage, different from that on the Lovering side. Where mostly flat Lovering had been an area of cattle and hay, pig, chicken and corn production, the Oka side had south-facing slopes on the escarpment that descended to the river. People had found fertile ground, suitable for orchards, market gardens, even vineyards.

They passed several farms advertising pick your own apples. It had been decided that bumping in a cart down a rough track behind a smelly tractor, then standing around while others went up ladders, wouldn't be enjoyed by the eldest member of their group. The vote was for the gourmet shop first, then a farm stand on the way back.

After being helped up the ramp at the shop, Marion settled herself in a store scooter with a large basket in front. This she proceeded to weaponize, zooming abruptly down an aisle, braking at the last minute to avoid anxious ambulatory shoppers, and filling her basket along the way with a copious quantity of provisions.

Bertie and Prudence sauntered along behind, discussing and selecting various choice oddments. "Well!" said Bertie, holding up a jar of preserved plums. "This store certainly rivals any in Westmount. Or anywhere downtown." He put the plums in their basket. "With ice cream, I think. Or custard."

Prudence selected fresh bread, a few cheeses and some paté. "For supper tonight. Come to The Maples." She added a pear *tarte Tatin*.

Bertie looked shocked. "*Buying* fresh baked goods, Prudence? Have you gone mad?"

She smirked. "I can't gallivant around with you all day *and* present a fabulous dessert at the end of it."

"I'm glad we're gallivanting," he said warmly. "What a nice word. I bet it's French. Let's look it up when we get home." They both paused, as if to better get the sense of what he'd just said or suggested. What if they *were* going home together?

Realizing they'd shared a thought made them shy and Prudence physically separated herself from him. "Now, where's Marion?" she murmured, finding her by the sound of her voice in an excited conversation with the gentleman behind the fish counter. A large whole salmon lay on the cutting board between them. The man held a large knife.

The conversation was in French and involved much hand gesturing and shrugging by both parties. At the end, the salmon was filleted, wrapped in brown paper and handed to Marion with a laugh.

"What was *that* all about?" asked Bertie, trailing behind Prudence.

"That, my dear, was about tonight's supper," snapped Marion, her cheeks flushed. "We had a bit of a disagreement about the best way to fillet a fish."

"Who won?"

"Who d'ya think?" was the response, from which, if they thought about it, they could infer anything they liked.

"What about your cheesy supper?" Bertie whispered to Prudence.

"It'll all keep till tomorrow," Prudence assured him. "I just hope Cathy doesn't have anything else planned."

Bertie smiled. "So, a possible three menus to choose from. I'm a lucky man." But the way his smiling eyes stayed fixed on Prudence's face hinted that a surplus of suppers was perhaps not the only reason he had to feel fortunate. Waiting at the checkout behind Marion, Bertie's hand found Prudence's and for once, she allowed the intimacy.

"Looking at all that food has made me hungry," Marion announced as they settled themselves in Prudence's car.

"I know," Prudence said. "Let's look for somewhere to have a picnic. We have all this food. We just need something to drink. And something to drink it from." The others were in agreement and that's how they found themselves a half hour later, sitting at a picnic table in front of a farm stall, with three cans of pop, three hot dogs and three greasy bags of french fries in front of them. (For there was a fast-food truck parked to the side of the farm stand and their noses seduced them away from Prudence's bread, paté and cheese.)

"We'll probably all die from some form of botulism," Bertie suggested, chomping heartily into his hot dog.

"Don't be ridiculous," said Marion, who'd been the one to first notice the food truck. "I've been eating this stuff all my life and it hasn't done me any harm."

The view was of rows of grapevines descending to a strip of forest by the river. "I can't believe they grow grapes here—in snowy cold Quebec," Bertie said, toasting the two women with his pop.

They munched their junk food. The sun shone. When they'd finished they packed everything away, including Marion, who was tired. Prudence bought a big sack of apples while Bertie paid for some bottles of soft cider and a bag of apple doughnuts, which they munched during the drive back to the ferry.

Prudence couldn't remember when she'd had a nicer day.

Prudence sat next to the living room table surrounded by apples. And cats.

The cats didn't actually *want* the apples. But they were intrigued by the long strips of peel that grew and grew, spiralling down until they fell into the bucket between Prudence's feet. So her mother had taught her, making a game out of seeing who could keep the curl of peel in one piece before the peeler accidentally slipped and cut it short.

Maybe the cats had missed her, she thought. Now she was working out of the house more, and gallivanting (she smiled at the word) with Bertie and Marion, the cats were receiving much less human attention than they would have previously, considering their owner Gerry worked mostly from home. "Some of you will be positively feral by the time Gerry gets back." She pointed the peeler at the boys—Winnie, Frank and Joe, and Ronald. "You four in particular." Winnie had his paws on the edge of the bucket and was peering in. Frank and Joe had a peel that had missed the bucket and were wrestling for it under the table, while Ronald sat, his little white face with its thin black moustache moving in time to the peeler in Prudence's hand.

The bucket tipped as she'd known it would; Winnie twisted away from it; and Ronald made his move, grasping a peel in his mouth and running off. For once Winnie didn't chase him. His dignity a bit ruffled (after all, he was the leader of this little gang), he sat calmly and licked a shoulder. The other cats ignored his discomfiture.

"I expect I'll be finding dried peel in odd places for a few days," Prudence mused.

She was going to make applesauce. Most of it would be frozen, but some she would give away, and some bake in loaves, which were just banana bread with applesauce substituted for mashed bananas. The rest of the apples would keep for part of autumn at least and would find their way into pies and muffins.

She thought of the storage space under the dining room floor, undoubtedly cooler than room temperature, but pushed the thought of going down there away with a shiver. And it would hardly be convenient to move the table and rug every time she or Gerry wanted apples.

She hummed as she worked. She would miss all this, she thought with a pang, if, say, she moved into the city. She paused and looked out the window. A Tuesday afternoon. Not much happening. And the view outside this window hadn't really changed in at least a hundred years, maybe more. Even before that, when the house had been the home of a trader, wouldn't the arrival of boats with goods have been an only occasional event?

*Then* there would have been some activity: the men walking down to unload goods; the women coming out of the house to watch. Or maybe they'd just have continued sitting by this window, continued with whatever task they were at. She smiled. Maybe they'd have been peeling apples, dreaming of all the good things they would make.

"And maybe there was a cat," she said to Bob, lounging on the window ledge. "And maybe he looked like you."

Bob, handsome devil that he was, blinked as if to say, "I doubt it" and laid one white-booted black front paw over the other.

When the phone rang, Prudence, thinking it might be Bertie calling to firm up a time for supper, rose cheerfully and went into the kitchen to answer it. "Hello!" she said heartily.

"Prudence?" said the somewhat taken aback voice of Lucy Hanlan.

"Lucy!"

"I've been calling you."

"We took the ferry to Oka this morning. It was such fun! How are you?"

"I'm fine," Lucy replied flatly. "But somebody else isn't."

Prudence put down the receiver. In a daze she slowly returned to the table, looking at the piles of peeled and unpeeled apples. Did she have enough peeled to start making applesauce? What had a moment before been a pleasure now seemed a chore. She began coring the peeled apples, then went into the kitchen, returning with the biggest pot she could find.

After a minute, she rose and walked to the front hall where the other phone and the answering machine lived. The light was flashing. She pressed play and listened to the two messages from Lucy, asking her to call, and the one from Cece Muxworthy, in which he said in a serious voice that he had something to tell her.

I'll finish the applesauce, she thought, then phone Cece. Anyway, I already know what he's going to tell me.

Marion had felt well enough to walk, so Prudence let her and Bertie into the house around six that evening. Despite her welcoming smile, her strained face told both her guests something was amiss.

"What's wrong?" Marion asked abruptly.

"Well," Prudence said reluctantly, "let's get settled first and, maybe, well, have a drink. I need a drink. I was thinking gin and tonic? Gin's all there is in the house."

"It smells fantastic in here, Prudence," commented Bertie, sniffing the air.

"I made applesauce this aft. I've got a container for you to take back to Cathy's." They settled in the living room, Marion and Prudence on the sofa, Bertie in a rocker. Prudence jumped back up. "Oh! The drinks!"

"You can make mine a martini," Marion prompted. "Hold the vermouth. Do you have any olives?"

"Um, I'm not sure. If we do, they're those ones stuffed with a bit of pimento. Are those okay?"

Marion gave her a look. "I can tell this is your first time making a martini. Yes, the green ones with the pimento are acceptable. In fact, in Canada, they're iconic, considering that when martinis became fashionable in the fifties, they were practically the *only* type of olive in most grocery stores."

"I think, judging by your expression, dear Prudence, that we'll make mine a martini as well," said Bertie. So only Prudence, inwardly shuddering at the idea of sipping straight gin flavoured with one or two olives, added tonic to her glass.

Once she was seated again, she took a healthy gulp of her drink, a big breath, and sighed.

"What's it all about?" Bertie asked, sounding mystified. "Are they okay in Europe? Is Gerry okay?"

"Oh. Well. Yes. As far as I know they're fine. No—" And she told them of the fire that had destroyed not only the Ménard, but the Lester home. And that Walter Lester was missing, presumed dead.

# 17

"Good God!" said Bertie. "Good thing—" He stopped abruptly.

"What?" queried Marion. "What could possibly be good about it?"

"Oh, well, you know. Good thing Mme Ménard wasn't home as well." He hastily added, "Too bad about the other fellow, though."

"Well, that's it," Prudence said in a worried tone of voice. "They've checked the ruins for his body and didn't find it. I know he's, ah, different, but I don't think he'd hide inside a burning house." She turned to Marion. "He'd have had enough sense to get out, wouldn't he?"

Marion shrugged. "I don't know him. You do. Was he asleep? No smoke detector? Smoke inhalation?"

"No, but no body," Bertie reminded them.

Prudence asked hesitantly, "Are people ever burned to just ashes? In a hot enough fire?"

Marion shook her head. "From what I've read about cremation, they still have to manually crush the bones so they can fit into the urns. You don't get ashes; you get ground-up bones."

Bertie gave her a look. "Thank you for that arresting image, Marion."

Then Prudence slowly said, "So he must have been frightened and ran away. But he rarely even ventures off his property. Where could he have gone?"

"I'm going to sound like a demanding old woman," said Marion, "but if I don't eat soon I'll become a grumpy one."

"Oh, my goodness!" Prudence said, standing up. "It's all ready. I'll put it on the coffee table. We can just help ourselves."

Soon they were eating good crusty bread, peppery paté, soft Brie and firm Oka cheeses, along with a few apples Prudence had quartered. Cats, who had been less than intrigued by the martinis, now crept closer, drawn by the smells of meat and cheese.

"Fantastic!" Bertie said, smacking his lips. "I could eat this every day."

Marion nodded agreement. "I often eat this kind of meal. No prep and no pots."

Prudence felt sorry for the woman then remembered Marion could always pop a TV dinner into the oven when she felt like a hot meal.

Min Min put a paw on Marion's leg and mewed piteously. "Whatever you, do, don't feed any of them. Please," Prudence begged.

Marion leaned over and said, "Sorry, Buster." Min Min, gentle soul that he was, subsided with a final heartrending meow.

Prudence asked, "Do you want dessert and coffee right away or—?"

Bertie and Marion spoke simultaneously. "In a while," said he while she said, "Now, please."

Prudence laughed. "Well, we can please everyone. I'll make coffee and bring Marion her tart and Bertie and I will wait a bit."

As she returned to the room after a few minutes, she heard Marion say, "…probably dead," then look up smiling to add, "Why, thank you, Prudence. It's been ages since I had a *tarte Tatin*. And with pears instead of apples. Lovely!"

Bertie watched Marion enjoy the crisp pastry, creamy pears and caramelized sugar topping. Then he broke. "Ah, maybe I'll have my dessert now too, Prudence. If it's not too much trouble."

She grinned at him and returned with the whole tart, plates and forks. "In case anyone wants seconds," she said. She and Bertie looked at Marion.

"What?" said Marion, shovelling in the last forkful of her portion. "What? It fell." They looked at the rug where Min Min was lapping at a bit of pastry.

They drank their coffee and talked of other things than the fire and Walter Lester. Marion was exhausted by 8:30 so Prudence drove them back to Cathy's. As she steered her car back onto the road, she wished it wasn't always to an empty house that she was returning.

Tomorrow, she thought as she tidied the kitchen. I'll think about it all tomorrow. Then, just as she fell asleep, she remembered Mme Ménard's cat.

"Well, somebody's been saved the task of pulling two houses down," observed Lucy grimly. She and Prudence were standing on the lawn of the house across the street from what was left of the Ménard and Lester homes. They'd met at Lucy's at nine then walked down from her house. Both were required to be at their jobs at ten.

"You're assuming they would have ultimately been bulldozed and developed?" Prudence asked.

"Yeah. At least we managed to shift almost all Mme Ménard's stuff to the church basement. Except the larger pieces of furniture."

Prudence thought of the big old armoire with the heavy sideboard on top of it from the Ménard kitchen, now reduced to ashes. That piece was older than we are, she reflected, and should have outlasted us all. "I guess M Ménard will be happy. No way his aunt is ever going to return to live in *that*." She added, "Happy first day of fall, by the way."

Lucy grunted.

A backhoe, operated by the younger Hudson, supervised by his father, was slowly pulling the blackened rubble of the Lester house onto the front lawn. The town's fire chief and an official were also watching. A dump truck waited.

Prudence nervously said, "They're sure there's no body in there?"

Lucy shook her head. "As soon as they heard the house was supposed to have one occupant, the firefighters did a search." She continued. "How am I going to feed the cat? Where can I put his food now? Even the porch is burned."

"Over by the fence?" Prudence suggested. "Put another box with a blanket in it and put the dish next to that? No, that won't work when it rains. What about a larger wooden box and put the food inside?"

"I'll figure something out," Lucy said resignedly.

Once the earth where the Lester house had been had been more or less scraped clean, the elder Hudson gestured to his son that it was time to turn the backhoe's attention to lifting the burnt mess into the waiting dump truck.

"Why don't we look for the cat over behind the café?" Prudence suggested. "I saw him there once before."

"Might as well." They crossed the street and carefully passed behind the dump truck. As they neared the rear of Coco Poco, Prudence saw Dan Bartram standing inside watching it all. She waved and he lifted one hand and let it drop before returning to some task.

"Luc, Luc, Luc," called Prudence, bending to look behind garbage cans and peering between buildings. They walked all the way to St. Pete's and its graveyard, then back. "He'll show up," she said, "when he's hungry." She wondered if the same could be said for Walter Lester. She hoped so.

"Not if he was burned to death on the front porch," Lucy responded gloomily.

"I think, as he was sleeping outside, he would have heard or smelt the fire and escaped. Don't you?"

"I really don't have a clue, Prue," Lucy said peevishly. "The whole thing is making me ill." They crossed the street to their former position and resumed watching the men working. The dump truck was full and slowly trundled away up Lucy's street.

Prudence said idly. "I suppose the ruins are well soaked with water and ready to dump safely."

Lucy said bitterly, "Yes. I think the fire department managed that much at least."

"Now, now," Prudence remonstrated. "Old wooden houses. Must be impossible to put out once the fire's got a good hold."

"Exactly." Lucy turned to her friend. "I watched the whole thing. What if it had been my house? And I sleep upstairs…"

"Ah." Prudence examined Lucy's miserable face. "Check your smoke alarms before you go to bed tonight. That'll make you feel better."

Lucy's brow cleared. "I will. I always keep spare batteries." They watched as the younger Hudson moved the backhoe to begin scraping at the Ménard house. "Gosh. Her vegetable garden and shrubs must be all burnt up." Lucy sounded sad.

The backhoe lifted and pulled, its scoop reminding Prudence of a human hand, a gardener's perhaps, digging in earth. How we make machines in our own image, she thought dreamily, mesmerized by its rhythmic rising, falling and dragging.

The mechanical arm lifted, lowered, then stopped, poised over its next load. The younger Hudson half-raised himself from his seat and peered over and around the scoop. He yelled something to his father who drew a forefinger across his throat. The son sat down, backed the machine away from the debris and cut its engine.

In the sudden silence that followed, his voice could be heard clearly, even across the street. "Found him," he said.

"Oh, *no*!" Prudence exclaimed. And took a step forward.

Now it was Lucy's turn to comfort her friend. "Come away," she said, grasping Prudence's arm. "Come away, dear."

"Oh, that poor man," Prudence repeated as Lucy handed her a second cup of extra-sweet tea. "If only—if only I'd paid more attention to him."

"You thought he'd be safe in his house," Lucy reasoned. "We all did."

"Yes, but I saw close up how fragile he was. How helpless. I should have—"

"Should have what, Prue? Taken him in? Adopted him?"

"No...but. If I hadn't been so busy gallivanting around with Bertie, so distracted, I might have…" Her voice trailed off as she realized how feeble this sounded. She drank her tea. "What time is it?"

"Ten to ten. Are you going to work?"

"Of course. My boss saw me just now, even if I wanted to call in sick."

"Well, I guess I should be getting along too. Doris has her own key but she'll be curious if I'm not there."

Prudence rose. "I'm sure everyone is finding out about the fire, if they don't already know."

"Yeah. Doris doesn't live far. She'll have heard all the commotion last night. Are you sure you'll be able to cope?"

Prudence took a breath and squared her shoulders. "It's what single women of our age do, Lucy. We cope."

When they walked past the scene of the fire, a police car and two officers had joined the group already there.

Prudence kissed Lucy goodbye and walked up the café front steps. The door was locked so she gently rapped on it.

Dan opened it quickly. "I was just getting stuff ready for opening. Also, it felt funny sitting in my office staring at all that. Why do you suppose the police have arrived? Do they suspect arson?"

"Dan, I have something terrible to tell you." Prudence took off her coat and came behind the counter where he was. "You know Walter Lester?"

"Yes."

"I'm afraid he's, he's been killed. He's been found in one of the burnt-out houses."

"That's awful. I mean, I didn't *know* him, just to see him wandering around in the front yard of their house. First his mother, then him." He ruminated on this for a second before adding, "Um, can you do a full day today? Till four?"

Prudence nodded but was distracted. Even as she'd said "one of the burnt-out houses" she'd wondered, why and how was Walter Lester in his neighbour's house?

Dan left by the front door, muttering something about a meeting. As she prepared herself for her first customer—Mr. Willis and Jazz would be along as usual any minute—she forgot her shock and her brain came alive.

Why *would* Walter be found in the house next to his own? Based on what she'd briefly observed of the relationship between the Lesters and their neighbour, he wouldn't have had a key with which to let himself into the Ménard house. Could Lucy have left the house unlocked by mistake after working there? And anyway, why go from one burning building to another? Unless —

At that moment a sharp rap at the front window alerted her to Mr. Willis, requesting his regular brew.

She brought it out to him and, as there were no other customers, sat down. "All right, Mr. Willis?" She leaned over to pat Jazz's soft golden head.

He nodded. "Terrible night, though. Roy Hudson told me they just found a body. And that Walter Lester is missing." Prudence nodded that she already knew. He drank and returned to retelling his personal version of events. "Heard the engines and came down the street to see. The Lester house didn't have a chance. Maybe if it hadn't been attached—"

Prudence said slowly, "You mean the fire started on Mme Ménard's side?"

"Yup. Just lucky it wasn't a row of attached buildings like they have in cities."

"Yes. Lucky." So Walter would have become aware that something was wrong when? Had he been asleep? Had he smelt smoke and checked his own house first? Had he heard the fire crackling on the other side of the attached wall? Perhaps he'd entered the Ménard house by breaking a window, tried to put out the flames.

Mr. Willis was speaking. "…and wonder what the insurance will make of it."

"Don't they pay if it's a fire?"

"Oh, yes. But this will be a complicated claim. Two attached houses. Fire starts in one. Have to know the cause of *that* fire. Was there negligence?"

"I heard Mme Ménard *had* let the house go a bit lately," Prudence said slowly.

"See? If the electrics were old, or her gas or oil tanks—my insurance company made me replace the oil tank for the furnace last year. Nothing wrong with the old one. In fact, when I rapped on it you could tell it was made better than the new one. If I press on the new one, it gives. Why—"

He was getting excited so Prudence interrupted. "You seem to know a lot about insurance, Mr. Willis."

"Should do. Worked in it for forty years. God, it was dull. Until you realized it was the lives of real people involved in all the claims, the forms, all the delays." He sipped his coffee. Jazz sat up, scratched one ear then circled and collapsed again. "Anyway, the Lester claim won't be processed until the cause of the Ménard fire is determined."

Prudence said softly, "I wonder if there's any one left to *make* the Lester claim."

"Yeah. There's that. If not, it'll be up to the government to fight it out with the insurance company." He heaved himself to his feet. "Anyway, mustn't keep you. Looks like you got a customer." As he and Jazz went down the stairs, one of the police officers came up.

"Hi," she said. "Can I get some coffees?"

"That's what we're here for," Prudence said and held open the door. With a feeling of satisfaction, she thought: a held-up claim. Hah! That'll rot M Ménard's socks!

# 18

After filling the young officer's order (apparently, being the youngest meant you had to buy coffee for your partner *and* the fire chief and town official *and* the Hudsons) of six regulars, three with cream, and sugar packets stuffed along with stir sticks in her pocket, Prudence kept busy with a regular stream of curious Loveringians, some gently, others not so gently, trying to pry information from her reluctant lips.

Many were uninformed as to there being a body in the ruins and Prudence didn't enlighten them. Yet it must be obvious to anyone who looked at the scene (as did Prudence when she ventured into the back in search of more freshly ground coffee—she found a few bags of something simply called AFRICAN BLEND—CLEAN DELICATE FLAVOUR WITH A RICH BODY AND ACIDITY—Dan must have been roasting), the scene which now sported a small tent around where she guessed Walter's body lay, two people in white suits going in and out of it, that someone had died. She wiped the previous special from the blackboard to write the African one with its notes and thought: those words—clean, delicate, rich—don't sound like Dan's; he must have been distracted by the fire.

At twelve-thirty she had a moment to herself and had just sat down to eat her sandwich when a rap at the front window alerted her of Mr. Willis's return. He jerked his head to indicate that she should come outside.

"Look what I found eating leftover chips and burgers behind the restaurant."

Prudence's mouth opened. There, shivering, dazed, and holding onto Mme Ménard's cat Luc, was Walter Lester.

The cat, obviously freaked out by the proximity of Jazz (who was too old to give a monkey's about Luc or any other cat) was struggling and digging its claws into Walter's thin arms. "Well, I'll be off," said Mr. Willis. Prudence pulled Walter into the café, thinking to herself, I won't make the same mistake twice, and vowed this time not to let him or the cat out of her sight. She flipped the "open" sign to its "closed" side.

First she gave him a coffee with extra cream and sugar in the largest cup the shop had. The cat, now finding itself in a dog-free zone, had jumped off Walter and was exploring. He received a saucer of milk as Prudence wasn't sure the richness of cream would be good for him. And he'd probably turn up his nose at soy milk. She also gave Walter the half of her sandwich she hadn't yet bitten into and a couple of biscotti from the big glass jar on the counter.

These requirements seen to, she sat for a moment and watched him eat. Who should she call? She settled on Cece Muxworthy. Walter already knew him and might be persuaded to go somewhere with him. And Cece could alert the authorities. Then she had a better thought. "Walter, do you mind coming into the back with me? Just for moment? You remember. It's a glass-walled room and we can see your hou—I mean, where your house was from there. Just for a second?"

Walter's eyes, still frightened-looking but certainly less dull from hunger, darted from side to side. "I guess," he said, standing up.

Leaving Luc lapping more milk (she had nothing else to give him—he'd hardly enjoy her partially eaten half a peanut butter sandwich) she preceded Walter into the back room. Taking him by the hand, she pushed open the outside door. "Hey!" she called. "I've got him!" When the assembled men turned, she continued, "This is Walter Lester! He's alive!"

She retreated with Walter back inside, phoned Cece from Dan's desk, and waved at the advancing police to come around the front.

"Now, Walter," she said soothingly, "the police are going to ask you what happened the night of the fire and then that nice Mr. Muxworthy—you remember? The one who's working on your mother's will, getting you money for groceries?—is going to come here and together we'll all figure out a place for you to stay. All right?"

The bell indicating someone had entered at the front jingled. The police. As they moved toward the connecting door, Walter said, "I'm still hungry."

And so Prudence found herself, once the police and Cece had arrived and were settled talking with Walter, across the street, ordering a double cheeseburger and large fries. And a plain hamburger, no bun, no condiments. When the fry cook, who looked like he'd seen everything, handed over her bag, he said, "Plain burger for your dog?" Prudence replied with a smile, "No, cat." And as she walked back with Walter and Luc's lunches, she realized she'd gotten twice as much food at the greasy spoon than she could have at Coco Poco for half the money!

The police questioned Walter in the back of the café and Cece took him to his house for a wash. "Until we think of something more permanent," he assured Prudence. Prudence turned the "closed" sign to say "open" and resumed business.

Walter had insisted on taking Luc with him and after a moment's thought Cece had shrugged and said, "It will amuse Bea. And our own cat." Walter left meekly without thanking Prudence for any of the food, while Luc looked over Walter's shoulder and blinked a few times. "Now what?" he might have been thinking.

Now she had good news to relate, she didn't hesitate to share it. She nipped in the back and called Lucy, and she chatted happily with her subsequent customers, until the third or fourth, an elderly woman with carefully coiffed blue hair, said, "But then who died?" Prudence shut her mouth tight again.

Who indeed?

As she worked that afternoon, foaming milk, adding flavourings, dusting with cocoa or cinnamon, and making change, all with a smile, she could think of only one person.

She considered going out the back and hailing the police again to tell them her hunch, but the café had already been closed once that day; she felt she couldn't do that again to her employer. She wondered if Lucy had heard anything through the gossip mill. For the first time she regretted she didn't own a cell phone. She could have texted like Ginger did without leaving her post.

When she saw Dan Bartram's car turn onto the street and heard him moving around in the back, she breathed a sigh of relief. It was almost four.

He entered the café and she asked, "How did your meeting go?"

"Oh, fine," he replied. "How about you? How was it in here today?"

"Actually, in terms of business, quite good. The crew out back bought coffee three times and lots of people were curious and came in. And I had to use some of the African blend from the back."

"What did you think?"

Prudence, who'd thought it tasted pretty unexceptional, remembered the notes. "Delicate. But rich. Nice." Liar, she told herself.

Dan looked pleased. "Yes. I think it's one of my best."

Prudence remembered the most important thing about the day. "Oh! I almost forgot! Walter Lester is alive!"

Dan looked mildly surprised. "How can that be? I thought you said—"

"Oh. Yes. There's still *someone* dead out there, but it's not Walter. Mr. Willis—one of our regulars—found him scrounging for food in the garbage and brought him to me. The police questioned him here. I hope that was okay?"

"Well, yes, of course." He smiled. "Especially as they were such good customers. Where is he now?"

"My friend Cece Muxworthy, the lawyer—do you know him?" He shook his head. "He's been trying to sort out Mrs. Lester's will, so he took Walter to his house till he can find a better place for him." A thought entered her head and she added, "May I use your phone before I leave? Then I'll be off."

"Yes, of course. Thank you for working a full day. You must be tired."

"I am. A bit." She took her coat and purse and paused at the connecting door. "But it's been interesting. See you."

"See you."

After her phone calls (one to Cece and one to Lucy who was thinking the same thing as Prudence about the identity of the body in Mme Ménard's house), Prudence talked briefly with the police out the back, two different officers now, telling them her idea. They listened courteously. Then she drove to Cece's.

The cats at The Maples were not impressed. *Another* cat come to live with them? The place was already bulging at the seams, many of them seemed to indicate by the haughty way they drew together, some of them pacing around the new arrival.

Another human wasn't a problem, though this skinny old man seemed a bit peculiar. Harmless, but peculiar.

"Now, Walter, I hope you like barbecue chicken, because that's what I picked up at the IGA. I'm cooking some wholesome vegetables to go along with it. You've had enough french fries the last day and a half."

Walter mumbled something, seemingly relieved that someone else was taking charge of his life. The grey and white cat crouched under his chair, its tail lashing to and fro. Walter could feel it thump on the rungs under the chair. He himself was glad there was just this one woman living in this big house. He didn't cope well with groups of people and the noisy big woman married to his lawyer had intimidated him. He'd been glad to get out of there, though they'd kindly provided him with clean clothes after his shower. Prudence was talking again.

"Just house- and cat-sitting for one of my clients. I don't *live* here. Chance would be a fine thing. Well, she—Gerry—is more than a client really. The niece of my oldest friend who's now deceased. Left her this house and twenty cats—can you believe it?" Prudence set the table and brought their supper. "There. Tuck into that."

Walter did. Enthusiastically. The woman ate then sighed, pushing her plate away. "That better?" He nodded. "Would you like an early night?" He allowed his gaze to flick over to the corner where the TV sat. "Oh. You want to watch the news or something?" He nodded again and got up, reseating himself on the sofa.

Prudence switched on the TV. Luc, after hesitating for a moment, made a dash for the sofa and launched himself into the safety of Walter's lap. As the comforting tones of the newscaster filled the room and Prudence cleared the dishes, other cats crept closer to the pair on the sofa. *Their* sofa.

Mother was the first to make a move, jumping stiffly onto the end farthest from Walter and turning her back on Luc. Jay followed Mother, curling into her broad marmalade side, then Blackie and Whitey joined them. Others seemed to find the hearthrug satisfactory while Bob, their leader, leapt onto the mantel and reposed attractively next to a bowl of apples, surveying his kingdom.

Prudence washed the dishes. She was exhausted. When the phone rang, she cursed, dried her hands and snapped, "Hello?"

There was a beat, then Bertie said, "Is everything all right, Prudence?"

"Yes! Why wouldn't it be?"

Bertie spoke gently. "Because we were supposed to talk this afternoon, to firm up dinner plans."

Prudence looked at the kitchen clock. Six-thirty. She and Walter had eaten early. "Oh. I'm sorry. I've already eaten, Bertie. And I have a guest." There was a pause. She continued, "We found Walter Lester alive today and bringing him here seemed the best solution. Cece Muxworthy's place is small and they don't have a spare bedroom. He's got Mme Ménard's cat and I thought…" She trailed off into the silence. "It's just until Cece can find a permanent residence for Walter."

"I see. I'm glad your, er, friend is alive. Good luck with all that."

"Good luck with all what?" She knew she sounded peevish but couldn't seem to control herself.

"All of it. Hey. I looked up gallivant. It means to go a-courting and—"

"I know what gallivant means," she said wearily.

"Oh." An empty space stretched between them. "Well, I better get going and rustle up a dinner option for Marion. You know how she gets when she doesn't eat."

"Yes." There didn't seem anything left to say so she muttered, "goodbye," and hung up.

Now she felt exhausted and *sad*. Great. So much for good deeds being rewarded. She went into the living room. Walter seemed oblivious to her. The news had ended and he was watching game shows, surrounded by dozing cats. All he needs is his meals and a television set, she thought. What a life.

She trudged upstairs, pausing to get sheets out of the trunk in the hallway, before entering the little room next to Gerry's at the front of the house. Probably this will be the baby's room, she thought as she removed the coverlet and blankets and made up the single bed. She wondered if Luc would sleep with Walter. Probably he'd feel safer with the quiet man than risk multiple contretemps with The Maples' regular denizens.

As she went back downstairs, she had a thought. "I'll bring him right back," she told a startled Walter when she plucked sleepy Luc from his lap.

The cat was limp and warm in her arms. She walked the length of the house, showing him where the downstairs bathroom was and plopping him in one of the seven cat boxes ranged in a row there. As she watched him tentatively sniffing and then scratching in the litter, she said, "What a fluke, eh, Luc? Walter and you finding each other. You're a lucky cat."

The cat paused in his search for the perfect patch of litter and looked up at her. What had she said, she wondered, to make him stare with those opaque yellow eyes? He soon went back to his business and she left him to it.

She returned to the hall and wilted when she saw the answering machine light flashing. Oh, no. Now what? One message from Lucy, asking her if she had any more news, and one from Edwina Murray, calling to see if Prudence could clean her house the next day, Thursday, instead of the usual Friday.

Lucy could wait. She dialled Edwina's number. "Edwina? Prudence here. Yes. I can do your place tomorrow. But I have a favour to ask in exchange." When she hung up the phone, she felt a bit better about her and Bertie.

She and Walter watched nature programs until ten when they went upstairs to their beds. She set her alarm for seven as she had to be at Edwina's by nine. But when she came downstairs the next morning, everything had changed.

"What on earth—?" She stood on the landing halfway down at the turn of the stairs. The upstairs cats, those who slept on Gerry's empty bed—Bob, Jay, Seymour and Lightning—plus the Honour Guard, hungry for their breakfasts, paused and swirled around her. A large skein of yellow wool that she'd been saving to knit a sweater for Gerry's baby had unrolled itself all the way down the stairs and along the foyer's floor to the front door.

"Cats!" said Prudence and stooped, began winding the wool around her left hand and elbow. Strangely, none of the cats tried to intercept the wool as she twitched it toward her, though Jay seemed to think about it, approaching the tempting object then backing away hastily.

When Prudence got to the front door, she found the sheer curtains, which guarded the windows either side of the door, had been rolled up and tucked into their curtain rods, the way she would do if she was going to clean the glass. Which she obviously hadn't done recently—and the curtains were thick with dust. She released them and they wisped downward. "They're all wrinkled!" she exclaimed, clucking her tongue and making a mental note to handwash and iron them before Gerry's return. She paused, suddenly discomfited. Had Walter Lester done this? He must have.

She quietly went back upstairs, utterly confusing the cats, who milled around at the bottom of the stairs, possibly wondering if, and for the first time, they were going to be offered breakfast in bed. Prudence put the wool back into her knitting bag in her room, then crept to Walter's door. Gently, she pushed it inward.

No Walter. But the bed had been made. "Huh," she said, looking around the room. Everything appeared to be as it should. "Huh," she repeated and went back downstairs to be greeted joyfully by the cats.

This time, as she passed the hall table, she looked at the answering machine. The light was flashing. She pressed play, thinking to listen to Lucy's message again. Dead air followed by a click. Then another similar message. Or rather, non-message. Then another and another and another. Prudence lost count and never made it back to Lucy's. She hadn't heard the phone ringing in the night. As The Maples was a large house, the machine was set to allow the phone to ring six times before it answered the call, to give the house's occupants time to leg it to answer if they wished. She had been tired but she doubted she'd have missed that many rings in the night.

Prudence stood in front of the machine and gazed at the portrait of the first Coneybear, John, Gerry's great-great-grandfather, who'd died in 1893. *Not* one of Prudence's ancestors, she was glad to say. The face was plump, self-satisfied; the lips thin, pinched, even cruel. She straightened her shoulders, turned and marched into the dining room where the cats who usually slept there stretched, some dropping from their perches.

She took two steps, then another, then stopped, staring around the room. Cat towels, which normally covered any upholstered surface in the room, and this included the many dining chairs ranged around the table as well as a few easy chairs, had been gathered and piled together on the floor. As Prudence herself would do if she was preparing to launder them. She was beginning to see a pattern.

Of course, the cats who usually sat on these towels weren't bothered by their absence. Brothers Kitty-Cat and Harley were sitting on the two chairs nearest Prudence. She clucked her tongue as she absently petted the huge black and white shorthairs. "Now I'll have to brush the upholstery before replacing your towels," she informed them. The cats blinked. They were probably thinking: not on our account; this upholstery is quite nice. And—breakfast?

Now Prudence turned to face the sideboard. As before, the drawers where she kept the cutlery were open. "Not all jumbled again?" she muttered as she cautiously looked in.

This time the cutlery had been sorted, some knives, forks and spoons removed from their fellows and placed together, and when Prudence picked these up and examined them, she noticed they were the ones that were the most tarnished, in need of polishing. "What the —?" she exclaimed and slammed the drawers shut. Crystal glasses on a nearby shelf tinkled. Someone was commenting on her housekeeping!

She better find Walter. God knew what he'd be up to in the living room, if that was where he was.

But when she arrived there she found Walter Lester sitting at the lake-view table, calmly buttering his toast, while a stream of hungry cats ebbed and flowed around his ankles.

"Walter, have you been, er, tidying parts of the house? Sorting cutlery? Taking towels off of chairs?" As she spoke, she realized how ridiculous this all sounded. She didn't mention the unravelled wool—that was almost certainly some cat's work.

He looked blank for a moment then shook his head. "My mother did all the housework. I worked outside." He looked at his breakfast. "But I can make toast. And tea. And sandwiches."

"Oh. Good. And did you notice the yellow wool on the stairs when you came down?"

He nodded. "I thought—I thought it was a cat toy. Or something." He got up. "I made a pot of tea, if you would like—I'm sorry. Should I have waited?"

She patted his arm. "No, no, you're fine. Sit down and finish your breakfast." She went into the kitchen and made hers, thoughtfully. He seemed honest, believable. But maybe he'd done these things in a trance? He *was* a bit different, though this morning seemed less shocked, more normal.

She sensed a furry tide coming in around her ankles and hurriedly dumped cat tins out onto plates. "You've been very patient," she told the cats.

"What?" asked Walter from the other room.

"Nothing," she called back. "Just talking to the cats." She was happy to see Luc bellying up to the cat plates for his share. "Well," she said, plunking herself down at the table across from Walter, "if you didn't move those articles and I didn't move them, who did? You don't sleepwalk by any chance?"

# 19

Dear Prudence and Cats, (and greetings to Bertie and Marion, of course, as you must be seeing lots of them),

Aberystwyth has a cool cliff railway ride up a nearby hill. We took it Monday morning. I was feeling tired so Doug made me lie down in the afternoon, then we took a leisurely drive north to our final Welsh stop—Llandudno. This is a Victorian tourist village, as we observed the next morning. Blocks of low white apartments are right on the beach and there's a pleasure pier with a domed building at the end, a bar, as it happens, or should I say, pub. Very British!

Our hotel there was a nice tall grey Victorian building with black slate roof tiles. Inside there's red cloth wallpaper and heavy dark furniture in the lounges. Dark wood staircase and railings. Our bedroom was more modern with a great view of the bay. The dining room also looks out onto the water.

Here I must mention the tinned grapefruit. At every single B&B or hotel where we've eaten breakfast, there they are: two large glass bowls, one with white, the other with pink grapefruit segments. It's tasty, I agree, but it must be some kind of required breakfast thing. It was the same in Devon but not in Ireland. Weird, eh?

That same afternoon we caught a matinée at a puppet theatre! I know! Right?! A permanent one. It's in a tiny theatre, ten minutes from our hotel, brightly painted inside in yellow and green and red. The marionettes were amazing. We saw *Sleeping Beauty*.

Early to bed again that night as we wanted to blast our way north to the Lake District. It couldn't have been easier. We almost made it in one go but I got hungry so we stopped in Lancaster at a pub for lunch. After Lancaster, the land became less industrial and more farmland. We were at Lake Windermere for tea and that is where you find me—in an internet café. More about the Lakes soon.

Much love, G and D

PS: Hope your visit with Bertie and Marion is going well.

PPS: To the cats: you are called *cath* in Wales, still pronounced c-a-t. Plural *cathod* pronounced—?

PPPS: (Is there such a thing as a third postscript?) I forgot to say we dropped into a place where they make sea salt—all different flavours, and we bought some for you and us, as well as a Welsh cookbook.

Well, that's something to look forward to, Prudence thought as she typed her brief reply—salt and another cookbook. Those are certainly Prudence-appropriate gifts. Then she felt ashamed. It was lovely Gerry was keeping her up to speed with their travels, trying to include her. And lovely that there would be presents to exclaim over on her friend's return. She mentioned Walter was staying at The Maples and why, but not the strange doings in the house in the night, nor, still, anything about the trap door's independent motion.

Gerry sounds cheerful, she thought. So, if she sent that on Wednesday and today is Thursday, another couple of days and she'll be in Scotland, I guess, then home. She sent her message and closed the computer.

When Cathy Stribling answered, "Fieldcrest B&B. How may I help you?" Prudence asked her to tell Bertie and Marion about the tea with Edwina Murray that Prudence had arranged at The Maples Friday afternoon. Then she felt bad about leaving Cathy out again and added, "And would you like to come too, Cathy?"

Cathy was delighted. "Yes, please. I haven't yet met her. Thank you, Prudence. Are you sure you won't speak with Bertie? He's right here. They just finished their breakfast."

"No, no," said Prudence hastily, still feeling ashamed from their previous phone call. "Tell him—tell him—I hope he has a nice day."

"All right then. I'm driving him and Marion to the British store later and they're going to find a place to lunch in Lovering."

"Lovely," Prudence said, hearing a note of artificiality in her own voice. "Get it together, Prudence," she mumbled as she hung up. "Walter," she called, walking through to the living room.

"Mm?" He looked up from petting Luc, who sat in his lap purring.

"Will you be okay if I go to work? It's just at the neighbour's house over there." She pointed in the direction of Edwina's house. "I'll be about three hours. If you need me, just walk over through the path from the backyard. You can go outside if you want to. It's a gorgeous day."

To all of which, Walter replied, "Mm. Maybe. Okay."

He seemed happy enough with the cats. Putting on an apron, she let herself out into the beautiful morning.

Small birds chirped from shrubs, their last clutches of the year preparing to leave the nest. A crow cawed from high up in the willow down by Gerry's swimming pool. Geese were already flying overhead, their honks signalling the beginning of the autumn migration, though Prudence knew they'd mass on the lake for months before finally leaving the region late November, even as late as early December some mild years.

So with all this life around her *and* the sun shining, why this bad feeling in the pit of her stomach? She smiled sourly as she walked through the thicket of raspberry canes and wild roses between Gerry and Edwina's properties. Good old Prudence, she thought, as usual, the life of the party.

With a shock, she realized the voice in her head was that of her former husband. Making an effort, she pushed it away and knocked at Edwina's back door.

Uncharacteristically, an hour and a half later, Edwina interrupted Prudence, hard at work mopping the floors, with the offer of a cup of tea. Thankfully, Prudence accepted. They sat in the attractive new kitchen and sipped. Edwina's dog Shadow had followed them in and subsided onto the floor nearby with an enormous sigh.

"Is he still depressed, do you think?" Prudence asked.

"Maybe not depressed exactly," Edwina mused. "More like: worn down by waiting for Roald to return. Every time someone knocks at the door, or a car drives by, he pricks up his ears, lifts his head. I wish I could do something for him."

Prudence examined the woman. She really did seem to be concerned for her dead husband's hound, and she also seemed less vague, less distracted. Knowing how Gerry got when mid-project, Prudence could understand how the months-long process of writing a book might sap one's empathy. "What time's the meeting tonight?" she asked. Edwina had confided the reason she needed to bring forward the house cleaning by one day was because she was hosting a meeting Thursday night of the executive committee for the local garden club, which she'd recently joined.

"Oh, seven-thirty." Edwina shot Prudence a keener than usual glance. "I suppose you're wondering why I've become a member of the club when I don't even do my own gardening?"

It was true. About the gardening. Upon her husband's demise, Edwina had completed her extensive renovation of the run-down house by hiring a local gardening company that specialized in dense plantings with lots of colour all the time. It was not a style Prudence particularly espoused, preferring the staggered elegance of the gardens at The Maples, where one perennial followed another and no annuals were used except for a few at the front of the house. (Which reminded her, she hadn't watered The Maples' geraniums in their wooden half barrels for a couple of days. Had it rained recently? And what about her own window boxes?) She realized Edwina was waiting for an answer and replied primly, "It's not my place to wonder, I'm sure."

"I'm writing a new book," Edwina said with a glint in her eye. "I usually start one in the fall. One in the fall and one in the spring. It's to be called *Murder Among the Dahlias* or something like that. So I wanted to see how a garden club, whose members include the murdered character and most of the suspects, works from the inside."

"You're very organized, aren't you, Edwina?" Prudence said admiringly. And monomaniacal, she thought to herself, and a bit devious. She suppressed a smile at the thought of the people who ran the garden club, some of whom she knew, unsuspecting that their little quirks and foibles were about to be mined by the keen and impartial mind of Edwina Murray as she served them tea and nibbles. She switched back to the subject of the dog. "Maybe Shadow needs a distraction. To get him to stop sitting moping in Roald's study all day."

"Well, you may have noticed, I got rid of all Roald's smoking stuff. Threw it away. Who'd want a second-hand pipe? And I've sold the pool table. I have a plan to turn that room into a kind of sunroom. Remove the southeast-facing corner and replace it with one of those glass conservatories. Nice to sit in in the winter. So I'm hoping, as his master's room changes, disappears, Shadow will have an easier time."

The dog at that moment gave another huge sigh.

"Mm." Prudence thought for moment. "I have, or used to have, a client who does canine obedience classes with her Shelties. There are also agility classes you can take. You can hire a private trainer or join a club, or both. It might bring you together."

Edwina looked down at Shadow. "He's already very obedient. Canine agility. Is that what it's called when they run and jump and slither through tunnels?" Prudence nodded. Edwina smiled. "Might be fun. And I could use the exercise, sitting all day."

Prudence said mischievously, "And you might get another book out of it—*The Dog Barked Twice*."

"No, that doesn't sound right," Edwina commented. "Oh. You're joking. Good one."

Hoping she hadn't been too familiar, Prudence rose. "I'll just finish the mopping and dust the living room, shall I?"

Edwina, who seemed to have disappeared down one of the many rabbit holes in her mind, looked up and said, "Sure. Okay. I'll leave the money in the usual place."

"See you tomorrow," Prudence said cheerily. Edwina nodded.

Prudence finished, took her wages from the little table near the back door, petted Shadow, who'd accompanied her, and left. Edwina, she guessed, was shut into her study, writing.

With the first half of the day accomplished, her mood had lifted, and, as she walked toward The Maples, she anticipated a quiet lunch. It was a shock, therefore, to see Walter Lester sitting in a comfy lawn chair staring at the lake. She'd briefly forgotten about him. "Walter! Everything okay?" He nodded. "Want some lunch?" He made as if to rise. "No, I'll bring it out here."

She made two peanut butter sandwiches, got a couple of packs of potato chips, poured two glasses of milk and loaded a tray which she took out to the picnic table. Walter shambled over. "What did you do all morning?" He shrugged and began eating. "Well, that's no good. Boring. Let's see. There are plants in tubs at the front of the house that need watering; the lawn needs cutting, and oh, yes, you could clean out the cat litter boxes for me. I'll show you later."

Walter's eyes brightened a bit. "I like yard work," he offered.

"Good! Now, let's enjoy our food and the view."

Various of the house's cats flitted here and there on their individual errands. Luc was bound to be out there somewhere. Walter didn't seem worried about "his" cat so Prudence relaxed.

Once she explained what to do, Walter proved a good worker, and when Prudence thought he could be left on his own, she drove to check her own place.

She wondered if the police had identified the burnt corpse in the Ménard house yet. Presumably any ID would have melted or burned; would car keys remain intact? Maybe there was a car parked somewhere in Lovering that had been in the same spot for a few days that someone would notice. The police know what they're doing, she concluded. They don't need my help. She parked in her driveway.

The plants in *her* containers certainly needed watering. She stuck a finger in one of the two window boxes. Parched. The geraniums' flowers were withered. She pinched them off and picked many brown leaves off the ivy. Maybe, with the first frost fast approaching, she should just dump them —

"Prue! I haven't seen you for *ages*! How you been?" Prudence found herself being hugged by Rita, her neighbour from across the street. "Time for a coffee?"

Prudence thought of Walter determinedly walking back and forth pushing The Maples' lawnmower. Probably, when he finished, he'd just sit back down and stare. "Better not, Rita. I just came for a quick look around. These flowers are almost done, I think."

Rita inspected the offending plants. "Mm. Shoulda asked me to water 'em. So whatcha been up to?"

"Oh, I cleaned Edwina Murray's place this morning, worked at the café yester—"

"Prue!" This iteration of her name boomed from across the road. The owner of the robust masculine voice, Charlie, crossed the road. "It's like you've moved away, Prue—we never see you." Charlie stood next to Rita, his arm casually draped across her shoulders. Unselfconsciously, Rita leaned into her husband's solid frame.

Prudence felt such a jolt of jealousy that for a moment she had to look away. "Uh, yeah, well, it's just temporary, eh? Gerry'll be back in about ten days and then *I'll* be back." She edged through the front door. "We'll catch up then, eh? Sorry. I've got lots to do." And she closed the door.

What a liar, she thought bitterly, as she surveyed the interior of the silent house. The refrigerator motor clicked on. She went to the kitchen and made a cup of tea. She carried the tea with her as she walked around the house.

She stood in the living room. There was a small sofa but Prudence usually sat in the one easy chair with a little tapestry-covered footstool in front of it when she read or watched TV. Next to the chair was the table with its single coaster and ceramic-lidded container for the Scotch mints she sucked when she was reading. There were the bookcases, the sole picture of her parents and her propped on one shelf, taken by someone else—she'd forgotten whom—on a summer's day out behind their farmhouse kitchen. Her father, rugged and beaming, his hand resting on his wife's shoulder while his other hand caressed the top of Prudence's head. Her mother, shading her eyes with one hand while with the other hand she held one of Prudence's. The three of them, linked.

And ten-year-old Prudence, smiling gravely at the camera, unaware that she was living the happiest time of her life.

She turned away, walked into the front bedroom, now office. It had used to be hers—it could be a bedroom again. What if Bertie and she—? What if they—? She didn't know if she even *wanted* sexual intimacy again. She wasn't sure if Bertie did. We could have separate bedrooms, she thought, rather desperately. But then, what would be the point?

Someone to bring you a cup of tea when you're tired or ill, a little voice said in her head.

Confused and sad, she returned to the kitchen and rinsed her mug. She dumped two watering cans of water in the window boxes, hoping for the best. As she exited, she missed her own phone answering machine's blinking light.

Something made her turn at the front door and look back. She approached the machine and listened to the one message—twice. Then she called the number, but the person was absent so Prudence in her turn left a message. Her curiosity about the message's contents occupied her mind for the short drive back to The Maples where Walter Lester and twenty cats—no, make that twenty-one—needed her.

Thursday evening passed much as Wednesday's had. Except there was no upsetting phone conversation with Bertie. She invited one more person to the next day's tea party—Mary—as a small thank-you for her taking Bertie, Marion and Prudence out to dinner. Mary accepted.

Mary would be a good guest. Between her and Marion, the conversational ball would be kept rolling despite any of Edwina's vagaries or awkwardness between Bertie and herself.

As she watched TV with Walter (Was this what life with Bertie would be like? Supper, dishes, TV?), she considered what she would make the next day. Scones, of course, perhaps those buttermilk oatmeal ones. And a cake. Her eye was caught by the blue bowl on the mantel and the red and green apples in it. Hmm. An applesauce loaf wasn't fancy enough, though she could make some apple butter to spread on the scones. And an old-fashioned apple cake full of big chunks was a bit hearty. No. she'd make a delicate iced sponge. Appropriate. Tomorrow. She would do it all tomorrow. She dozed on the sofa then went early to bed.

As she crawled under the covers and the Honour Guard Plus One (the Plus One being Mother) disposed themselves about her person, her mind returned to dwell on the oddness of the message on her home's phone. It had never happened before: that that person had called her; always it was she, Prudence, who initiated contact. What could have happened? Could it be simply a social call? But the person had said—what had she said? "That several strange occurrences had made further communication necessary." And she, the caller, had apologized but said it might really be for the best that they meet.

Like the proverbial squirrel in its cage, or hamster on its wheel, Prudence's brain went round and round. The answer eluded her. All was a mystery. All, including human relationships; and she fell asleep considering hers with Bertie.

She'd sent Walter out to deadhead flowers and rip out obviously extinct tomato plants. She gave the house, the public parts, anyway, a quick vacuum, dusted in the living room and cleaned the downstairs bathroom. Then she made her cake and left it to cool. The scones she would whip up at the last minute.

Apple butter! That could take hours if she started from scratch. She thought for a moment then got some of the frozen applesauce out and set it to thaw slowly in a pot on the lowest temperature. It already contained cinnamon so that was okay. She set the timer for a half an hour and called Walter for lunch.

As she was preparing their sandwiches the phone rang. Cece Muxworthy had a place for Walter to stay. In downtown Lovering at a retirement home. And having a cat wasn't a problem. The timing couldn't have been better for Prudence. Of course she would have included Walter at her tea party but it would no doubt be nicer if he wasn't there. Just her friends.

She paused uneasily, thinking, Mary and Cathy, and even Edwina could hardly be classed among her *friends*. Oh well, she thought, maybe they will be someday.

Walter didn't seem bothered when she told him he was moving again. "And you'll be back in your old neighbourhood and I can look in on you when I'm at work. The building is across the street from the café. In fact, I'll come see you tomorrow on my break." If I get one, she thought. She hoped Ginger might eventually again make an appearance at their shared workplace.

After they'd eaten their meal and Walter and Luc had left with Cece, the house seemed a bit emptier.

She stood at the stove stirring the apple butter. When it was a rich golden brown, she strained it through a sieve and put it in the fridge to cool. She iced her sponge a pale pink. At a quarter to two she made the scones and was just taking them out of the oven when she heard a car pull into the small circular driveway in front of the house. She saw Mary Petherbridge walk by the kitchen window.

Prudence dumped the scones into a tea towel-lined basket and returned them to the now cooling oven. She removed her apron and let Mary in.

"I thought I'd be informal and come in through the side entrance. After all, I *did* grow up here." The lack of any acidity in Mary's tone kept the remark from being offensive.

"Welcome," Prudence said quietly.

"Sorry I'm a bit early. But I was coming back to Lovering from an appointment and misjudged the time. Doesn't it smell nice in here! All applish and cakey."

Another rap at the side door announced the arrival of Edwina, who'd probably just taken the short cut from her back yard. "Hello, Prudence. Hello, urm—"

"This is Mary Petherbridge, Edwina. You met before, here, in the spring."

Edwina obviously didn't remember Mary but pretended it was all coming back to her. "Oh, yes, you're Gerry's—"

"I'm Gerry's aunt, Miss Murray." They shook hands.

"And Mary is also my cousin," Prudence offered.

"Ah," said Edwina. The tall woman moved restlessly. The tiny kitchen had become crowded.

"Would you like to —?" Prudence gestured for them to go through into the living room. "I'll just be a moment. Do sit down." She walked past them toward the front door, as she'd just heard another car arrive and park behind Mary's.

Nervously, she patted her hair and opened the door. Cathy and Marion stood there. Cathy was beaming; Marion not so much. Cathy spoke first. "Oh! It's so nice of you to invite me, Prudence. I'm eager to meet Miss Murray. Is she already here?"

Unseen by Cathy, Marion grimaced and raised her eyebrows. "Hi, Prudence."

Prudence stepped past them to look in the driveway, then re-entered the house.

"Bertie sends his regrets," Marion said quietly. "He has to supervise the installation of a new vanity or something in the art gallery bathroom. It got wet when the toilet tank leaked and now the wood is warping. Apparently the owner is a delicate flower who can't deal with 'rough men.'"

Prudence could see Marion knew more about Bertie's no-show than she was telling. They both knew if things were good between Prudence and him, he'd have phoned her instead of leaving Marion to break the news.

Prudence looked away and swallowed, trying to clear the sudden constriction in her throat. "Well," she said, ushering them into the foyer, "he doesn't know what he'll be missing."

# 20

To say Prudence felt awkward during the ensuing hour and half would have been an understatement. What would have been a great pleasure if Bertie was there—serving him and the others her homemade delicacies and listening to quiet conversation—felt flat without him.

And Mary's remark of, "Oh, where's Bertie?" in a disappointed voice as Prudence removed the sixth table setting, hadn't helped, though Marion soon distracted her, talking about people of consequence they both knew. But Marion without Bertie also seemed subdued, though a flash of her usual critical mind gleamed when she described the miserable lunch and awful service they'd received at one of Lovering's restaurants the previous day.

On the waitress: "She acted like she was doing us and the owner of the place a huge favour by just showing up and told us this long story of how she doesn't *have* to work, she just does it to get out of the house!"

On the food: "Bland fillings on stale bread *and* it took ages to appear. We'd waited so long, we gobbled it up but, really, we should have sent it back and left. Didn't bother waiting around for dessert or coffee. Terrible!"

Then she subsided as Mary turned her attention to Edwina, who'd been chatting with a star-struck Cathy about Edwina's latest book *The Case Against Norman Crumbles*, which had just come out. Mary went on and on about the book and how she, Mary, had suspected the killer all along but had never quite been sure, thus defining, in Prudence's mind at least, a well-written mystery.

"And what's the next one called, Edwina?" asked Cathy.

"*Wild Blood*," Edwina replied tersely. "It'll be out next spring."

"Oo, sounds exciting," said Cathy. "What's it about?"

"I can't explain exactly. My publisher doesn't want me to give things away before publication. But it's generally about the relationship between a woman and her adult son and how it can go so wrong."

Prudence, who knew what the basis for the plot was and even the people involved, shivered.

Edwina continued. "Would you like to hear a bit from the book I've just begun writing?"

"Oh, yes!" squealed Cathy.

"How interesting," drawled Mary. "Like watching a painter at work."

Edwina rummaged in the cloth shopping bag that seemed to do service as her purse and produced a small sheaf of papers. She frowned as she licked her fingers and thumbed through them, putting them in some kind of order. While this was going on Prudence took note of the cats. They were being very good, as if they knew a certain etiquette was required at a ladies' tea party.

Actually, the more rambunctious ones were elsewhere, probably outside, where the pace of life was swifter, and that left the quiet, old cats to politely saunter into the room, perhaps rub gently on some stocking-clad shin, receive the caress that usually followed, then find a quiet place from which to observe the consumption of tea and dainties.

Edwina now seemed ready. "All right." She began to read.

So, this must be a rough draft of *Murder Among the Dahlias* Prudence thought with some amusement. Edwina had decided to open with the meeting of the garden club executive at one of their member's houses—a device to introduce some of the main characters and the tensions between them. And who knows: maybe the victim and murderer?

As Edwina read, Prudence became aware of Mary's growing discomfort, Cathy's rapt attention, and Marion's interest. The character descriptions were concise and cruel, and also fairly easy to recognize as those of local ladies. In fact, they were the Lovering Garden Club executive to a tee. A club of which Mary was probably a member.

When Mary drew in her breath sharply and Marion gave a bark of laughter at a particularly vicious (though somewhat comic) verbal exchange between two of the characters in the privacy of the bathroom of the house in which they were meeting, Edwina ceased reading.

Cathy urged, "Oh, don't stop!"

Mary muttered, "Perhaps you'd better," but whether she meant stop reading to them or writing any more, Prudence couldn't have said. She herself was wondering whether Edwina's membership in the garden club would survive the publication of this book. No wonder the woman had few friends.

"Well, perhaps that's enough," said Edwina and folded her papers.

"It's very funny," commented Marion, with a wicked look in her eye.

"Is it?" asked Edwina.

"I see you write the first draft by hand," said Prudence, trying to change the subject. "Is that what most authors do? Somehow, I have a picture of them at a typewriter, or now, I suppose, a computer."

"I can't speak for other authors, but I do believe most of them nowadays write the first draft on their computers. I prefer to hand write. I don't know. It just flows that way for me."

"I can't wait to read the whole book when it's finished," said Cathy.

"Cathy is a talented caterer, Edwina, and she runs a successful B&B, just across the way." Prudence hoped this would channel the conversation away from *Murder Among the Dahlias* once and for all.

"Yes, Edwina," Mary chimed in. "Perhaps the book after *Murder Among the Dahlias* could be set at Fieldcrest. *Murder Between the Bedsheets*." She snickered.

Cathy actually clasped her hands. "Oh, Miss Murray, I would love that. I mean, if you ever want a tour, I would be happy—"

Edwina half-closed her eyes. "A bed and breakfast murder. Hmm. I'll think about it. But not until next spring when this one's written. Otherwise, I'll get confused."

"Prudence, this sponge is most delightful," Marion interjected. "What have you put in the icing? Almond extract? I thought so. May I have another piece?" And to Prudence's relief, she launched into a long story about being on a committee for some big charity do and how the famous caterer had let them down at the last minute—a nervous breakdown or divorce or some such negligence on his part—and she'd had to scramble to find a replacement—and so forth.

Prudence relaxed and cut Marion a generous chunk of cake. To the rescue again, she thought and smiled at her favourite guest. She hated to think what Edwina's cruel pen could do in describing little plump Cathy, never married, mid-fifties, running a romantic weekend getaway for mostly couples, mostly younger than she, not to mention her doting relationship with her opportunistic dog, the greedy Prince Charles. She felt protective of *them*; of the ladies of the garden club, not so much. Edwina should call *that* book *Tough Tulips*, she thought.

She took a moment to ask Mary, "Aren't you a member of the Garden Club?"

Mary flushed. "Haven't been going since—" she said gruffly.

Prudence could guess since what. Mary must feel shamed by her husband Geoff's "accident." Not to mention her daughter Margaret's actions. She, Prudence, could sympathize with shame. "More tea?" she asked gently. When the pot was discovered to be dry, her guests took this as a hint, and rose to leave. By their relaxed chatter as they loitered, she realized her literary afternoon had been a success.

Then she was shaking hands and seeing them out various doors. As she folded Marion into Cathy's car, the old woman leaned close and whispered, "Call him," before pecking her on the cheek.

Prudence went back inside and fed the cats.

"And would you like anything with your coffee?" The customer shook his head, so Prudence entered his purchase in the cash register. "Thank you," she called as he left.

The chalkboard still read AFRICAN BLEND from Prudence's previous shift but the bag of coffee on the counter read QUETZALCOATL'S GIFT. Hmm, Prudence thought, Dan's usually on top of this. She erased the board, trying to remember what the Mexican blend's tasting notes were. "Look on the bag, dummy," she muttered, and added WITH A HINT OF CHOCOLATE.

*Four* yummy mummies were in residence in the back half of the tiny room, three of them with strollers, one with a toddler who kept wandering into the front half of the room where Prudence was trying to work.

Trying, because the toddler's mother seemed to be only half paying attention to her child's shambolic trajectory and Prudence was in a state of fear that it would be lurking by the front door to be hit if and when the door suddenly opened. So Prudence was constantly dashing from behind the counter to redirect the little person back towards its mom, at which point "Mom" would notice, thank Prudence, and lovingly chastise (that is to say, not at all chastise) and caution her charge.

It was wonderfully peaceful when they left. Prudence felt she could breathe again. She tidied where they'd been sitting, served Mr. Willis his small regular, and sat down inside the café for a quick break.

At which point the door chimes tinkled. "Ginger! I'm so glad to see you! Are you okay?" This query was occasioned by Prudence's noticing Ginger's puffy eyes and general air of misery.

Ginger turned to hang her coat from one of the hooks by the door. "I'm all right," she muttered. "You?"

This asking how *Prudence* was, was so unusual it took Prudence a moment to reply. She tried for jocularity. "Oh, well, you know, had a fight with my boyfriend."

This distracted Ginger. "*You* have a *boyfriend*?"

"You don't have to sound so surprised. It has been known."

"What's his name?"

"Bertie."

"Bertie?! Is he named for the puppet?"

"As in Bert and Ernie? Ah, no, for a prince actually. *Are* you okay?"

"I've had a fight with almost everyone I know this week, including *my* boyfriend. And I'm in trouble at school."

"Tell me," coaxed Prudence.

So, while they washed plates and cups, Ginger unloaded her teenaged woes. Afternoon customers began arriving, and Prudence, for once, was able to leave to take a proper lunch.

She crossed the road to the block of apartments where many of Lovering's elderly lived. She rang the number Cece had given her, and was buzzed in. "Number fifty-one," she murmured, looking at signs with arrows. Down one long hallway she trudged, passed through a common room full of cast-off odd chairs, sofas and tables, and through a door into another wing. "Number fifty-one!" she said triumphantly. The apartment door was open a crack so she knocked then pushed.

Luc came skittering out, turned one way, was stopped by a door, turned back, pranced past her to the closed door at the other end of the hallway, then returned to sit at her feet. He groomed a raised paw, passing it over one eye.

"Walter?" Prudence said and opened the door all the way. At the far end of the room (which wasn't very far) Walter Lester was seated on a small doily-and-afghan-draped couch. Too many houseplants hogged the light from the only window. Furniture lined the walls leaving only a small passageway to where he sat. The TV was on. As Prudence entered, he muted it and rose.

"Well, this is cozy," Prudence began. "Luc was in the hallway. Does he often zoom around like that?"

Walter nodded. "He's used to going out. I tell him it's temporary—the hallway."

Wondering how long it would be before the neighbours complained, Prudence simply said, "That's nice. What do you mean—temporary?"

Walter looked around him at the little room crowded with a lifetime's worth of ornaments, photos and unfinished crafts. "The lady who lives here is just away for a few weeks. Mr. Muxworthy knows her and he said it was temporary. Maybe my house will get rebuilt again and I can go live there—next to Mme Ménard and Luc."

"Mm." Prudence couldn't see any of that happening, not with developers and Dan Bartram competing for the lots. Even if the insurance company paid out for the fires, was it enough to rebuild? Considering today's prices for materials, compared to when the little houses had been built, how could it be? She'd have to remember to ask Mr. Willis.

She snapped out of her reverie and remembered she was on her lunch break. Sitting down at the card table that separated the kitchenette (one cupboard with a bit of counter below it whereon a kettle, toaster oven and hot plate jostled for room) from the living area, she pulled out her sandwich. "Could you make me a cup of tea, Walter?"

He made a pot and joined her at the table. "My mother would have sold our house."

"Really? Why?"

"She said she could get more money if she sold it and we moved into an apartment. Like this one, I suppose."

"Would you have liked that?"

Walter looked into his mug. "No. I like cutting the grass. I like having a porch."

"Mm. Well I really hope you'll have those again, but you must be patient, you know. It takes a long time to get insurance money and then a long time to build a house." He looked uncertain. "But meanwhile, you have this nice place to stay." He looked away, muttering to himself.

"She talked to that man, Mme Ménard's nephew."

"She did?"

"She said they had made a deal."

Curiouser and curiouser, Prudence reflected as she walked back to the café. At least Walter and Luc are okay now. Temporarily. Though Walter had looked a bit more vague than usual…

"There was a guy here, asking for you." Ginger said, looking up from her phone. A middle-aged couple sat at the back of the room quietly sipping from large bowls.

Prudence's heart leapt before she realized Bertie would hardly take one train in to Montreal Friday just to return on Saturday. Especially when he and Prudence weren't getting along. And when his and Marion's holiday was to end Sunday. Would he?

"Tall man? About sixty?"

Ginger's attention was back on her phone's screen. "Nah. Not *that* old. Forty-five or so, medium height."

"What did he want?" Prudence asked, thinking the mystery man sounded like every police detective she'd ever met.

"Wouldn't say. But he seemed angry. Rude, even."

That Ginger would notice rudeness when she herself—Prudence bit back the uncharitable reply. "I hope he didn't disturb the customers." There was no reply. "So, what? Did he leave a phone number?"

"Nah. Said he'd be back."

"Today?"

Ginger shrugged. Oh, great, thought Prudence, now I have to look forward to an angry man popping up sometime in the future when I'm at work. "Bloody hell," she muttered. Then, "Need any supplies? I'll just go into the back—" She smilingly edged around the couple, having to walk between them to access the door. This is really unacceptable, she thought. No wonder Dan wants to get his hands on extra space.

She moved between the coffee roaster and the grinder, accessing large, stacked boxes of napkins, stir sticks, packs of sugar and sweetener, putting them in a smaller empty box. Then she sat at Dan Bartram's desk and looked up Lucy's street.

The blackened mess that had been Mme Ménard's house had been removed. Now Prudence could see how large the two combined lots made the space. If Dan bought it, he could build a coffee *factory*, she thought. And if the other developer persisted, bought the land from Walter and Mme Ménard, *he* could build a multiple dwelling unit, two triplexes next to each other, if he liked.

Past the flatness of the empty lot, Mackenzie Street continued up its slight rise. Lucy's house was too far and set back but Prudence could see her hedge.

Her gaze dropped to the desk in front of her. Dan Bartram was as neat about its top as he was about everything else in the room. A pile of papers was weighed down by a large purple crystal; another pile was clipped together—a Post-it note scribbled "Done" stuck to the top sheet. Without meaning to, she read the top sheet's contents.

It looked like an order form; customer copy was printed at the bottom. Another roaster; an automatic coffee bagger. Hmm. *Those* would be hard to fit in this little space. There was barely enough room for the—

Prudence's eyes returned to the empty space where two little homes—one happy, one unhappy—had been, and where a man had lost his life. Her head turned to the left. Dan Bartram turned his car into his reserved parking spot. He alighted, caught sight of Prudence and gave a wave.

She slid the box of supplies to cover the papers. "Hi, Dan," she said as he entered, and stood up. "Just replenishing stock."

He smiled. "Not trying to take over my job, are you, Prudence?"

She laughed, as the situation seemed to demand, and returned to Ginger and her customers.

The afternoon dragged. Clients were few so Prudence dusted and wiped all available surfaces. Ginger texted away. A few people came in around three, no doubt feeling, as did Prudence, a mid-afternoon slump in energy.

She was just fixing herself a double cappuccino (That'd perk her up, if anything could!) with her back turned away from the public, when the door chimes jangled. As Ginger was dealing with a group of three cyclists in their tight shiny costumes, this one would be Prudence's responsibility.

The tall man gave her a grave look. "An Americano, please, Prudence," he requested.

She turned to the espresso machine and filled his order. "No charge," she croaked, as she handed it over, her voice inexplicably failing her. Then, with a glance at Ginger, she amended, "I mean, my treat."

"Oh, thank you very much," he said. The cyclists departed, to drink their espressos on the porch.

"Ginger," Prudence said quietly. "*This* is Bertie." Ginger's eyes widened. "We're going to sit on the sofa for a sec."

For a short time, Prudence and Bertie sipped their drinks in silence.

"Good," Bertie said, lifting his up and nodding.

"How is the vanity? I mean, how did the installation go?"

He waved a hand. "It went. She didn't really need me." For a moment he looked sad. "But I was okay with being there. How was your tea party?"

"Oh. Nice. I was disappointed not to see you there. You could have called."

"I didn't think you'd miss me, to be honest. And Marion was capable of delivering my regrets."

Another silence. Ginger, not interested in what older people might get up to, was again engrossed in her phone.

"So," said Prudence, putting down her cup.

"So," said Bertie, draining his. "I should—"

Whatever Bertie should or should not have done was, at least temporarily, put on hold. He saw Prudence staring at a man who'd just entered the café. A man in a shiny gold suit with pointed shiny light brown shoes. A man who was looking at Prudence with an obviously angry face.

"That's him," Ginger was beginning, when the man took a step toward Prudence. She and Bertie rose, Prudence gaping. Not dead but alive!

"You! You think you can wangle your way into my aunt's affections? You think you can get control of her and her money away from me? You and your lawyer? You better think again!"

He took another step in Prudence's direction. Bertie stepped in front of the speechless Prudence. Cece Muxworthy must have had had his "discussion" with M Ménard regarding Mme Ménard's health and care.

Dan Bartram appeared from the back of the store. "What's all the—?" He stared at the man. "You!"

The door chimes jangled again and all heads except the man's turned. His eyes remained fixed on Prudence.

Lucy Hanlan entered the shop and blurted out, "Prudence! He's alive! M Ménard's alive!"

Then the man in the shiny brown suit turned. "You, too, are in my way. I'm warning you!" Lucy stepped back from the door as he left. He slammed it hard. The door chimes jangled then grew still.

# PART 5
# ACCEPTANCE

Night. When a cat's life intensifies. When nerves are hyperstimulated and interactions fraught with possibilities. Night, when stealth is made easy by shadows and the blindness of people, intent on their own business.

Now he sat next to and partially under the dumpster behind the hamburger place. Raised up on two long pieces of wood, the smelly box made a good spot from which to regard his house. Or—where he thought his house had been.

It hadn't been easy sneaking out of the big building where he and the skinny man were sharing one tiny room. He'd first had to wait by their open door for the sound of someone opening one of the hallway doors, then dash through that without the person noticing.

He'd shadowed them down some stairs and around a corner until they opened a door with a light glowing above it. At that point, the person, a little old woman, lit a cigarette and, as Fluke exited the building, nodded and winked at him, saying, "I won't tell if you won't tell."

Not that he understood the words, just the tone was enough for him to understand she was complicit. He'd circled around the front of the big building, smelled bitterness and old grease, and crossed the main road.

His house had vanished. Even the front yard's iron fence. He crossed his quieter road, keeping low to its dark surface, and crouched near the only bit of cover, the garbage cans behind the bitter-smelling, glass-walled building. Though now he knew it also contained quantities of milk for cats, the place had gone up in his estimation.

Light shone from the milk place where a man moved about, going from one object to another, bending, lifting. Soon, the sour odour intensified. The smell of burning reminded Luc of the house fire.

*As if he could forget, staring at the flat blackened piece of earth. There was where his front porch with its comfy chairs and, lately, blanket-lined box had been. There was the living room where they used to watch TV. There was the kitchen where they ate.*

*He trotted over to what had been the vegetable patch. Plants had been flattened, trodden into the earth, but still the smell of leeks, tomato leaves and herbs lingered. At least here the horrible smell of ash was partially obscured.*

*And he found the iron fence, laid at the back of the property. It was a familiar point of reference. He lay next to it and meditated.*

*Funny that the milk woman had known his first real name, had said it. Funny she spoke the same choppy tongue his first person had, who'd named him Fluke. Fluke because, as the first person, a young man, never tired of telling people, it had been a fluke that made him pull his motorcycle over, one beer-sodden evening, for a piss by the side of the road, where he discovered three kittens, two dead, one alive, and tucked the live one inside his leather jacket, to be taken home and fed coffee creamer.*

*That had been a fun life, eating tuna and egg salad, pepperoni and cheese from the meals the young man brought home. He was always ready for a game of footsie, only roared with laughter when the kitten Fluke dug his claws and fangs into his thick socks. He'd roll up sandwich wrappers and toss them for Fluke, drop empty cans for the kitten to roll.*

*He seemed to understand cats, letting Fluke out at night all through his first summer so he could court females and fight and define his territory. And he was always happy to see him, to let him back in the next morning for a meal and a good long sleep while the man was away.*

*Except—one evening the man hadn't come back and Fluke— hungry, afraid—had prowled the one-room apartment yeowling, until two people—a crying woman and a very sad man—appeared and gathered up all the young man's possessions.*

*They'd fed Fluke and put him outside and when he returned and scratched at the door, there was no one to let him in.*

*That had been a bad time; he let his thoughts turn into a doze and then into a deep sleep in order to forget it.*

*He was woken by the sound of feet on gravel and looked up to see the man from the bitter-smelling yet milk-filled place standing looking at where the two houses had been. His hands were on his hips and he was grimly smiling the way the old neighbour woman had used to smile before she threw something at Fluke or shouted at his woman.*

*As he watched, the man turned and paced the length of the lot, taking exaggerated long steps. Then he turned right and paced the depth of the lot, stopping next to the flat fence.*

*Fluke kept very still. The man smelled bitter, like his building. He took a little book out of one pocket and made a note in it. Then, muttering, he walked back to his building and went in.*

*Fluke wondered if his woman knew about the fire. Would she come to look at the scene and find him? He hoped...*

*He remembered those bad days after the young man had disappeared. He'd wandered the neighbourhood, scrounging garbage, hunting birds and mice. He wasn't a very good hunter, not like the wild cats who got angry when he infringed on their territories. That was how he'd lost the chunk out of one of his ears. And become a better fighter.*

*People in the area knew him; some even knew his name from hearing the young man tell his finding story so many times. And so it had happened.*

*One evening—it must have been the same time of year as now—when the days shortened and nights grew colder—he happened to enter her garden when she was working in it. She was talking to herself, but in a different smoother tongue than that of the young man. Or maybe she was talking to her plants. Then she noticed him. "Fluc?"*

*It had sounded funny the way she said it, not the "Flook" he was used to, but he didn't mind. He had trotted to her. "Fluc," she'd said more gently and picked him up. He'd curled up as small as he could in the crook of her arm. Her head had bent down. And that had been it.*

*She'd just been beginning the first of their many conversations when the back door of the house next door was violently opened, slamming against the outside wall. The mean old woman appeared, uttering threats over her shoulder.*

*She noticed them and they froze as she shifted her malevolence toward them, cursing. There followed a heated conversation, utterly confusing to the cat, as each woman spoke mostly in their own tongue: the neighbour loud and emphatic; his new woman softer but no less intense.*

*When it seemed there was nothing left to say, the neighbour entered her house and he and his woman theirs.*

*Over the next few days, he went from Flook to Fluc, pronounced in her own way, until finally, to Luc. She even trickled a little water over his head at her kitchen sink, which he found odd, but not frightening. "Luc. Luc. Luc," she intoned, and neither of them had looked back.*

*Now he was aware of the coldness of the night. He furtively crossed the road toward his new place. As he hunkered down by the same door he'd left by, he wondered how long it might be before the skinny man noticed he was missing.*

# 21

Dear Cats (and Prudence)—har,

You would love the Lake District, Prudence. So many little villages, narrow roads, hills; so many ice cream stands, though coming in late September as we have, some of them are starting to shut down. So many cats! Leisurely crossing streets, disappearing under parked cars, sunning themselves in windows. (I realize that ice cream and multiple cats may be more favourite things of mine than yours. Sorry!)

Our B&B is a working farm in the northern part of the district. Our host and hostess are busy people—breakfast is at eight as they have already been up doing chores with animals and continue after mealtime, when they eat with us. It's all very homey. (We are some of their animals, I suppose. Cash cows?)

We've seen Wordsworth's house and Beatrix Potter's farm where she produced some of her stories. We've taken the steamer to the head of Lake Windermere and back. We've eaten Kendal mint (Meh! I prefer chocolate any day!). And I've daydreamed about which farm Arthur Ransome might have stayed at as a child and which is Wild Cat Island. Doug never read the Swallows and Amazons books so is immune to this particular delight.

Anyway, tomorrow we drive to Scotland, to Edinburgh. Scotland is going to be a whirlwind—we want to fit so much in. Will write when we can.

                                      Much love,
                                    Gerry and Doug

Yes, thought Prudence. I definitely like the sound of the Lake District, especially the farms. But I wouldn't like living somewhere that was so very flooded with tourists half the year.

She typed her short reply: about Cece finding Walter a more suitable if temporary place to stay; how she was going to visit Mme Ménard the next day; and how, also the next day, Bertie and Marion were taking the noon train back to Montreal.

Things she *didn't* talk about included her belief that Walter needed a mental health check-up; how frightened she now was of M Ménard; or how she felt about Bertie and Marion leaving Lovering. She summed up her mental state: worried, afraid, sad. Add disappointed. That she and Bertie had mucked up a perfectly good friendship by wandering into some romantic no-man's-land.

As she made her supper, she wondered if the relationship would be able to get back on its former friendly footing once Bertie was in Montreal and she was back in her own little house.

With a sigh she took Volume Two of Virginia Woolf's biography, which began with the author getting engaged to Leonard Woolf, and went up to bed.

Sunday, Prudence was invited by Cathy Stribling to a farewell brunch for Marion and Bertie, so church was out of the question. She dressed with care in a pair of beige dress pants, a cream blouse and a rusty tweed jacket. A paisley scarf in autumnal colours protected her throat from the slight chill in the air.

She listened to the bell calling worshippers to St. Anne's Church, then turned her back to it and walked over to Fieldcrest.

The road was quiet as Prudence picked her way along its side. Cracked and potholed, it was showing its age. The air was still and a slight mist rose from the earth in patches. It's cooling, she thought.

As she walked into Fieldcrest's driveway, she noted Prince Charles snuffling among the foundation shrubs. As she watched, he appeared to tear off a choice leaf and eat it. "Grazing as usual, Charles?" she asked humorously.

The prince's head snapped upwards and swivelled. He was by no means a watchdog, seemed more annoyed at the interruption than anything; nevertheless, he raised his muzzle and let fly. "A-roo-roo-roo-rooooo-gla!" He lowered his head and glared.

"Really, Charles? Arugula?"

Charles made up his mind, that tangerine-sized organ he kept above those other more important body parts—his olfactory receptors, tongue and saliva glands. Humans, especially female humans, equalled food possibilities, and delicious odours *had* been wafting from his own house for hours. He followed this woman around to the back of the house.

Prudence knocked on Cathy's kitchen door and opened it, poking her head in. Charles flumped past her up the three steps, pushing the door wide. "Need any help?" Prudence asked the busy cook within.

"Oh, Prudence, you're meant to be a guest! You should have come to the front door! Bertie would have let you in."

Prudence, only now realizing that avoiding him was probably why she'd come around to the back door instead, fumbled for an excuse. "I figured you could use a hand. That's all."

"Well, now you're here, you can carry this and this through to the dining room. But then stay there! I'm nearly ready."

Prudence obeyed, taking a covered dish and basket of fresh hot rolls down the house's long central hallway, passing the closed basement door with a shudder. These last two weeks marked the first time she'd been in this house for almost a year, since she and Gerry— But she didn't care to revisit those memories today. "Good morning," she said cordially to the two who were already seated at the large table.

"Good morning," Marion said politely.

"'Morning," was Bertie's terse response.

From the brief ensuing silence that occurred before Marion, indefatigable socialite that she was, rescued the conversation by informing them how she'd slept, Prudence inferred that they had been talking about her.

"I can feel the weather changing in my bones," Marion said. "For the first time since coming here I felt cold getting into bed last night. Not that there weren't enough covers," she added, as Cathy entered bearing the main course.

"Ta da!" said their hostess, removing the lid off a large flat dish. "*Oeufs bénédictine*! With hash browns!" She took the cover off the dish Prudence had brought in and opened the towel around the rolls. "*And* whole-grain rolls."

"You spoil us, Cathy," Bertie said pleasantly, offering the basket to Prudence.

"Yes indeed," agreed Marion heartily, helping herself as Prudence passed the basket on. "Fresh rolls! I never rose above—" and here she named a well-known commercial brand of prepared dough. "These are delicious."

Charles, who'd followed on stumpy legs and with clacky toenails in Cathy's wake, parked himself between his mistress at the head of the table, and Marion who sat to her left, and focused on Marion's right hand.

The rest of the meal was handed around and they began to eat.

"Do you need a ride to the train?" Prudence asked. She was seated on Cathy's right and directed her question at Marion across the table.

"Cathy said she'd take us," Bertie said from the foot of the table, in that same pleasant tone.

Cathy looked sharply from Prudence to Bertie. "And what time is that, Bertie? The train's at twelve thirty? Oh, my. I find I'm busy at that time after all. Perhaps Prudence better take you, if she doesn't mind." She shot a glance at Prudence.

Bertie covered his mouth with his napkin and seemed to cough, though Prudence could have sworn that underneath the cough he'd said, "Clumsy."

"I don't mind," Prudence said quietly. "We should leave around twelve. That all right?"

"Perfect!" interjected Marion, letting the last bite of her roll drop to the floor. "I'm already packed. Now, let's enjoy this wonderful feast. Cathy, how on earth do you get all the egg yolks to stay liquid?"

As Cathy leaned forward, preparatory to giving Marion some culinary tips, Prudence looked down the table to where Bertie sat. He didn't seem hungry, was pushing his cut-up food around his plate. He caught sight of her glance and flushed, then began shovelling food in like the train was already at the station. He wiped his lips and placed his napkin next to his plate.

"More of anything, Bertie?" Cathy inquired.

"Maybe some coffee." He passed his cup to Prudence so she could fill it from the nearby pot. Their fingers touched and it was Prudence's turn to flush.

Bertie sipped his hazelnut vanilla as Prudence finished her meal. As she was using her napkin, he leaned forward and asked, "Would you enjoy a little walk around the grounds, Prudence? If you've finished."

While Cathy and Marion watched, Prudence, her cheeks now flaming, pushed back her chair. "Sure. Thank you, Cathy. Everything was delicious."

They walked to the front of the house and let themselves out.

Fieldcrest was a large enough property that it took a few minutes to walk slowly around it clockwise. "It's a wonderful old house," Bertie said. "I've enjoyed staying here."

"Oh," was Prudence's witty reply, and, "Good." She looked at the house at that moment, knowing those were the living room windows. Two heads hastily drew back from inside one window. Cathy and Marion must have *raced* from the dining room.

They reached the back of the house where woods and fields were visible. "Cathy's a lucky woman to own such a place," Bertie hazarded.

"Yes," Prudence assented. They were approaching the dining room windows. Prudence looked up. This time Cathy and Marion stayed in position by a window. Marion winked. And Prudence made up her mind. "Stop," she commanded. He stopped. She gestured with her left hand to a driveway parallel with the main road where Cathy's four-car garage was. "If we go this way, there's a lane. We can go up it a fair way before we encroach on the house owners' privacy."

"A fair way, you say." Bertie smiled. "Just what I want to talk about."

It was a few moments' walk up the shrub- and tree-lined dirt road before, as the trees ended and fenced pastures were revealed, the old farmhouse came into view. A few moments to walk up and back but it sufficed.

Prudence and Bertie were holding hands as they climbed Fieldcrest's front stairs. "Shall I tell them or will you?" he asked.

"You do it," Prudence said. They let themselves in.

"My dear ladies," Bertie began, as Cathy and Marion were revealed now lounging in the living room. "You must be out of breath dashing from one side of the house to the other."

"Yes? Yes?" Marion said impatiently from the sofa.

"Miss Prudence has done me the honour of agreeing to be engaged to be married." He puffed out his chest and hooked his thumbs in his armpits. He began his oration. "At this moment, it seems to me—"

"Oh, shut it, you idiot!" Marion interjected. "Come here, both of you!"

# 22

Lucy was too busy sewing Mikado costumes to accompany Prudence to the Chestnut Nursing Home. After dropping Bertie and Marion at the train, Prudence drove straight there.

The same scene of old people dozing; the same dour receptionist greeted her. In her overlarge tote bag she'd packed a toothbrush and paste, a washcloth, a small basin, soap, nail scissors and a towel.

As she rode up in the elevator, she planned what she would say, or rather, ask. Cece had begun the legal proceedings, having already visited Mme Ménard; now Prudence would have to pursue the personal ramifications.

This second visit, she was somewhat less affected by the misery exhibited on the fourth floor of the home. You never think it'll happen to you, she reflected. If I ever thought I'd wind up here—"*Bonjour*, Mme Ménard!" she exclaimed as joyfully as she could.

Today, that lady was on her back. She slowly turned her neck toward Prudence and mouthed *bonjour*.

Prudence held up her tote. "I thought you might like a sponge bath? Yes?"

Slowly Mme Ménard nodded, a smile trying to rearrange slack facial muscles. Prudence left the room with the water carafe and, trying to look as if she belonged, marched off to find hot water.

She carefully bathed the poor lady and washed and combed her hair. Then she settled her in a more upright position in the bed where she promptly fell asleep.

That was fine; Prudence had all afternoon. She walked to a nearby doughnut shop, bought a coffee, thought for a moment, then went back and bought another one. Mme Ménard might enjoy a good cup of coffee for a change. Probably the home's coffee was dreadful.

When she returned, she settled herself by the bed and gently woke the patient. "Mme Ménard, I brought you a coffee." After the first sip, Mme Ménard's eyes closed in satisfaction and she exhaled deeply. Prudence continued. "Taste good?" Again, the woman tried to smile. "You know the lawyer Mr. Muxworthy is looking into your nephew's curatorship with a view to you taking back some control?"

Mme Ménard nodded. "So, I'm here to talk a little about the selling of your house. I mean, before, when there was a house to sell."

The woman's eyes had filled with tears. "I'm so sorry, Mme Ménard, about your house. Certainly your furniture is gone but almost all your linens and dishes are safe in the church basement."

Mme Ménard struggled to speak. "L—L—L—"

"Luc? Luc is fine. He was found by Walter Lester, of all people, and they're both in an apartment in the seniors' residence in Lovering." Prudence was struck by an idea. "Would you like me to bring Luc next time I come?"

Mme Ménard almost managed to smile. She certainly did with her eyes.

"All right. It's a deal. Now, I need to know whether you ever intended to sell your house."

Mme Ménard shook her head slowly.

"That's what I thought. Did Mrs. Lester want to sell *her* house?"

This time, the woman nodded as vigorously as she was able.

"Ah ha. And did she discuss this with you?"

Again, she nodded and this time the tears filling her eyes were of anger. "L—l—l—"

Prudence was confused. "Something about Luc?" She'd thought they were done with that topic.

Mme Ménard shook her head. "Lef—le—lef—m—ee."

"Lef—me? Your left knee?"

This time when Mme Ménard shook her head, she also managed to make a clicking sound of, Prudence guessed, annoyance.

"I'm so sorry. Is this something to do with Mrs. Lester?"

Mme Ménard nodded. She raised her right hand a little from the bed, flinging it once, twice, toward the floor.

"Mrs. Lester threw something?"

The woman flung the hand again then brought it shakily to her own chest, pointing.

"Mrs. Lester threw something at you?"

Mme Ménard shook her head. This time she timed the two hand gestures with the two syllables. "Lef—me."

The light dawned and Prudence said in a hushed voice, "She left you? On the back lawn?"

The woman nodded and lay back. She closed her eyes.

Prudence sat in her chair and finished her coffee. She turned what she'd just heard over in her mind.

Madame Ménard had had her stroke and fallen in her backyard. Mrs. Lester had come out for some reason, seen her, seen she was still alive, and left her to die.

But that—that was—evil! Certainly a kind of murder. A murder of negligence. That wicked woman! She must have reasoned that with her contrary neighbour out of the way, her house would be sold and she, Mrs. Lester could sell her own, and get a good price for it. On its own, it was practically worthless; twinned with its neighbour, it made part of an attractive package to whomever bid the highest for the plot.

"And she had lots of money in the bank!" Prudence muttered. "So she did it because of greed."

Mme Ménard stirred in the bed. Gently, Prudence helped her slip down under the covers where she went back to sleep. Prudence quietly left the room.

When she returned to The Maples around four, it was time to feed the cats supper. She made a cup of tea, took it and the last oatmeal scone into the living room, and had a good long think.

She made two phone calls that evening, with the result that she found herself with two appointments for the next day. Both of them were to be life changing.

Prudence returned to The Maples and made her lunch, thinking over what the real estate agent had said. "It's a nice little house, Mrs. Crick, and I'm sure I can sell it, but you have to realize it's a buyer's market right now and there *are* only two bedrooms, one bathroom—and the overall lot is quite small. I would suggest starting the listing at—" And here she named a figure which sounded about right to Prudence, who knew perfectly well what prices similar houses on her street were selling for. Then the agent had added, "But you might have to settle for less." And named a figure considerably smaller than the first.

Prudence kept her counsel. The agent wanted a fast sale and her commission. Prudence wouldn't *have* to accept a low offer. She knew the house had been well maintained. She thought it would be perfect for a young couple starting out, or a singleton, or an old couple. She wasn't worried.

After her lunch, she gave The Maples a brief tidy, finishing in the dining room. Her second appointment would be at three o'clock in that room and she wanted everything to be ready. She strolled around the room, a few cats in attendance, and looked for anomalies. There weren't any today.

She went back into the kitchen and quickly made an applesauce loaf. "You're not hosting another tea party, Prudence," she chided herself. It's just something to do, her inner voice responded, until she gets here.

At ten to three she heard a car pull into the driveway. Her guest had chosen to park behind Prudence's car at the side of the house, so naturally she knocked at the side porch door.

"Hello, Mrs. Smith," Prudence said, and ushered the medium through the kitchen and living room, into the dining room.

"What an interesting house," Mrs. Smith said quietly as she took off her coat and set it and her purse on a chair. "*Full* of emanations. Do you sense them?"

Prudence nodded. "Sometimes. This is the room where most of, er, the happenings have occurred. Will you sit down, Mrs. Smith?"

"I'll just walk around for a moment, if that's all right." Prudence herself took a seat in the corner and watched Mrs. Smith's perambulations. Mother sat by her feet.

The cats—the older ones—were *very* interested in this visitor. The younger, more harum-scarum ones like the boys, Ronald and Jay, took one look at her and skittered away. Harley and Kitty-Cat, who regarded the dining room as theirs, and who were even now lying each on a towel-draped chair pushed half under the table, sat up and followed Mrs. Smith with their eyes.

Seymour and Lightning physically followed the medium, stopping when she paused in front of the wood stove and looked into the convex mirror, and when, on the opposite side of the room, she opened then shut the sideboard cutlery drawers.

Mother came over to sit next to Prudence while Bob roosted at one end of the dining room table, his white-tipped black tail lazily flapping on its surface.

Mrs. Smith pointed at Lightning and Seymour. "These two are extra sensitive, but all cats are. To spirits, I mean. And this house is full of them." She was near Prudence when old Min Min stretched up on his hind legs, putting his paws on one of her knees.

She picked him up. He became limp in her arms then reached one paw up to her chin, and Prudence thought she heard Mrs. Smith say softly, "Yes, I'm sorry," though she had no idea why she was apologizing to the cat. Min Min gave a piteous little meow and Mrs. Smith gently returned him to the floor. She turned to Prudence. "I'm ready."

They sat at the opposite end of the table to where Bob was. Before she took her seat, Mrs. Smith leaned toward the centre of the table, putting her hands flat on its surface and waiting a moment. She seemed satisfied and took her seat facing Bob with Prudence to her right. Prudence wondered if Mrs. Smith had sensed the trap door directly under the centre of the table.

Prudence was an old hand at this and extended her left hand toward Mrs. Smith's right hand. "Please put your other hand flat on the table," the medium requested, and did likewise. They waited with eyes closed and Prudence heard Bob's tail slapping the table.

Mrs. Smith spoke. "Prudence Crick is here. She is ready to speak with you." There was a pause and Prudence could no longer hear Bob's tail. She guessed the other cats were similarly poised, waiting.

"Yes?" said Mrs. Smith. Then, to Prudence, softly, "Your mother is here."

Prudence felt her heart beating. She opened her eyes. She hadn't tried to communicate with her mother in the half-year since her husband, Alex, had died, for fear of confronting *his* spirit. She cleared her throat but knew better than to speak.

"She wants you to know that you're doing the right thing." Mrs. Smith addressed Prudence quietly. "Do you know—?" Prudence nodded.

"She's been trying to get your attention here in the house, moving objects, so you would communicate with her. She wants you to know—." Here Mrs. Smith paused as if trying to make out the words. "To let you know it's all right to let go of it, all of the past."

Prudence felt the tears come to her eyes. And to think, just this morning she'd put her house, her parents' house, up for sale. "Ask her about the trap door."

Mrs. Smith focused a moment and repeated, "Prudence wants to ask about the trap door." She waited then addressed Prudence. "Your mother says that's about something else. She made the door open and close to get your attention, but there's some other event or events connected with it. She doesn't know what exactly but it's nothing to do with you. Or her." She waited a bit longer. "She's going, Prudence. She says she loves you."

By now Prudence was crying. "Tell her I love her too, and Dad."

"She says she knows, Prudence. They know." Mrs. Smith took a deep breath and released Prudence's hand. "I don't think, my dear, that she'll be back."

Prudence found a tissue and blew her nose. "Tea, Mrs. Smith?"

And Mrs. Smith said, "Please."

Over their Earl Grey and slices of applesauce loaf in the living room, carefully observed by the now relaxed cats who'd followed when Prudence headed toward the kitchen, Mrs. Smith made conversation about some of the old houses she'd been in and what she'd sensed in them. Min Min climbed into her lap while Mother took possession of Prudence's.

"So many times it was simply a place where people had been born and died and left their essence behind. A mixture of normal human emotions. Like in this house, though I know you had an experience outside of the house involving a murdered spirit." When Prudence simply nodded, Mrs. Smith continued. "But at one place there was a terribly sad spirit, that of a woman who married without her father's consent and was disinherited.

When she died, she came back to haunt her father's home. I felt her presence. I and others at the séance heard what sounded like beads hitting the floor, as if a necklace had suddenly broken.

"At another house, a historical house run as a museum, I was just visiting as a tourist. When I got to the doorway, I felt such a strong sense of evil, physically pushing me out the door, I couldn't go in. I went home with a migraine and spent the night throwing up. Later I found out that it was generally believed that about a hundred and fifty years ago, that house was occupied by some who were believed to be werewolves and that packs of them had been seen running along that stretch of the Ottawa River."

A bit taken aback by the gothic images, Prudence commented, "You must have to be careful where you go."

"Oh, it's no good being afraid. I learned that long ago. Afraid of either my being able to sense the spirits or the spirits themselves. I have to go on."

Mrs. Smith made this statement in such a quiet, non-dramatic voice that Prudence's already considerable respect for her went up. "Mrs. Smith," she began.

The medium held up a hand. "I know what you're going to say, Prudence," and her eyes twinkled. "And *not* because I'm a medium, but as an observer of human nature. I know we won't be in touch again. I contacted you simply because your mother kept slipping into sessions I was holding with other clients." Her eyes twinkled again. "And it was becoming annoying."

"A very determined woman, my mother," Prudence stated.

"Like her daughter," Mrs. Smith said, and toasted Prudence with her teacup. "I hope you'll be very happy in your new life, whatever you choose it to be."

When Prudence related it all to Bertie on the phone that evening after supper, she found the eerie happenings at The Maples easier to explain than she'd feared. "My mother messed things up—the trap door she opened and closed, the mixed-up cutlery, the wool trailing down the stairs, were her trying to show me I was confused—they were random. Then, the second time she manifested—the signals were more organized. The cutlery had been sorted; dirty curtains rolled up. She was telling me to get on with it! Get on with my life. She was showing me there were resolutions to what was bothering me. I should have known it was her trying to communicate with me, but I thought it was something to do with The Maples."

"And?" asked Bertie.

"And what?"

"And what were you so confused about that your mother's spirit had to come back from the dead and reassure you?"

"Oh. Well, not just about you and our future together. I mean, I'm still not sure what our future will be, but I'm sure about you."

"I'm glad to hear it." Here followed reassurances on both sides of the most private nature.

"No," Prudence continued. "I feel like I need to change more than my marital status." She hesitated. Perhaps she would save the fact that she'd put her house up for sale for another day.

"You're in the process of changing jobs, too," Bertie reminded her. "No more housekeeping."

"Well," Prudence said, thinking of Gerry with the new baby coming, "not much housekeeping."

Bertie enumerated. "So, one: changing marital status and two: modifying work. Lessening work, I hope, to spend more time with me. Speaking of which, when are we next to meet?"

"Well, Gerry and Doug get back next weekend. I need to clean this place really well. And I'm working three or four days this week. After that? Perhaps I'll visit Walter and Mme Ménard again."

"I think it's really lovely you've involved yourself in their lives, Prue."

"You didn't at first," she reminded him.

"No, well, I was jealous. Of the time you were giving them."

"All right. I should give the cats here some attention too. I haven't groomed them once this whole time Gerry's been away!"

"Scandalous!" he agreed. "See you soon. I love you."

"Love you," she echoed, and hung up.

She got a cat brush and steel comb, and, in a dream, wandered about the house, trapping, grooming and releasing mostly reluctant cats. There was little resistance though. They knew better than to try to deflect Prudence once she'd determined to do something.

Apple blossoms, she thought, as her head touched the pillow. Apple blossoms smell like apples. And, satisfied with this random revelation, she instantly fell asleep.

# 23

Prudence hummed as she cleaned surfaces in Coco Poco. She'd slept like a log, as though her body and mind, worn out from vacillating about Bertie, were relieved she'd given in. It was a beautiful day, she'd just taken Mr. Willis his eleven o'clock coffee and had a word with him, and life seemed full of promise.

"Somebody's happy," Dan said with a smile, entering from the back of the café.

"Oh, Dan, I wanted to tell you—now my friends have finished their vacation in Lovering, I can be more available here. If you need me."

"That's good to know," he said absently, pushing the sofa tighter to the wall. "I hope to have some good news shortly that might very well mean more hours for you."

"What?" She sat down in one of the chairs.

"We may be expanding sooner than I thought. M Ménard has accepted my offer for his half of the lot out back." He moved to the blackboard and began composing the day's special.

"He has?" Prudence couldn't keep the dismay out of her voice. "But how? His aunt's not dead."

"No," said Dan, "but the way he explained it to me, he's got the curatorship of her property. Anyway, he says she's eager to sell." He wrote: THE CLASSIC—FRENCH HAZELNUT VANILLA—OURS IS THE —

"I don't think that's true," Prudence said firmly.

He stopped writing. "Eh!? What do you know about it!?" He sounded startled that his barista had an opinion about his business dealings.

"I don't think she wants to sell. I know she didn't want to sell her house. We—"

"You've talked to her? But Ménard said she can't talk! That she's in a vegetative state!"

Prudence gave him a hard look. "Then how does he know she wants to sell?"

"*I* don't know! Maybe they talked about it before her stroke. She did have a stroke, right?"

"Yes. But her speech and movement are slowly coming back and if we could just get her into rehab—" Prudence hesitated. "I may not have mentioned it, but I was helping someone from St. Anne's Church clean out the contents of Mme Ménard's house before the fire. And I happened to meet M Ménard. He didn't strike me as being very interested in his aunt's well-being, so I visited her. He's stuck her in a residence when she should obviously be in a rehab facility."

"So?"

"So I hired a lawyer."

"You did what!?" Dan appeared to be gobsmacked.

Prudence herself felt taken aback at his reaction. "I hired Cece Muxworthy to ask M and Mme Ménard separately a few questions, and when he was satisfied I was right about her condition and her nephew's indifference to it, he filed a request to review M Ménard's curatorship. If that's granted—"

Dan clutched his head. "If that's granted, I have to start all over again."

Prudence felt bad for him. "I'm sorry. But I think you should also know that I had a word with Mr. Willis—you know, the old gentleman with the black dog who comes every morning for a coffee on the porch. Did you know he used to be an insurance agent? Anyway, Mr. Willis said if Mme Ménard's house, which caught fire first, is proved to have been a straightforward fire not due to arson—"

"Who said anything about arson?" Dan's voice rose and he looked bewildered.

"It's just something Mr. Willis mentioned as a possibility. Arson or negligence. So when Mme Ménard's claim is settled, then Walter Lester's will probably follow. Walter seems to think his mother's insurance will pay for him to rebuild his house, which is his wish. Mme Ménard may never be well enough to live alone again, but there's nothing wrong with Walter."

Dan slowly sat down on the sofa and let his head sink into his cupped hands. "So I'm completely and utterly—" The chimes jangled announcing the arrival of the first of the yummy mummies. Prudence rose and helped the woman get her stroller over the doorsill. When she turned back, Dan must have retreated into his coffee-roasting lair. She finished the coffee note on the blackboard with the word she guessed he'd been meaning to write: BEST.

As Prudence prepared the customer's beverage (a double caramel cappuccino with no-fat soy milk and a chocolate-dipped almond biscotti on the side), she thought, gosh, I may have busy-bodied myself out of a job.

The mummy was joined by another. Two older women came in and sat together on the sofa. The conversations of the two groups blended with one another.

"Well! That was a brisk exercise class!"

"Did you? I ordered *my* yoga pants from them too. They took ages to—"

"Did you *hear* Frances? Huffing and puff—"

"Oh, I know, *and* half the time you get the wrong—"

"Tee-hee. Not half as bad as Monica. She's gotten so *fat*!"

"Rylan! Give me that! That's Aiden's!"

"Wah!"

"Well, I don't like to—"

"Is it? He has so many. Just the other—"

"Waaaaaaaah!!!"

"Oh, for heaven's sake, shut up!" It took a second before Prudence realized she hadn't said the words aloud. She got out her lunch and quietly ate behind the counter. She heard Dan's car reverse then leave. She went into the back, excusing herself to the customers with a smile and saying, "If you need anything, just rap on the door." She breathed a sigh of relief when said door snicked closed and she was alone.

All those years cleaning houses spoiled me, she thought. I only ever had to put up with one person at a time and they usually didn't want to chatter with the help. She thought with gratitude of Gerry silently sketching her cartoons and Edwina writing away in her study. But that's why people meet in cafés, you fool, to chat with friends.

She realized Dan had had the glass in the back door and the two damaged panes along the side replaced. It made all the difference to the lovely room. She looked up the street and tried to get the sequence of events straight in her mind.

Mme Ménard has a stroke. She lives but now her nephew is in charge. Then Mrs. Lester dies, which puts Walter in charge of that house. There are three interested parties that she knows of—she paused. No, only two really, as M Ménard doesn't want to develop the land, does he? No. He wants to sell it to those who do.

So, two interested parties, some developer and Dan. There may be more but let's work with what we've got.

The next thing is, the houses burn down. Walter says, and Mr. Willis agrees, that Mme Ménard's side of the building is where the fire started. And then a body is found in the ruins on that side. Possibly that of an arsonist hired by M Ménard was the theory Prudence and Mr. Willis had cooked up between them. Prudence was proud of it. She re-examined it.

Ménard had control of his aunt's house and would have had a willing ally in selling both properties if Mrs. Lester had lived. This according to Walter. Her dying was really an unfortunate coincidence from M Ménard and Dan's points of view and a fortunate one for Walter. Which left Ménard trying to make a deal with Walter so he could perhaps then sell the two lots as one, to either a developer or Dan, and take the middleman's profit as well as Mme Ménard's share. But as Walter had left the scene after the fire, only to turn up under the protection of Prudence and Cece Muxworthy, M Ménard must be struggling to bring his plan to fruition. Good, she thought with some satisfaction.

But if he knew about her involvement with Walter or where Walter was (and nothing he'd said made her think he did), he'd be even more angry at them—at her. Suddenly, she felt very alone.

Back to the two prospective property buyers, Dan and—

Rap! Rap! Rap! She jumped and hurried back to her duties.

After placating the customers (The older ladies wondered if it wouldn't be too much trouble if they could each have another cappuccino but this time could Prudence split one into two quite small portions? It was delicious, but the caffeine! And the mummies were irritated as there was no low-cal all-natural sweetener at their table.), she was surprised to hear another knocking, this time gently, on the porch window. That's odd, she thought, Mr. Willis doesn't usually come here *twice* a day. She stepped outside.

"Hi. Can I get you something?"

Mr. Willis waved a hand and shook his head. "Nah. Just wanted to let you know: buddy of mine still works at Ménard's insurance company. I asked him to confirm or deny arson as a cause of the fire."

"And? And?"

Mr. Willis nodded.

"Hah!" said Prudence with satisfaction. "And? Any details?"

"He said a burnt-out lawnmower had been found behind the Lester house."

Prudence nodded. "That makes sense. Mrs. Lester liked Walter to keep the outside neat."

Mr. Willis spoke slowly. "But—a melted gas can was found near the body inside the Ménard house."

Prudence sucked in her breath. "No!"

He nodded. "They'll be questioning Walter. At least about where he kept the gas can. If he kept it outside, anyone could have—"

"Taken it," Prudence finished his sentence. "And set the body on fire to try to hide a murder. Oh my!"

"Yeah. But that's a leap. More likely our arsonist tripped and fell after he started the fire. In either case, it's getting interesting." Mr. Willis licked his lips. "Almost makes me wish I was still working. Almost."

"I should get back," Prudence said. "Thanks for sharing all this with me. How will it end, do you suppose?" She shivered.

"Goose walk over your grave?" Mr. Willis asked sympathetically.

Prudence stared. "That's the second time that expression has come up recently. No. I mean, we guessed someone hired a pro to burn down the houses. A pro wouldn't murder someone, *then* set fire to the houses, would they?"

Mr. Willis looked doubtful. "Not unless the pro was caught in the act and afraid of being identified. Arsonists don't usually murder. They just like fires. Well, as you say, you better get back in there. Be seeing you."

"See you," Prudence said absently, and returned to the fray.

Various clients disturbed her peace and she was more than grateful when Dan Bartram stuck his head through the connecting door at four and said she could go. She crossed the street to Walter's residence. There's a gas can we have to discuss, she thought grimly.

But when she buzzed his number there was no answering buzz and when she drove back to The Maples there was a message from Cece Muxworthy saying the police had taken Walter in for questioning in the murder of an out-of-town property developer, one Christos Santorini.

It was an anxious Prudence who fed the cats that afternoon, made a pot of tea, then nervously paced from room to room.

She checked the computer but there was no message from Gerry. She deleted a lot of spam and closed the computer.

She wasn't hungry but opened a can of Gerry's revolting ravioli and, once it was heated, wolfed it down.

She turned on the news and watched with part of her mind while the other part jumped from one wild supposition to another. Could Walter have—? No! She denied the possibility of that gentle soul killing a man then burning his corpse. And though Walter might be anxious and fearful, he wasn't stupid. Would he really want to burn down his own house?

"What are the police thinking?" she wondered aloud to the cats, who, thankful she'd finally stopped her previous aimless wanderings, were mostly all clustered around her in front of the TV.

It had been dark for hours. Prudence got up and turned on more lights in the house. When the phone rang, she rushed to the one in the kitchen. "Cece?"

"It's me," said Bertie. "I hope it's not too late. I was doing an inventory at a client's house and just got in. You're expecting a call?"

"Yes." She breathed out a huge shuddering breath. "Oh, Bertie, I wish you were here. Things are becoming complicated."

"What things?" She filled him in on the day's events and her theories. "Prudence, call the lawyer yourself, if you're so worried. Then make a cup of weak tea and go to bed. Promise?"

She calmed. "You're right. And I promise. Thanks, Bertie. It did me good to talk."

"All right. I'll call you tomorrow. Or you call me. Whichever. Goodnight, dear."

"Good night." She immediately dialled Cece's number and got his wife Bea.

"Prudence! How are you?"

"I'm fine, thank you, Bea. Is Cece there?"

"No. He's out with a client. Can I take a message?"

"Yes. Ask him to call me at any time when he gets home. Thank you."

Prudence made the weak tea, trudged upstairs to bed, got out the Woolf bio and began to read. She finished the tea and slid down under the covers. Another hour ticked by as she fretted. She got up, went downstairs, cleaned the cat boxes and brought a slice of applesauce loaf back up to bed.

The phone rang after eleven. Prudence flew downstairs. "Cece?"

"Yup." He sounded weary. "I got him out, Prudence, but it wasn't good."

"What do you mean?" She sank down onto the chair next to the foyer's phone table. Mother slowly hopped down the stairs, stopped on the lowest one and watched.

"Walter admitted smashing the windows of the café."

"What!?"

"But he says he did it because M Ménard told him that that would drive Dan Bartram away. It seems Ménard's been working on Walter for some time. Telling him he wanted to buy Dan's building, not Walter's."

"But Walter told me his mother was ready to sell their house. But I don't know to whom."

"His mother, eh? Funny. When his mother was mentioned was the only time he clammed up. He got a strange expression on his face, too."

"How strange?"

"Kind of inward looking. Almost smiling."

"Geez, Cece, that's a bit creepy, isn't it?" He agreed. "I guess it's understandable that Walter wouldn't grieve her death too much. Theirs was a fraught relationship. She was abusive, from the sound of it. Is Walter back at the apartment?"

"Yes."

"Oh! I almost forgot. Where was the gas can kept?"

"On the Lester back porch."

"Oh. Good. Accessible to anyone."

"Which I pointed out to the police. Look, Prudence, I'm pretty tired. I'd be happy to talk with you again tomorrow, if you like."

"Thanks, Cece. We'll see. And on Walter's behalf, thanks again. We'll talk soon."

"All right. 'Night."

"'Night." Prudence slowly put down the phone. Something had been said that hadn't made sense. What was it? She looked over at Mother, staring from her step. "Well, Mother, I'll never be able to sleep now." She went to the living room, switched on the TV with the volume low and lay on the sofa. The next thing she knew, it was Wednesday morning.

# 24

Prudence stood sleepily, watching water turn to coffee, the white ceramic cone balanced atop her cup. The water was slow going through the paper filter. She was poking around in the sludge in the filter with her spoon when somehow her hand knocked the cone sideways, sending coffee and grounds everywhere. "Oh!" She stood frozen as coffee oozed from the counter down the front of the drawers and lower kitchen cabinets. "But I hardly touched it!" she wailed. "I'm not in the mood for this this morning," she informed the world.

Cats, finishing their breakfasts, were beginning to leave the kitchen. As she crouched, wiping the cupboard fronts and floor, she came in contact with a few of their furry bodies. Jay was the most curious, following every motion of Prudence's hands. Prudence calmed. "Oh well, just an accident, eh? Eh, Jay?" She reached out a coffee-soaked hand and petted the cat's head. Jay pushed into her palm then walked away so Prudence's hand stroked her back, finishing with her tail. She took a deep breath and rose to her feet. The thing that had been bothering her rose to the surface of her mind.

As she reboiled the water and got out a tea bag—easy, almost foolproof—she wondered why M Ménard would tell Walter he didn't want to buy his house. Well, obviously, to goad Walter into smashing Dan's windows. Dan, who openly *did* want to buy both houses. Who made no secret that he was eager to expand out the back of his property. Had Ménard just lied to Walter to incriminate him? *To blame him for the subsequent fire?* Prudence felt ill at the thought of such conniving, such callousness, as to use a mentally fragile older man whose mother had just died. But wait, she thought sourly, there's more. Ménard had also told Walter that he wanted to buy the old house in which *Dan* had his business. Was this just another lie or could it possibly be true?

Dan *did* appear to have an awful lot of meetings that took him away from the café. And he'd appeared to recognize Ménard when the man showed up there angry at Prudence. Could Dan have been meeting Ménard? Or this property developer Christos, Christos something? Or could all three men have been plotting together to get rid of the occupants of the Lester and Ménard houses?

Prudence took her tea into the living room and sat at the table, gazing out at the lake. What on earth am I doing, she thought? What's it to me?

You're acting like Gerry would. If Gerry was here, it would be *her* doing all this supposing, while you played calm, rational Prudence. Her internal dialogue continued:

What do you mean, "played"? I mean, what do *I* mean? I *am* calm. I *am* rational. Just not lately. I'll do nothing. It's too complicated. Walter, Ménard, Dan, Christos San— San—. I'm putting them all away. In a box.

Her eyes widened. Four men. A four-sided problem. A square. Where each side joined to the next there was an angle. This problem was all a matter of figuring out the angles. So that's what she proceeded to do. Or almost do.

She sighed and got up. Groceries. She needed to restock Gerry's pantry and fridge. She made a list and drove to Lovering. She decided to visit Walter before she shopped; see how he was after his interview with the police. I'm just checking on his well-being, she assured herself.

She parked on the street across from Coco Poco. Happening to glance at the place, she saw Dan at the café's one front window.

She gave a wave and he lifted a hand in reply. Then she crossed the street to the seniors' residence.

She buzzed Walter's apartment and, after waiting what felt like a long time, heard the intercom crackle into life. "Who is it?" Walter Lester asked in a low muffled voice.

"It's me, Walter, Prudence. Can I come up?"

He said something that sounded like "Uh," and buzzed her up. When she got to his apartment, the door was closed, and, judging by the sounds on the other side after she knocked, locked. The door opened slightly and Walter peered suspiciously through the crack. He was holding Luc and part of the cat's grey and white face also appeared.

"Hello, you two. May I come in?" Prudence edged past Walter and into the kitchenette. Boxes of cookies and crackers had been left open on the counter, along with a jar of instant coffee, the sugar bowl and a host of dirty dishes. "It's not the season for them, Walter, but if you leave food out, ants might come."

She was not expecting his response. "Will if I want to!" he slurred, his voice still lower than usual. Luc jumped from his arms and came to rub against Prudence's ankles. Walter slouched into the living room and sat down in front of the TV—some game show was playing silently.

Talking quietly to the cat, Prudence began to tidy and clean the kitchen area. "Well, Luc, how do you like life in an apartment? Miss your friends?"

The cat gave her legs a final caress with his tail then trotted over to Walter and curled in his lap.

When Prudence went to put things away in the cupboards she found an empty pill bottle lying on its side. Clozapine, she read. No idea what that's for, she thought. "Walter, do you need to get this medicine refilled?" He looked over with hooded eyes then shrugged.

The pharmacist's number was on the label. Prudence asked to speak to the pharmacist herself and used a quiet voice. "I'm with Walter Lester and he seems to be out of Clozapine. Does he need a renewal? And—he's acting withdrawn, surly. Should I be worried? Oh? Okay. Thank you very much."

She hung up and addressed Walter. "Someone from the pharmacy will walk your pills over right away. Meanwhile, I'll make some tea, shall I?"

"Maybe I don't want to take my pills."

This was said with such weariness that Prudence was touched and approached him. "Have you been on them long?"

He appeared not to have heard her. "*She* always stood over me to make sure I'd swallowed them." Tears came into his eyes. "She said I was bad either way but at least when I took the pills, I was controllable bad." He looked up at Prudence. "I just didn't want to be bad anymore. I thought—I thought—"

Prudence felt her body become very still. She remembered Cece had said the only point in the police interview when Walter shut down was when his mother's death had come up. "What are you trying to say, Walter?"

Walter seemed to be lost in a dream. He slowly lifted his head and said, "Eh?" She repeated the question. His eyes refocused. "I saw her. I saw her stand over Mme Ménard. She bent over and said something. Then she came inside. I moved back from the window so she didn't know I'd seen. Then she told me she was dead. But now I know she was lying. If it hadn't been for me being so afraid—" He clenched his fists.

"There, there," Prudence soothed. "Mme Ménard is strong. She survived the stroke and she's starting to recover."

Walter didn't appear to hear her. He was nodding his head. His body started to rock forward and back, which disturbed the cat. It moved to one arm of the easy chair. "So, when she got sick, I went into her room because she was making a sound, like she couldn't breathe. I leaned over her. 'I hate you,' I said. And 'I hope you die.' Then I went downstairs and sat on the front porch. I felt so guilty. When I went back upstairs, she was dead. That's all." With these last words, his rocking ceased and his attention was drawn back to the TV where a person dressed as a banana was jumping up and down next to a giant turning wheel. When the wheel stopped, the jumping of the banana became extreme, and Prudence felt a chill as Walter turned to her with shining eyes and quietly said, "He won."

Prudence waited until the pharmacy assistant arrived with the medication, gave Walter a pill with a glass of water, and fed the cat. Shaken, she let herself out and drove to Cece's where she told him all she suspected about both Mrs. Lester's behaviour toward Mme Ménard in her time of crisis as well as Walter's toward his mother in hers. She was done taking responsibility. Someone else would have to support Walter Lester. She was out of her depth. She felt a load shift as she left Cece's and went to park at the grocery store.

As she sat in the car, collecting herself, she realized the morning had passed and she was hungry. Going to buy a peanut butter and sweet pickle sandwich with a bag of chips, Prudence? She made a face. No. She would treat herself to a proper lunch out.

She walked to the closest restaurant, one she'd heard about but never visited. Gerry had said they had great grilled cheese sandwiches. So be it.

But when she opened the menu, she found nary a cheesy concoction on it. The chef had had a conversion. Prudence read descriptions of various Asian-fusion dishes. She chose pork dumplings in broth.

As she dipped her spoon in for the first taste, she was hailed by someone just coming in. "Prudence! What are *you* doing here?" As usual, her cousin Mary Petherbridge grated on her nerves, implying Prudence was the last person she expected to see in a moderately upscale restaurant.

"What are *you* doing here?" she snapped and took that first taste.

Mary looked taken aback, realized her mistake, and had the grace to blush. "Sorry, Prudence. I didn't mean it *that* way." On seeing Prudence's raised eyebrows, she said, "Okay, okay, maybe I did. A mimosa, Christine," she said to the approaching waitress. "Mind if I join you?" When Prudence still didn't respond, Mary said, "Ah, come on, Prudence. You know I don't have any filters. Never had. Never will." She paused with her hand on the back of one chair.

Prudence waved a hand. "Oh, go on then." Before she resumed slurping her dumplings she said, "But why is that? About the filters, I mean?"

Mary flushed. "I was the least favourite child, that's all. Mother had her darling firstborn Gerald. Father had baby Maggie. And I was invisible. So I taught myself not to care."

"I see." There was a pause. "These dumplings are very good."

"They are, aren't they? I like the peanut sauce they drizzle over the top. I will have—" She stabbed the menu mid-page with one pointed red nail for the hovering waitress's benefit. "Gerry back yet?"

"This weekend," Prudence managed, her mouth full.

"Going to miss living in that big old house?" Mary queried, sipping her mimosa.

"It'll be nice to get back to my own little place."

"Which is up for sale, I see. I drove by there this morning."

Wow, that was fast work, Prudence thought. She'd seen the agent yesterday morning and already the woman had a sign up. With a pang she wondered what Rita and Charlie would think of her not telling them. She better phone Rita —

"So where are you going to move to?" Mary sounded genuinely interested. Her lunch—a fried noodle nest containing a poached egg surrounded by big chunks of vegetables—looked good.

"I—we—haven't decided. It just seemed time to make a change."

"We? Are you thinking of moving in with Bertie?"

Prudence pushed her plate away and leaned back. "Actually, Mary, we're engaged."

Mary's mouth sagged in surprise. "To be married? I didn't think people got married anymore, never mind engaged first. You should put a notice in the *Lovering Herald*. That'll make the town sit up."

"You mean something like: 'Prudence Catford Crick, daughter of Edward and Constance Catford, widow of noted bank robber Alexander Crick, and Albert Edward Smith, son of the late Annie Smith, are pleased to announce that despite all odds, a late middle-aged woman can find someone to care for her'"?

Mary cackled. "I think I've underestimated you all these years, Prudence. Yeah, something like that, only leave out the bit about Alex. And why are you still using his name? What's wrong with plain old Prudence Catford?"

"You're right," Prudence said slowly. "Okay." She lifted her water glass to clink against Mary's mimosa. "To Prudence Catford. From here on in."

"To Prudence Catford," laughed Mary.

They drank. "Dessert?" asked the waitress.

"Just coffee."

"Coffee, please."

"About The Maples," Prudence said. "Did you know there's a whole other room under the dining room?"

Mary leaned back and looked at the tablecloth. "Oh, you found that, did you?"

"I had to push the table and rug out of the way when the wood stove was installed."

Mary looked surprised. "Gerry's put a wood stove in the dining room? I didn't notice it at your tea party. Nice."

"You came in through the kitchen door, remember?" Mary nodded. Prudence waited, then asked her again. "So what was the basement room for?"

"Oh, I guess for storage back when the house was a store."

"So your family never used it?"

"I remember it was opened to be cleaned out once when we were small. There was a trap door and we three clustered around to see it opened. We were excited. Well, you would be if a room you never knew existed suddenly appeared in your house."

"When was this?"

"Oh, I guess in the fifties. Maggie was tiny and Ger was a teen, with me in the middle. Anyway, they let us all go down on a ladder. It was so disappointing. Just barrels and boxes and lots of dust. I got out of there pretty quick. I didn't like being underground.

"The other two stayed there a while, making up stories about hiding from bad guys, or bad guys hiding in the room and popping up in the middle of the night. I remember Maggie had a nightmare—we were still sharing a room—about something coming to get her. And she'd brought her cat Snickerdoodle down with her during the day and in the dream she was crying that the cat was in the hole and couldn't get out. My mother had to find the cat and show Maggie it was fine before she'd go back to sleep. The next day the room was emptied, cleaned and shut up."

"And never opened since?" Prudence asked idly.

"Only once since then, that I know of." Mary flushed and played with her cup. "Over the summer of 1990, during the Oka crisis."

"Really? I remember that. It was weird having so many police in Lovering."

"And soldiers hiding in the shrubbery," Mary said dryly. "Literally."

"So why open the cellar then?"

Mary's flush deepened. "In 1990, I was forty-seven. Geoff was fifty. We were fighting a lot. I had made a mistake, and he was disappointed, sad. Then the situation across the river evolved to the point where we heard the Mohawk couldn't buy groceries. So people on this side started to donate stuff and needed somewhere to store it before it could be ferried across."

The light dawned for Prudence. "Oh. That's what Maggie was doing out in the garden at night."

"What?"

"She told me she met Winnifred, you know, that old lady that used to live next door to The Maples, outside one night in the garden. Winnifred asked Maggie why there were helicopters flying across the river at night. Maggie told her. But Maggie would normally stay on the screened porch at night—because of the mosquitoes."

"The mosquitoes at The Maples *are* legendary," mused Mary. "So, you think Maggie was outside waiting for someone to arrive to pick up groceries?"

"Am I right?"

"It started that way. The Mohawk rowed across. But once it was a teenaged girl and her little sister, and Maggie got so *mad*. That river's deep with dangerous currents. And helicopters flying overhead. Anything could have happened to them. After that she and Geoff took the groceries across themselves."

"I wonder why she didn't want me to know."

"Probably wanted to protect you. So you wouldn't be implicated if they got caught."

"And you never—?"

"Come *on*. It wasn't something *I'd* be likely to be a part of. Can you see me in a rowboat?"

Prudence looked at the immaculately groomed woman across from her. "Er, no. I guess not."

"But it brought Maggie and Geoff closer," Mary said grimly. "It confirmed for him, for all of us, what a good brave person my sister was. And that made me very jealous. I thought—he was always so relaxed when she was around." Prudence looked away from her cousin's grimacing face. Mary continued, "Anyway, they rowed groceries across from The Maples a couple of times before the crisis ended. Geoff and I patched up our marriage, and everything returned to normal."

"Well, I hardly know what to say, except, thank you for telling me the history of the cellar. I went down there and it's still empty. Just spiders."

Mary was silent for a moment then quietly said, "I'm glad about your engagement, Prudence. Congratulations. Enjoy it." Her tone changed. "Now! You must let me get this lunch as an engagement gift to you."

They parted amicably. Prudence got her groceries and drove back to The Maples. There, Bertie phoned her with some interesting information.

"So what's the good news, Prudence?" asked Lucy. "I'll be right with you, Madame," she called. "Make it snappy, Prue, I've got a customer waiting."

"I heard. You almost deafened me! I nearly dropped the phone! Can you get M Ménard to meet you at the café tomorrow?"

"I suppose."

"I'll take a break and then I'll tell you both together."

Lucy groaned. "You're going to make me wait till tomorrow?"

"You'll survive," Prudence said lightly and said goodbye.

Everything's going to work out, she thought as she made her supper. Everything's going to be fine.

# 25

And the next day, the last of September, everything seemed to promise a good day.

Prudence woke up cheerful, despite the sound of a gentle rain falling on The Maples' tin roof. She succeeded in making the perfect cup of coffee and had time to leisurely sip it before leaving for work.

When she entered the café, Dan was tidying up from making himself a large French hazelnut vanilla. He seemed tired and retreated to the back room with little comment. Prudence shrugged and got on with her tasks.

Around eleven Mr. Willis tapped at the window. He had nothing new to report from his insurance contacts. Jazz strained at the leash. "It's the cooler air. He needs to keep moving. Like me." He winked at Prudence and left with his coffee.

At eleven forty-five Lucy arrived, full of curiosity about what Prudence could be going to tell her and M Ménard. "But you say I'll like it?"

"Oh yes," Prudence said, handing her a small cappuccino. "First—Bertie and I are engaged."

"What? Oh, Prudence, that's wonderful! Congratulations! I'm so happy for you!"

Prudence blushed. "Thanks, Luce. We'll talk more about it later, eh?" She took a piece of paper out of her purse and pushed it across the counter. "Read this."

Lucy did. "But why do we—?" she was beginning to say, when M Ménard entered.

He checked his watch then addressed Lucy. "What's so urgent it couldn't be said over the phone? I've had to drive all the way from Quebec City."

"Lucy," Prudence said calmly, "may I?"

Lucy nodded.

"M Ménard, we and others worked swiftly and efficiently to clean out your aunt's house for you before the fire. Thankfully, by then we'd sorted her possessions and removed them, except for the large items, into storage."

"So?"

"So, the agreement was that St. Pete's would sell the items and benefit from the sale."

"Yeah, yeah."

"Do you mind—?" and here Prudence handed the piece of paper to him. "Would you mind reading and signing this paper confirming that? A lawyer has suggested a formal agreement is best. To protect the church."

He scowled. "Same lawyer who's trying to take away my curatorship of her?"

Prudence smiled a thin dangerous smile. "That's the one."

He signed. "That it?"

"Almost. Lucy, if you would sign as a witness. And I'll sign. Good!" She folded the paper and returned it to her purse. "Now. I'd like to take this opportunity of telling you that I will *not* abandon your aunt to spending the rest of her days in that inadequate and inappropriate residence."

"Yeah!" Lucy had found her voice.

Prudence continued, "And so the church will not be selling all Mme Ménard's worldly goods."

Lucy turned to look at Prudence. "We won't?"

Prudence shook her head. "First of all, she might make a full recovery and decide to rebuild her house. Then she'll need her stuff again."

M Ménard scoffed. "That's not going to happen. I've already—"

Prudence's gaze sharpened. "You've already what?"

He smiled unpleasantly but kept silent.

"M Ménard, it doesn't matter if you've sold your half of the lot. You'll never get Walter Lester to sell his."

"Think so? I will as soon as I find him. I know something he doesn't want told. I saw—" He stopped, realizing if he said what he'd seen, his power over Walter would be gone. For the first time, Ménard looked uncertain.

"If you mean you saw him kill Christos Santorini and set the body on fire, you're lying."

Ménard's eyebrows rose in incredulity. "How could I have seen him do that? Though he may well have done. That night I'd driven back to Quebec City to my home. My wife—"

Lucy looked confused. "Prudence, what—?"

Prudence held up a hand. "It'll become clear in a moment, Lucy. So how did Mr. Santorini get into the house?"

"Because I gave him a key! He wanted to look at the appliances, the gas stove, the furnace! So when his men tore the place down, he'd be able to direct them properly!" He was getting angry. "So who else could have killed him but Lester? I grant a good defence lawyer might get him off if he claims he thought Santorini was an intruder, but still—" A look of contempt overtook his face. "Considering his mental history—"

Prudence interrupted. "So, considering his mental history, you bullied him into breaking the café windows, didn't you? He told me you said if he broke the windows, Dan Bartram would get so discouraged, he'd give up his idea of expanding the business and move away."

"Sheesh!" Lucy said. "That was mean."

Ménard tried to bluster his way out of it. "He's lying! He's lying!"

"And," Prudence added, "we have only your word Mr. Santorini was alive when you drove away to Quebec City. You could have hired an arsonist to burn the houses down—and hide the body."

"How on earth would I have been able to find an arsonist so quickly?" He stopped, aware that he had admitted the possibility he *could* have found one, just not that fast.

Prudence said coldly, "I have no doubt you'd be able to condone an act of arson, if you thought it necessary."

"This is too much! I'm leaving!" He turned and had his hand on the doorknob when Prudence's next statement made him pause.

In a soft voice, she asked, "Don't you want to know the other reason the church won't be taking the profit from selling Mme Ménard's things?"

He looked at her warily.

"I have a friend," Prudence began. "A friend who deals in antiques. So I asked him to have a look at some of Mme Ménard's, er, objects, the ones that seemed unusual to me."

Ménard was silent but Lucy said excitedly, "Prue, is this the good news?"

Prudence continued, "My friend took one of the objects away with him and consulted another dealer who specializes in Asian artifacts. And guess what?"

Lucy said, "What!? What!?" Ménard had gone very still.

"There's a white jade bowl from the *Qianlong* period, *with* the imperial mark, indicating it was ordered by an emperor of China. Mme Ménard had it on top of her armoire in the kitchen. Next to the little ornaments you used to get free in boxes of tea."

"You mean that clunky uneven thing I said would make a good doorstop?" Lucy's voice was high. Ménard looked sick.

"Yeah, that one," Prudence stated with deliberation. "Anyone want to guess what it's worth?"

"Don't be so mean, Prue!" Lucy wailed. Ménard licked his lips.

"Let me see if I can remember." Prudence looked up at the ceiling. "Oh yes. Between five hundred and seven hundred and fifty. Thousand."

Lucy's eyes bulged. Ménard let out a slow breath.

"Plus there are three other jade objects, also valuable. So the expert figures up to a million five for all four." She concluded by saying, "Probably considerably more than you would have received for your aunt's land, wouldn't you say, M Ménard?"

He walked stiffly to a chair and sat limply in it, saying nothing.

Prudence felt a bit deflated. It hadn't been as much fun to twit the man with his mistake as she'd thought.

Lucy, meanwhile, was fizzing with excitement. "Oh, Prue, how wonderful for Mme Ménard! She's well off now! Where is it? Where's the bowl?" Ménard looked up.

"All the objects are in Montreal. With you-know-who's friend. In his safe."

Ménard rose and advanced on the two women, his fists clenched. "Tell me! Tell me where they are, you stupid woman!"

Prudence flinched, turned to get away and happened to look out the café's front window. "Oh look, M Ménard," she said in a tone of real surprise, "the police have arrived. Just at the right time."

Ménard turned to look. He stepped away from Prudence and Lucy. "Did you call them?" he asked through clenched teeth.

Prudence shook her head.

"*I* called them," Dan Bartram said, peeking through the connecting door as the police entered the café.

"Oh, good thing!" said Lucy. "Did you hear everything from the other room?"

He nodded. "Pretty much." Prudence watched the two officers come warily up the outside stairs then opened the door for them.

Lucy addressed the police. "Officers, I'd like to make a complaint that this man—" She pointed at Ménard, who had turned an unattractive shade of pale green. "This man was threatening me and my friend just before you arrived."

"Is that so?" the shorter officer asked Ménard.

"I—I—"

"I'm a witness to that," Dan said calmly. "At least, I was listening from the back room and heard him threaten them and I don't see anyone else in here."

The police officer gave him a careful look. "And you are?"

"I'm Dan Bartram, the owner here."

"Ah." The officer seemed surprised. "Okay then." He turned to the taller officer. "Better call in for another car. In a minute." Then he addressed Dan. "Dan Bartram, I am arresting you for the murder of Christos Santorini," and snapped on a pair of handcuffs.

Before he was taken away through the front door, Dan turned and said to Prudence. "Sorry, Prudence. I guess this means you're out of a job."

Prudence and Lucy sat on the café sofa, each with a cooling coffee on the table in front of her.

"I suppose it's true?" Prudence asked Lucy dully.

"That you're out of a job? I'd say so."

Someone tried the front door, which Prudence had locked after the police had taken Dan and Ménard away. She got up wearily and unlocked it. "We're closed," she said to the two yummy mummies who'd just wrestled their strollers up the stairs.

"Your sign says you're open," one of them accused.

"My mistake." Prudence reversed the sign. "Go away." She closed the door and heard them angrily clunking their strollers back down the stairs. "You think Dan killed the property developer?"

"*He* called the police. And not just to get Ménard off our backs. Though that was nice of him. I think he wanted to confess. He seemed very calm."

"Hmm," said Prudence. "Maybe it was an accident."

"You mean, like—what's his name?"

"Santorini."

"Like Dan pushed him and he hit his head?"

"Yeah."

"You really like him, eh, Prue?"

Prudence nodded. Lucy shook her head. "But what about throwing gasoline around and setting the house on fire? Knowing Walter was probably asleep next door? *That* wasn't an accident."

"No. You're right. It's terrible. Just terrible. But why did he do it? Did M Ménard tell him he'd already sold to Santorini? Or did Dan see a light in the house—he told me he worked late sometimes—and surprise Santorini? And *he* told Dan he'd bought it? And Dan got angry." She concluded sadly, "It must have been something like that. Maybe he has debts—" She remembered the bills she'd seen on Dan's desk for new equipment. "Maybe he's overextended." She looked around her. "Well. I suppose I'd better, uh, close up. For good."

They left the building together. Standing next to Prudence's car, Lucy said comfortingly, "You'll find another job, Prue. Don't worry."

Prudence nodded and drove away.

She travelled past The Maples and on to her own house. Someone had pulled out the withered summer annuals and replaced them with miniature yellow mums. She crossed the road and knocked on Rita's door.

"Prue? We were worried. We saw the for-sale sign go up and didn't hear from you! Come in! We're just having lunch."

"Hi, Rita. Hi, Charlie." Prudence sat down at the kitchen table as Rita brought her a bowl of pea soup. "Sorry I didn't call you. Quite a lot's been happening. Did you plant those mums?"

"Charlie did it."

"Eh?" said Charlie.

"I said, you planted the mums at Prue's."

"Oh. Yeah. They were on sale at the hardware. I thought, she's never going to sell that house with dead flowers out in front. Curb appeal, Prue. Curb appeal."

Prudence smiled at him. "Thanks, Charlie. You guys are the best neighbours." Then, turning to Rita, she announced, "I'm getting married."

Many squeals from Rita, and muttered congratulations from Charlie later, Rita made grilled cheese sandwiches and they discussed Prudence and Bertie's future.

"It's all up in the air," Prudence said. "We might live in Montreal, in Lovering, or somewhere else. All I know is, I need a fresh start. I need to leave my parents' house."

"Oh, I don't care where you go," said Rita, "just as long as it's not *too* far away. Don't want to ask Charlie for *too* many rides to visit you. I just might have to go get my own driver's licence."

Looking aghast, probably at the idea of his wife tootling around in his beloved pickup truck, Charlie hastily reassured her. "Happy to drive you anytime, Rita. You know that."

"Huh. There's a lot of grumbling sometimes, when I want to get my hair done, for example." She winked at Prudence. "We'll see."

Prudence made her goodbyes and let herself into her little bungalow. She walked from room to room, looked out the kitchen window where her father's last garden had been, then back into the hall. No phone messages. She gently closed then locked the front door.

"Are you kidding me? You've been working for a confessed murderer and arsonist?"

Prudence nodded. Bertie and she were snuggled on the living room couch with assorted cats wedged in around them. A fire crackled in the open hearth. Other cats basked on the rug.

As soon as Prudence had phoned him with the news of Dan and Ménard's arrests, Bertie had hopped on the next train to Lovering. Prudence had hurriedly bunged a frozen quiche and some baking potatoes into the oven and prepared a salad, then picked him up. Now, supper over, they relaxed.

"So," Bertie said slowly. "What about the café?"

Prudence sighed and shifted her legs to a more comfortable position. "What about it?"

"Well, I've been thinking," he drawled. "And I quite like the idea of leaving my dusty antique shop and moving to the country. For the sake of my allergies."

Prudence swivelled so she could look into his face. He was smiling. "You'd do that for me?"

"Well, I know you're a country girl, and you're looking forward to Gerry's baby. You can hardly babysit if we live in Montreal. I'll rent out my shop or get a manager and just pop in once or twice a week. We could go picking on the weekends."

"I put my house up for sale," Prudence said dreamily, gazing at the fire.

"Huh? When?"

"As soon as we got engaged."

"Now it's my turn to say: you'd do that for me? Give up your home?"

She sat up and looked at him. "It's not for you. It's for me. It's time I let go of the past. Not forget it. Just—not wallow in it."

"Amazing. Perfect sense," he said, reaching for her hands. "So, would you like to run a coffee shop with me?"

Prudence's jaw dropped. "Really?"

"Really. It's a nice little business in a sweet location. Once we get rid of all the coffee roasting apparatus in the back, knock down the wall between the two rooms, and introduce some of your *spécialités desserts*, we'll make a killing."

Prudence looked doubtful. "But Dan said people came because he roasted the coffee on the spot. And it *is* good."

"Pish! The guy was a fanatic. And look where it got him. It's a huge time suck roasting it yourself and you can buy perfectly good coffee wholesale. *Our* emphasis would be on the desserts."

"You sound like you know what you're doing," Prudence said slowly. "I'll think about it. Oh. We're low on wood."

"I'll go."

"We'll both go." They let themselves out the side door and stood for a moment breathing the cool damp evening air. The rain had stopped but the grass and shrubs were still wet. They heard a shout from Edwina's house and turned to look.

There, in the glow of a couple of floodlights shining down from the back of the house, was the acclaimed author, on her hands and knees, trying to coax an immobile Shadow into a length of plastic pipe.

Bertie and Prudence exchanged quizzical looks and went down the stairs onto the lawn. "This looks like it'll be worth wet shoes," said Bertie. Prudence shushed him.

They watched as Edwina gave up on that skill and instead, using treats, tried to coax the dog up one side of a steeply angled platform and down the other side. Shadow was halfway up when Edwina made the mistake of giving him a treat. He took it and jumped off the side of the platform.

"*No*, Shadow!" they clearly heard. "You must continue all the way up. Let's try it again."

As Edwina began walking up the platform herself, leaning sharply forward, while the dog sniffed a shrub, Prudence said with a smile, "I've seen enough." They got their wood and went back to their fire.

"I don't think I've seen this one before," Bertie said uncertainly, pointing to a grey and white cat with a notched ear, sitting grooming wet fur in the centre of the hearthrug.

"Bertie, meet Luc, Mme Ménard's cat." A shadow passed over Prudence's face as she remembered that where Walter Lester was, he couldn't have a pet. Then she brightened and added, "He was chasing Bea and Cece's cat all around their place and Cece was afraid Bea would get tripped up. She has MS, you know. So I said I'd take him. Just until Mme Ménard recovers."

"And if she doesn't?"

"Well then, he'll be ours. Okay?"

"Okay," he said, kissing her.

"Which reminds me, I want to take Luc to visit Mme Ménard tomorrow. Will you help me smuggle him in?"

"I'm your man. Cat smuggling it is."

"And I'm buying a piano," she said firmly.

He did a double take. "You are full of surprises today, Prudence Crick." He nestled closer.

"That's Prudence Catford," she corrected. "From now on."

Dear P and Cs,

I want to tell you all about Scotland but have left it too late. We fly out tomorrow and I'm exhausted. I'll just say that of all the places we visited, Scotland was the most beautiful, the most amazing. Even the cities were fascinating. And I can't begin to describe the beauty of Skye, Glen Elg, the castle of Eileen Donan. We need more time! We've agreed we'll come back someday if we can. For now, you'll have to wait to hear about it from us in person and look at all the sketches I made. Much love. See you soon.

G & D

Luc looked from the woman to the man and back again. They were talking about him. He heard his name. He preened on the hearthrug.

He'd sorted out the male cats of this house—all except the black and white top cat lounging on the mantelpiece above him. Well, that was satisfactory. He couldn't be expected to walk in and be top cat right away.

The females were no problem—easily dominated, all of them—except for the tailless one. Her sense of self was too strong for him and anyway, she only had one friend, the small black one-eyed male who ran away when Luc wanted to fight. Their position in the group was so low he could ignore both of them without loss of face.

Luc shifted from licking his right shoulder to his left. No, this place suited him. The food was served at regular hours and the cat flap was an improvement on his old woman having to let him in and out all the time. These people had mentioned her name as well.

He felt a twinge of longing for her. He still hadn't sensed her death. She must be somewhere.

He paused in his grooming and listened. A dog barked. The people made the fire burn higher.

He settled himself on the rug, closed his eyes, and waited.

# ABOUT THE BOOK

This note will be a bit higgledy-piggledy.

First, I must speak about Trudy Frey, to whom I have dedicated this book. I met Trudy many years ago, over thirty, when we found ourselves taking an evening yoga course at Riverdale High School in Toronto. Everybody in this particular class clicked, each with the other, and for a few years the annual end of spring term yoga party was held in Trudy and her husband Karl's beautiful backyard not far from the school and where I lived. When I broke my ankle, kind Trudy, newly retired, volunteered to give my big dog Honey a daily walk—and it was February! Over subsequent years, I enjoyed many suppers with Trudy and Karl until they left Toronto and I left Ontario, but we kept in touch by telephone and letter. Trudy was my biggest fan, always encouraging and giving words of praise to the "cat" mysteries. Karl went first and my dear friend Trudy died in the fall of 2021. She will be missed.

Second, I must mention my childhood piano and singing teacher—Mrs. Etta Ballands. She was my first music teacher and lovingly opened the door to the mysteries that have entranced me for most of my life.

Third, I must tell you that of the five places Gerry and Doug visit in *The Cat Looked Back*, I have been to two: Ireland, to visit my friend Maggie and her daughter Clodagh; and Scotland, which I fell in love with in the company of my friend Helmi, and of which I have written extensively in my three Chronicles of Deasil Widdy books. For the other areas' details I have relied on the trusty internet and a lifetime's interest in Great Britain and Ireland, their history and geography.

Fourth and most important, I must thank my daughter Yasmine.

I began *The Cat Looked Back* in August, 2020, and broke my left arm in October, about three-fifths of the way through. Yasmine took over the care and feeding of our two moggies, Jackie and Sandy, and husky Mata, as well as me! She drove me to appointments, did any cooking or housework required, *and* kept up her part-time job as well as studies. So, despite my injury and a brief delay while I got over the initial shock, I was able to write and finish the book.

So thank you, Daughter. You are the best.

# ABOUT THE AUTHOR

Born in Montreal and raised in Hudson, Quebec, Louise Carson studied music in Montreal and Toronto, played jazz piano and sang in the chorus of the Canadian Opera Company. Carson has published sixteen books: *Rope*, a blend of poetry and prose; *Mermaid Road*, a novella; *A Clearing*, a collection of poetry; *Executor*, a mystery set in China and Toronto; *In Which: Book One of The Chronicles of Deasil Widdy*, historical fiction set in eighteenth-century Scotland; book two, *Measured*; and book three, *Third Circle*; *The Last Unsuitable Man*, a psychological thriller; and her Maples Mysteries Series: *The Cat Among Us*, *The Cat Vanishes*, *The Cat Between*, *The Cat Possessed*, *A Clutter of Cats* and *The Cat Looked Back*. Her second collection of poetry—*Dog Poems*—was published in 2020; her first of haiku—*The Truck Driver Treated For Shock*—in 2023.

Her poems appear in literary magazines, chapbooks and anthologies from coast to coast, including *The Best Canadian Poetry 2013, 2021 and 2024*. She's been short-listed three times in *FreeFall* magazine's annual contest and won a Manitoba Magazine Award. Her novel *In Which* was shortlisted for a Quebec Writers' Federation award and the ReLit awards in 2019. She has presented her work in many public forums, including Hudson's Storyfest, and in Montreal, Ottawa, Toronto, Saskatoon, Kingston and New York City.

Louise lives in St-Lazare, Quebec, where she writes, tends her pets, and gardens.

Eco-Audit
Printing this book using Rolland Enviro100 Book
instead of virgin fibres paper saved the following resources:

| Trees | Energy | Water | Air Emissions |
|---|---|---|---|
| 4 | 7 GJ | 2,000 L | 257 kg |